D0758231

Darkest Light

Also by Hiromi Goto

Half World

Chorus of Mushrooms

The Kappa Child

The Water of Possibility

Hopeful Monsters

Darkest Light

Hiromi Goto

Illustrations by Jillian Tamaki

RAZORBILL
an imprint of Penguin Canada

Published by the Penguin Group
Penguin Group (Canada), 90 Eglinton Avenue East, Suite 700, Toronto, Ontario, Canada M4P 2Y3
(a division of Pearson Canada Inc.)

Penguin Group (USA) Inc., 375 Hudson Street, New York, New York 10014, U.S.A.
Penguin Books Ltd, 80 Strand, London WC2R 0RL, England
Penguin Ireland, 25 St Stephen's Green, Dublin 2, Ireland (a division of Penguin Books Ltd)
Penguin Group (Australia), 250 Camberwell Road, Camberwell, Victoria 3124, Australia
(a division of Pearson Australia Group Pty Ltd)
Penguin Books India Pvt Ltd, 11 Community Centre, Panchsheel Park, New Delhi – 110 017, India
Penguin Group (NZ), 67 Apollo Drive, Rosedale, Auckland 0632, New Zealand
(a division of Pearson New Zealand Ltd)
Penguin Books (South Africa) (Pty) Ltd, 24 Sturdee Avenue, Rosebank, Johannesburg 2196, South Africa

Penguin Books Ltd, Registered Offices: 80 Strand, London WC2R 0RL, England

First published 2012

1 2 3 4 5 6 7 8 9 10 (RRD)

Manufactured in the U.S.A.

LIBRARY AND ARCHIVES CANADA CATALOGUING IN PUBLICATION

Goto, Hiromi, 1966–
Darkest light / Hiromi Goto.

ISBN 978-0-670-06527-1

I. Title.

PS8563.O8383D37 2012 jC813'.54 C2011-906595-9

Visit the Penguin Canada website at **www.penguin.ca**

Special and corporate bulk purchase rates available; please see
www.penguin.ca/corporatesales or call 1-800-810-3104, ext. 2477.

ALWAYS LEARNING PEARSON

To Koji Tongu;

you shine.

Prologue

Long, long, long ago, before mortals began to inscribe mortal religions onto stone tablets and parchment, there were Three Realms: the Realm of Flesh, the Realm of Spirit and Half World.

For aeons it was a time of wholeness and balance; Life, After Life and Half Life were as natural as awake, asleep and dreaming. All living things died only to awaken in the dream land of Half World. There, mortals arose to the moment of the greatest trauma they had experienced in the Realm of Flesh. In Half World they relived Half Lives, until through trial and tribulation they worked through their worst suffering. Wrongdoings, doubts, fears, terror, pain, hatred, spite, all the ills of mortality had to be integrated and resolved before they could rise from physical fetters into light and Spirit. Once in the Realm of Spirit, all material cares disappeared. Spirits existed freely, unbounded by mortality and pain, untroubled by Flesh, in a state pure and holy. Until eventually their light began to grow dim, and they were called back into the Realm of Flesh once more. For without connections to Life, Spirit too passes away.

Thus, the cycles were in balance.

There is no account left of what led to the severing of the Realms. No one knows if it was the work of Spirits who grew aloof and righteous, if it was a trapped Half Worlder maddened into perpetual pain with no hope left of light. Perhaps it was a mortal who dreamt of becoming a Spirit without ever leaving Flesh. But the Three Realms that had been balanced and entwined were ripped asunder and locked into isolation.

Mortals, trapped in perpetual mortality, died only to be born again into Flesh. Trapped in this unchanging cycle, they grew bleak and despairing. Violence, wars, environmental destruction accreted as time passed. When the mortals died, their Half Spirits could not move on to Half World. Instead they were born back into Flesh without ever transcending their suffering. With no Half World to work through their troubles and no Spirit to raise them, mortals descended ever deeper into turmoil. Atrocities proliferated and hope began to fade.

Half World, locked into perpetual psychic suffering, spiralled into madness. No Life ever to be born, unable to die, the Half Lives cycled through eternal nightmares. The great transformative powers of Half World, meant to bring redemption after suffering, instead began to form monsters.

The Spirits, cut off from mortality and Flesh, began losing all memory, all knowledge of the other Realms. Growing cooler and more distant, they forgot they were part of a greater pattern.

Their lights were fading, slowly, one by one. . . . So little was left of them they cared not of their own demise.

The Three Realms were in great peril. The Realms were very close to dissolution.

Who stepped forward to answer the call? What brought forth the hero?

At this most needful time a young mortal girl bravely crossed into the nightmare Realm of Half World. The girl sought only to save her mother, lost and broken. The child, ignorant that she had been miraculously born of Half World parents, knew not that her actions determined the continued existence or dissolution of the Three Realms. . . .

The monstrosities of Half World: the maimed and the twisted, the hopeless and the lost, the creatures turned to evil. . . . The girl of flesh faced them all. She met evil and overcame evil without destroying her own Spirit.

She became more than she had been. She saved the Three Realms and the ancient unbinding was rewoven once more.

But prices are paid, whether deserved or not. Life is bound with pain and grief, even as it is bound with joy and pleasure. The young girl's beloved mother could not return to the Realm of Flesh. And though she wished the burden be passed on to another, the young girl carried back into the Realm of Flesh a Half World infant born to Life. . . .

It is said that the sacred cycle, renewed, is not yet wholly stable. That something is left undone. . . . The Half World infant, as is true for all mortal beings, has the potential for both good and evil.

An infant grows from child to youth—and what will he wreak when he comes into power? The future is never fixed and the fate of the Realms is at stake. The choices of the Half World boy, who turns into a man, are the doom and hope of Half World.

from *The New Book of the Realms*

Introduction

Ilanna and Karu walked in the eternal twilight of Half World. The onion domes and pagodas, skyscrapers, wooden huts, pyramids and cathedrals cast uneasy shadows upon them. The ground rumbled beneath their feet as a subway train roared to nameless destinations. The odd auto rickshaw *put-putted* past them in a cloud of black exhaust. People, creatures, they shambled along garbage-strewn streets, some slinking indoors while others crept under cardboard tents, settled into doorways.

From the darkness light began to flicker; gas lamps, candles and open fires in rubbled alleys. The smell of rotten meat roasting was pungent and sour.

Ilanna's eels were hungry. They were always hungry.... They slid around her cool, wet, slender torso, twined around her pale neck and snapped their jaws beside her ears as she and Karu walked down a broken street.

Ilanna was cold. The wet fabric of her dress clung to her icy flesh, seawater streaming down her body, leaving a wet trail behind her. Perpetually.

Snick. Snick. Snick. Thankfully, the sound of the eels' sharp little teeth made it difficult to hear what Karu was saying. He'd been yammering, off and on, for half an hour and Ilanna was bored and hungry along with her eels.

The feathers on Karu's head ruffled with agitation and his large curved beak clacked loudly with each word. "We don't need him back. We've been doing fine without him since he was taken. What kind of leader can be overcome by a *girl*!"

Ilanna raised one eyebrow, but Karu did not notice.

Click, click. Rilla's slender teeth were too close, too loud, by her right ear. Ilanna pushed the eel's head away.

"Retrieving him from the Realm of Flesh is a waste of time. I don't know why you bring it up now. If the Three Realms were separated once before, it can be done again. And *we* will be the ones to do it, to rule Half World," he yammered on and on.

He had a nice human body—lean, smooth, dark. Ilanna could appreciate that. But she really couldn't stand the words coming out of Karu's bird-brain. She eyed his neat clean feathers, the reptilian quality of his eyes, his nervous head motions. No, she was not fond of his bird-brained thoughts, but she suspected that even if he had a human head she wouldn't like those ideas any better.

The little eel inside her mouth lashed about, scraping its tiny sharp teeth against the tender flesh of her inner cheeks.

Ilanna stared down at the eels that had replaced her arms so very long ago. With their slick, tapered tails wedged into her gaping shoulder sockets, they kind of looked like arms from a distance. Graceful, fluid, eely arms....

It had taken many Half Lives to train the eel that had replaced her tongue to do her bidding. But at least she could talk.

There were benefits to having eels instead of arms, Ilanna thought. Monstrous men left her alone. No one imagined her easy prey.

Hungry! Lilla, on the left, snapped too close to the side of Ilanna's face.

She shivered. Ilanna had grown to love her eels, she did, but she knew that if she didn't feed them soon, they would, perhaps sorrowfully, consume her.

The edges of her Half World *wavered.* A flicker between solid and immaterial. Ilanna shuddered. Clenched her will, seized it, and her world held solid once more.

Her cycle was calling her back.

Despite Karu's bird-brained arguments, Ilanna knew that only Mr. Glueskin had the capacity to stretch the limitations of their Realm. He was the first to break out of his own Half World cycle, and he was the one who had plucked her from her torturous suffering. Mr. Glueskin had taught her how a Half Life could be extended—so that it could be stretched into something of her own. He had taught her how to eat. She owed him, for teaching her this.

And she needed him....

Something caught against her icy feet. Ilanna glanced down. Barnacles grew on her toenails, and a piece of newspaper had snagged on the rough edges. Angrily she kicked the rubbish away.

Once, she had managed to tear herself out of her own cycle, without Mr. Glueskin, after he'd been stolen away from their Realm. But the wear of suffering, the pain and the torment when she was thrown back into her original pattern—she knew she didn't have the capacity to free herself, over and over again, as Mr. Glueskin was capable of doing. He was so powerful, so wonderfully creative and sadistic. At least he *had* been, before that disgusting girl from the Realm of Flesh had plucked him away from her. Ilanna shivered. Rilla and Lilla twined around her midriff and squeezed. She would do anything to resist the nightmare of her cycle.

"There are different ways to overcome the patterns of Half World," Karu croaked. "Mr. Glueskin found one way. So there must be other means. Are you listening to me?" he snapped. He continued talking without waiting for Ilanna's reply.

Her sad little end had happened so very, very long ago, Ilanna thought. Her lover had betrayed her. Had tied her to an anchor and thrown her into the sea, deep, deep into the icy green depths. The penetrating cold of death. The eels reached her first, to tear the flesh from her arms, to eat her tongue.... She had woken in the Half World sea, even the stripped bones of her arms gone, and in their place two large eels attached to her shoulders. Where she once had a tongue, a small eel was fixed to the root.

She had still been tied to the anchor.

There Ilanna remained, eaten half alive, eternally, by flounders, skates, eels and octopi. Giant-clawed crabs, the fury of shrimp, the snapping, ripping teeth of sleeper sharks.

Ohhhhhh, they were never sleepy. She cycled through betrayal and death, betrayal and death, until she knew nothing else.

Eels. She learned the language of eels.

Snick, snick, snick. Lilla, the eel on her left, sliced tender cuts into her icy earlobe.

Ilanna jerked her chin to the side. "Stop that," she chided.

"What?" Karu snapped.

"Darling." Ilanna's voice was slick with cool affection. "Don't be like that. Come here."

Karu, hissing, nonetheless stepped toward her. Too close. She could smell the powdery, musty smell of his feathers. He must be ready to moult. So messy. She had never liked his beak.

Rilla and Lilla swirled once around his arms. Smooth, slide, wet. Karu shuddered. Ilanna could see the human skin on his arms pimpling with revulsion and longing. The ruffled feathers on Karu's head began to flatten as he lowered his head to press his soft cheek on the top of her head.

"We will lead Half World together." His voice was fierce. Harsh.

Why couldn't his voice have been sweet, Ilanna wondered. Such a shame....

"The two of us," Karu rasped. "We will crush the Realm of Flesh and dissolve the Realm of Spirit. Half World will be the only world and we will hold dominion for eternity."

Ilanna slowly tilted her head from side to side. If one could get past the smell, his feathers felt so nice.

If only he'd keep his beak shut.

The eels shuddered. Ilanna could feel their tails writhing with excitement in her shoulder sockets where she once had arms.

"That tickles," she murmured.

"What?" Karu went still.

Ilanna sighed. He was such a coarse bird man, after all. She'd had to make do with him as her lover, but oh, how he paled in comparison to Mr. Glueskin.

Karu broke away and strode on, debris crunching beneath his calloused bare feet. "If he were meant to lead us once more, he would have returned on his own. But where is he? He is not of us any longer."

Ilanna knew Karu was wrong. For a while now, she had *felt* something. Far off, so faint, barely noticeable. Lately the feeling had been growing stronger....

He was calling her. She sensed it with her entire being. And just as she knew he was coming into his power, she knew her own was waning. She would be thrown back to the worst of her Half World cycle again. Back to the moment when she had been betrayed, thrown into the sea, where she first met her lovely eels....

She was not going back.

Ilanna's large dewy eyes narrowed into slits. That human, Melanie, had ruined everything! Since she had come, Half Worlders were no longer trapped in their Half Lives. Those who cycled in suffering eventually turned to Spirit, turning into brilliant colourful spheres of light, to fly, fly away.

Not her! This is *my* Half World, Ilanna thought. And no one will take it away from me! What did she want of Spirit? Give her Half Flesh to feast upon, give her Half Life to control. She wanted nothing of a cycle that promised only future death and future suffering. A future where nothing of hers was through choice. She could be born to a wretched family. She could choose a violent love. She had no faith in a better outcome. She'd chosen Half World and she wanted it back, the way it was, before that girl ruined everything. Only Mr. Glueskin had the strength, the evil, to lead Half World back to its glory. And she would bring him back.

Karu clacked and clacked his curved beak with great agitation. Just like an octopus.

She loathed octopi.

A blast shook the ground, and Ilanna and Karu staggered. Bits of rock, cement, a cloud of dust raining down. Dogs began to howl, infants cried.

The staccato burst of gunfire. The *crump*, *crump* of far-off grenades.

Somewhere an enormous beast moaned, vibrating the dark skies, and a man screamed, frantic. A siren began to wail, warning of a blanket of bombs to come.

People in buildings quickly turned out their lights. Closed shutters, dropped blinds, blew out smoky candles. The city grew darker still.

Clop, *clop*, *clop*, *clop*.

The sound grew nearer and louder, accompanied by the ringing jangle of metal.

Ilanna shook her cold head, seawater flying from the tips of her hair. The sound was so friendly, she laughed aloud.

Clop, *clop*, *clop*, *clop*.

Ilanna turned around.

In the flickering light of the street lamp, the girl on the horse made a pretty picture. She rode astride it, like a boy. And she wore trousers and leather boots, her slender hands holding the reins tightly.

She had left without a coat, such was her hurry.

Charming, Ilanna thought. Poor darling.

The girl's eyes were swollen and her tears shone upon her

cheeks. She dragged the back of her hand under her nose, sniffling loudly. "Rowan!" she called, her voice breaking. "Rowan!" She gulped back a sob.

"Tut, tut, tut." Ilanna made a comforting sound. "Look at the poor child, trapped in her stupid suffering."

The young girl's eyes slid over Ilanna and Karu as if they weren't there. The girl hadn't discovered how to break out of her Half Life pattern. She was caught, repeating the greatest trauma suffered during her short life, forever looking for Rowan, until she finally attained Spirit. Or discovered the power of eating Half Flesh....

"She looks tasty," Ilanna whispered. "Do you want to eat horse?" she asked Karu.

The horse pricked his ears toward Ilanna and waffled the air with his great nostrils. Some animal Half Life left inside him could sense danger, even if he couldn't see them.

Rilla whipped toward the horse's muzzle, snapping her gleaming teeth in warning. The horse yanked his head to the side and clattered three steps backward, the girl squeezing her legs and shifting her weight to stay atop her mount. She pulled on the reins so that the horse backed away from them further. The girl blinked nervously as she turned her horse around. She dug her heels into his sides and they clattered away into the darkness. "Rowan," she continued calling. "Rowan."

"Look what you did!" Ilanna snarled at Rilla.

Lilla, equally vexed, hissed wetly at her sister eel.

Rilla snapped back.

The eels suddenly dove toward each other, twining faster than the eye could follow, snapping wildly, barely missing taking chunks of black flesh from each other's bodies.

"Stop it!" Ilanna screamed.

Karu began to laugh, a hoarse croaking in the back of his throat.

Something stirred in a black doorway.

The eels, feeling the movement on the tiny hairs of their skin, froze. They stared into the impenetrable darkness with gleaming eyes.

Ilanna licked her lips with her black tongue.

The *rustle, rustle* of newspaper ... the scrape of wooden clogs against cobblestone.

"Little mouse," Ilanna called out in a soft, sweet voice. "Come out, little mouse."

Her eels silently untangled from each other and stood poised, S-shaped, fairly quivering with anticipation.

A dirty little boy crawled out from under the pile of paper. Mucus had dried in clots around his nose and dark circles cupped his large stunned eyes. All the buttons had been lost from his little jacket and his stockings were torn, his knees abraded. The sad little boy looked so much like the girl who sought Rowan that if he'd been older they would have passed for twins. Much too late, he raised his arms toward the sound of fading hoofbeats.

Ilanna wondered what kind of death was part of the boy's dreadful little cycle. Maybe he was caught by slavers and sent off to a house of pain. Maybe he fell into a canal and drowned. He and his sister caught in a loop, he perpetually lost, she forever searching. Until finally, somehow, they surpassed their suffering and passed into Spirit. Or they took control of their pitiful Half Lives by killing and consuming.

Ilanna snarled. The eels quivered.

"Don't." Karu's voice was rough.

"What!" Ilanna spat.

"We needn't eat children—there are animals: rats and cats. That girl must be his sister. She's looking for him...."

"Don't be a snivelling weakling," Ilanna hissed.

The little boy, unable to see beyond the loop of his own suffering, stared at the darkness in the direction his sister's horse had gone. He began to cry.

Karu ground his beak with agitation.

Ilanna licked her lips with her little black tongue. "This one has fresh energy. I can smell it. More energy to keep me going that much longer." She swallowed hard. "What does it matter anyway, bird, beast or human! Once eaten, they all return to the start of their Half World trauma once more. We're not *killing* him. He's dead already!"

The little boy was beginning to crawl back into his futile nest of paper.

"So leave him to his pattern." Karu's voice was low. "There're plenty of other things to eat."

Ilanna's eyes widened and she began to smile. "Karu, my darling ... is this a show of *compassion*? Does the little boy remind you of your own little trauma? Maybe your amnesia is beginning to fade. Maybe you're starting to remember—"

"Enough!" Karu roared.

The eels, in a frenzy of hunger, plunged.

The little boy didn't have time to scream.

Karu, crossing his arms, turned away from their feasting.

Who is the weak one? Ilanna sneered, as she lowered her head. For all his bird-brained talk about becoming a new leader of Half World. Why did he not eat? Idiot! She was hungry. At least that's what she called that desperate, hollow feeling inside her.

There were no physical needs to be met in Half World—no one needed to eat or drink, sleep or dream.... But Mr. Glueskin had discovered that eating other Half World creatures extended your own cycle. *Ohhhh*, he was such a wise and creative thinker! The little orphan boy's unfinished cycle added time to her own.... And she'd grown fond of the taste of flesh.

Rilla and Lilla gorged, and Ilanna snarled to stake out her share.

She dragged her mouth across her ragged shoulder, leaving a dark smear on her pale flesh. She smiled, her white teeth stained with black blood.

Ahhhhhh, so much better. She throbbed with power and satiation. Now, now she would go and fetch him. Her saviour and her lover.

He was almost fully ripened. She could *feel* him, the threads of his dark desires, stretching across the Realms. Longing to return to the place of his birth.... Surely he could feel her too. Ilanna shuddered with her need. They were meant to be together.

She wanted him. He was the only one who could keep her from returning to her suffering, the only one with darkness great enough to disrupt the patterns of Life, Half Life and Spirit.

She would find him. And she would never let him go.

Chapter One

The late Sunday afternoon light shone tawny gold upon the mounds of pomelo and Chinese pears. The large old-fashioned plate-glass window was speckled with dust from the inside, exhaust fumes from the outside. Behind the store counter Gee tilted back against the wall onto the back two legs of the wooden stool. A flop of thick black hair fell across his eyes as he gazed out from behind the strands at the luminous beams of dust. His popo no longer had the energy to keep the storefront windows clean—but the dirty glass did something beautiful to the light.

Gee supposed most sixteen-year-olds would resent the boring job, especially on the weekend, but he didn't mind so much. His homework was done, and he had no friends. It had been very clear since playschool that he would never have friends. An early life of solitude had shaped him profoundly. He was never lonely. Once, his grandmother brought home a dog, but it ran away after three days. She did not bring home any more pets after that.

Gee's longest companion, apart from his popo, had been disquiet. When he was very little he didn't know what the feeling was called, but he always knew it was there, and sometimes it would flare up with the darkest light, so much so that he'd be filled with trembling. He never knew if this trembling was fear or excitement. He did not want to look at it so very closely.

For a while, there had been Older Sister. But when he was eight she moved out, across the country, to go to graduate school. She'd visited once a year as she completed her studies, but after that she never came back. Five years, he thought, was a long time not to visit. But she must have her reasons. She phoned once a month and sent postcards when she was on archaeological digs, but really, she was a stranger to him. Sometimes he felt bad for Popo, who spoke of Melanie often, with much love and admiration, but mostly he was glad to have his grandmother all to himself.

Both he and Older Sister had been adopted by Popo—Older Sister when she was already a teenager, and Gee when he was still a baby. Older Sister had been through troubles, that was certain, but they were such Bad Troubles that they were never spoken of. As for Gee's adoption, he knew there were irregularities. His grandmother had told him he must never get in trouble with the law, because she didn't have proper adoption papers for him, and they would take him away. When Popo told him this, the disquiet inside him roared like a fire. Always serious, cautious and quiet, Gee had stared intently into his grandmother's resolute eyes and nodded. He was very, very careful.

The bell on the door jangled as a customer came into the store. It was Ms. Carlson, the librarian from the community centre.

"Hullo, Gee. Good to see you helping your grandma," Ms. Carlson said. She said the same thing every time she saw him at the counter. Gee ducked his chin, a kind of greeting, and reached for his sunglasses.

Oh—he'd left them upstairs, on the dining room table. He let his long dark hair fall over his eyes. Maybe his best friend was disquiet because of his eyes. With his irises as dark as his pupils, almost everyone's reaction to them lingered somewhere between fear and disgust. What with his pale, pale skin and his dark eyes, he knew he repelled people somehow. And this knowledge had formed him, too.

Ms. Carlson had known him since he was a child. She was always careful not to show her distaste. He could hear her open the sliding door to the refrigerator. The motor hummed louder as she decided between fresh tofu or deep fried. Popo hated it when customers kept the refrigerator door open too long. "Do they think Rainbow Market is here to pay for their indecision?" she would snap, loud enough for them to hear.

It always made a small smile twitch upon Gee's thin lips.

Something white flickered in the corner of his eye. Low to the ground. Gee swung his head toward the darker recesses of the store where the stairway to their upstairs home was located.

Nothing was there.

Must be sunlight reflecting off a passing bumper, Gee thought.

Ms. Carlson finally let the fridge door slide shut and moved toward a basket of ginger.

A Neo Goth girl stood nearby, reading the information on the packets of different miso brands. Gee had never seen her before. He would have noticed. She wore heavy black boots with numerous silver buckles that jangled like Santa's reindeer. Black fishnet stockings on skinny legs. A torn white T-shirt and a black skirt fluffed out with layers of red crinoline underneath. Jagged black hair. Eyeliner.

Gee shook his head. He didn't understand why some of the kids tried so hard to stand out as different when they could just blend in with the other ducklings. How they would go out of their way to draw attention to themselves. Gee didn't have that option. His clothes were nondescript. Jeans. Black T-shirt. A loose, dark-grey jacket. But his clothing could not mask his features.

At first the Neo Goth kids at school had been drawn to his striking looks. They'd thought he was one of them until they realized that his white skin wasn't makeup, but was his natural complexion, and that he wasn't wearing contact lenses. After a few awkward starts at conversations they had pulled away, as if they couldn't stand to be around him. Like he gave off a kind of smell. He was avoided by everyone thereafter.

The doorbell chimed wildly before ending with a bang as two teenage boys burst into the store. A boozy cloud roiled outward as they began to guffaw.

"Oops!" one boy said, before they burst into drunken laughter again.

Gee's lips twisted. They looked familiar—had they been in his Phys. Ed class in grade ten?

Winston Chang and Tad Rivera.... Gee lowered his chin. They were trouble in school, and he didn't want their trouble in his grandmother's store.

The boys, pushing each other and laughing, approached the counter.

"Uh—a pack of matches and, uh, filter papers. Oh, and, uh, one BonusFun 50/50 Chance for Life! ticket," Winston demanded, a waft of booze escaping his lips. "Buddy," he added, for friendly effect.

Gee did not look up to meet his eyes. "You have to be nineteen in order to buy a lottery game ticket."

Winston fisted money out of his pocket and threw the bills on the counter. Tad snickered at his elbow. "I'm paying for it, just give it to me. That's your job, boy," Winston said.

Darkness unfurled in Gee's gut and he grew very still. He breathed carefully. Slowly. He did not want to become angry. Gee could sense the Neo Goth girl approaching the counter, an aura of indignation flaring from her body.

"It's against the law for us to sell lotto tickets to anyone who's underage," Gee explained. "Unless you can show me some I.D."

"Can you believe this shit?" Tad, shrugging dramatically, turned toward the girl. "We're paying customers!"

"Heeeeey." Winston peered at Gee's downturned face. "You go to our school! You're that freak who doesn't talk! Are you a Re-tard?"

Winston and Tad laughed, batting at each other's arms as if they'd just told some wonderful joke.

"Why don't you leave?" the girl snapped. Her cheeks were flushed with feeling. "Go on!" She thrust out her chin. "You're not welcome here!"

"Get a load of the dyke!" Winston sneered. "You're the one who isn't welcome!"

"Do you know where you *are*?" the girl shouted. "This is the gay area of the city, you stupid fuck! This store is called Rainbow Market, moron!"

Gee observed them as if they were part of a social experiment. The young woman was so marvellously angry. He wondered coolly at her passion. What must it feel like, he thought, to be able to let yourself go like that? He'd always known that he must never, ever lose control.

"That's enough of that." Ms. Carlson used her librarian voice. "Boys, I think it's time for you to move on." She sounded calm, but her eyes darted from side to side.

She was right to be nervous, Gee thought. The air quivered with tension, and he almost smiled. Instead he frowned beneath his flop of hair. None of it was funny, of course.

The Neo Goth girl seethed with anger and outrage. She was practically crackling with it. Winston Chang's hands on the glass countertop were turning into fists.

"Time for you to go," Gee said in a low, quiet voice. He did not raise his head, only stared at his own pale, slender hands. "Now."

"Not even man enough to look me in the eyes, you little faggot," Winston whispered. He reached across the counter and grabbed the lapel of Gee's jacket.

You fool, Gee thought, raising his chin. You have no idea.

He deserves everything he gets, a dark voice inside him crowed. *You didn't do anything, but he came asking for trouble!*

Gee began to smile. He opened his eyes wide and stared into Winston Chang's startled hazel eyes. You see, Gee thought, you think you have someone figured out, but really you know nothing about them at all....

Winston's hand fell from Gee's lapel. His Adam's apple bobbed, a muscle twitched in his jaw, but he could not break his gaze.

Gee could almost feel the expressions morphing across Winston's face. Micro-seconds of emotions. Confusion. Anger. Uncertainty.... Social experiment, Gee thought. It's all a social experiment.

"What the hell are you staring at?" Winston hissed, testosterone tinged with fear.

Tad, confused, darted glances between Gee's and Winston's face. Time was stretching, elastic slow motion. Gee could sense Ms. Carlson raising her hand, palm outward, as if she were trying to stop traffic. The Neo Goth girl dug into her bag, rummaging around for something.

What will happen now? the dark voice inside Gee crowed. *Something bad....*

I should stop staring. Gee's thoughts felt as if they were coming from far, far away. I should stop staring. But beyond Winston's pupils, from deep inside him, something would begin to rise to the surface and Gee didn't want to miss it....

At high school, Gee always walked away from trouble. But not in the store. Because Winston had entered *his* world, had he not? *Why should you be the one to look away?* the dark little voice inside him whispered. The voice he never spoke aloud. The one he must control.

"Come on," Tad laughed, but there was something forced to the sound. "Let's get out of this shit store."

Gee continued staring. And Winston could not tear his eyes away. There, Gee thought, almost tenderly. There. The edges of the boy's own darkness. Everyone had it inside them. What you could do with that power. What—

"What's going on!"

Gee blinked. Shook his head. His grandmother charged toward them, a field hockey stick in one hand. Ferocious.

"Awesome!" the Neo Goth girl breathed.

Fingers shaking, Winston retrieved his money from the counter and shoved it back into his pocket. "Come on," he said to Tad. He glared at Gee with loathing. "See you at school, faggot."

Popo raised her field hockey stick ever so slightly. "Homophobia is unacceptable. Get out of my store. Never come back!"

The two boys began to laugh once more as they shoved each other through the door. "Old dyke bitch!" one of them shouted before they roared away in a retro Hummer.

Gee wanted to kill them.

The bright glint in Popo's eyes dulled, and she seemed to deflate. The field hockey stick fell to the floor with a clatter. She rested her hand on the counter and closed her eyes.

"Popo!" Gee cried, and ran to slide his arm around her back.

Popo flapped her hand in front of her as if batting away a fly. "Popo is fine. Popo is just a little dizzy from running and all the excitement."

Frowning, Gee guided her behind the counter so that she could sit on the stool. A puff of air escaped her lips. It was almost a sigh.

Gee stared at his beloved grandmother's face. Her eyes were closed and something twitched in her temple. He gently placed his slender hand on Popo's forearm.

"It is nothing, child," she said quietly, without opening her eyes. "Popo just feels a little tired today. Please get some water."

Gee knew she didn't mean a bottle of water from the store. Without bothering to remove his downstairs shoes he ran up the steep, narrow back steps, taking three at a time, to their living space above the shop. In the small neat kitchen he half-filled an empty jam jar with lukewarm water from the kettle.

Popo's hands trembled, ever so slightly, when she raised them. Gee watched the thin skin in her neck move as she swallowed the water. The lines upon her cheeks, the wrinkled ridges on the bridge of her nose, the corners of her eyes. The slight tremor in her hands....

Something torqued inside his chest.

She was old.

Gee took a step backward. How could he not have seen it before? How long had she been this way? Something bulged and twisted, an emotion he could not name—only that it was unpleasant, and that he didn't like to feel it. He quickly quashed whatever it was and returned to the grey neutrality he preferred.

"Those ignorant boys." Ms. Carlson shook her head as she set down soy milk and tofu on the counter. "Are you all right, Ms. Wei?" The kind librarian's voice quavered. "Are you okay, dear? They were just dreadful!"

Gee's popo waved her right hand, letting it flap up and down. "Ms. Wei has seen far worse. Ms. Wei only feels a stitch from running." She managed a fierce smile before closing her eyes.

That odd little emotion spasmed inside Gee's chest once more.

"We can call the cops!" the Neo Goth girl said indignantly. "There are anti-hate laws! We don't have to just take it. We can—"

"No police." Popo's voice was resolute.

The Neo Goth girl scowled. "How can you let them treat you like that? How can you just let them win?" She glared at Gee as if it were somehow his fault, but he kept his face averted. "They'll just do it again with someone else. Unless they're stopped. Unless they're taught a lesson!"

No one responded.

Shaking her head, the girl marched out of the store, the many buckles on her boots jangling loudly. She closed the door so hard that the plate-glass window shook.

"Oh dear," Ms. Carlson sighed. "Such an afternoon it's become." She shook her head sadly and peered at his popo's face with something like compassion. Something like pity. And then her gaze turned toward Gee's face. The moment she caught his eyes, she jerked her head the other way.

Gee rang her purchases through the till. "Five dollars and thirty-five cents, please."

Chapter Two

Gee stared at his plate, the eggs scrambled with diced mushrooms and spinach and drizzled with soy sauce. The clink of Popo's chopsticks and the sound of her slow chewing seemed too loud. Rain pattered against the windows.

Popo flipped a page of the book she was reading and held it down with her left wrist, her chopsticks in her right hand. She stopped chewing for a moment, her eyes narrowing as she read a passage. She laughed aloud, then resumed chewing once more.

Gee stared at his mug of clear chicken broth. It had grown cold and a wrinkled skin of fat floated at the surface. He hadn't brought a book to the table.

After Gee had entered kindergarten he'd stopped talking so much, even at home. His sister had already left, choosing to live on campus. And Ms. Wei was no stranger to silence. So they often read books while they ate their meals, sometimes silently pointing to a page to share interesting tidbits. A brief flash of a smile.

Gee gazed at his bowl of rice, cooked with too much water. The scrambled eggs, the broth, the soft rice....

There used to be juicy steak, crisp gai lan, whole steamed crab. Crunchy stir-fried broccoli with fresh water chestnuts, tonkatsu and bamboo shoots. Asparagus sautéed in sesame oil, chewy king oyster mushrooms and plump, firm prawns. His mind's eye flickered from images of meals past through to what meals had come to be.

It wasn't that Ms. Wei was trying to save money.

Everything on the plate now was soft....

"Not hungry, Grandson?" Popo asked gently.

Gee picked up his bowl of rice and scooped some grains into his mouth with the chopsticks. It took a long time to chew the small portion, to swallow.

The old woman's eyes widened and she stuck her hand into her sweater pocket. She pulled out a worn postcard and held it toward her grandson. "Look what Popo found in the mailbox!"

He let his chopsticks clatter upon his plate.

The postcard felt silky. On its front was an old illustration of some kind of tropical lizard. He turned it over and recognized his sister's messy scrawl. A Peruvian stamp. Postcard in hand, he left the dining room table to put the kettle on the stove and tap out brown twiggy stems of tea into the pot. He read the message in the kitchen while he waited for the water to boil.

> Ola. The dig goes well but staking pain every day.
> Have they taught you about irony in school? (If not,

watch the original Twilight Zone television program.)

Be well.

M.

Gee read it twice, then tucked it into the back pocket of his worn jeans.

She never left a return address.

He rarely thought of her as *Melanie*.... It seemed at once too familiar and too distancing to think of his adopted sister by her first name.

He took the tea out to his grandmother and she nodded her thanks.

They sipped noisily, the nutty brown aroma filling the quiet night.

"Popo," Gee finally said.

"Yes, Grandson."

"Is there a way to contact Older Sister?"

"There is no need to contact Older Sister."

"But what if there's an emergency?"

"If there is a need, Older Sister will know to return." His popo's tone was final.

Frustration roiled inside of him. There were so many things unsaid. *How* would Older Sister know when to return? Why was Popo so certain? What did she know that she wouldn't tell him, had never told him?

"That girl was right, you know," Gee muttered.

"What? Speak more clearly!" Popo exclaimed.

"That girl, today, in the store. She's right. We shouldn't have let those shits win!"

Gee wrapped his long fingers around his cup, glowered at the brown tea. The heat through the ceramic made his skin feel moist, slightly sticky. He could feel his grandmother's gaze.

"You are troubled, Grandson," Popo said gently.

Gee stared into the woody brownness of his tea. The reflection of his long pale face rippled. He did not like how it looked.

He could feel his grandmother's concern, and resentment churned inside him. "There're just so many things that aren't spoken, Popo." He looked up, flipping his hair to the side so that his dark eyes were exposed. He stared, hard, into his grandmother's eyes, and she met his gaze fully. The only person who ever could. "How will Older Sister know when she's needed? Why can't we call the police to report on those jerks from school? What do we have to hide?"

Popo swept the last grains of rice into her mouth and set her chopsticks down. "Why ask these questions now, Grandson?" She sipped her nutty aromatic tea, slurping loudly as if nothing troubled her.

"Because you're old," Gee said flatly. "You're old, and without you, I have no one. No one to answer my questions."

Popo sighed. She rubbed her palms over her closed eyelids then set her hands upon her lap. "Popo has not had a girlfriend for a long time." She smiled as she shook her head. "And her siblings are a bunch of old homophobes. Indeed, Grandson. We are a very small family."

Gee had the grace to look away.

Popo's last girlfriend, Glenna, had moved out when he was eight years old. Glenna and Popo had quarrelled. About what, he didn't know, but he was upset with Glenna and had stared at her every time Popo wasn't in the room. On the seventh day, behind closed doors, Glenna had told Popo she had to choose between her and Gee. Don't force me to choose, Popo had said. Glenna had chosen for her.

A wave of guilt lapped at Gee's consciousness. Was it his fault that they were so isolated? Was it his fault that his popo didn't have a girlfriend? That Older Sister never came home?

You know it is, his dark inside voice crooned. *Whose else could it be? Your grandmother's? She's the only one who loves you. And once she's gone, you're going to be utterly alone, with no way of knowing who or what you truly are. Disconnected from your past, nothing in your future. Oh, boo hoo hoo!*

Gee quelled the darker feelings, pushing them deep inside him.

Popo looked sad and tired. It made her look even older.

"I'm sorry, Popo," Gee muttered.

She shook her head. "No need to apologize for asking questions, Grandson. Questions are good. But not yet.... Not ready, yet."

"Who's not ready for what?" A stickiness caught in the back of his throat. He could scarcely swallow.

Popo looked up briefly to rest her gaze upon the row of bookshelves just beyond Gee's head.

He twisted around. What was she looking at? He scanned the neat rows of books on the shelves along the wall. A small white sculpture sat upon an ancient tome that was set horizontally atop several vertically placed books. The edges of the sculpture were worn smooth with age, but there was something vaguely catlike about the shape. Gee had never noticed it before. Odd, he thought. Popo seldom bought things unless they were food items or books. And she always placed the books vertically on the shelves.

He turned back toward his grandmother, but she was no longer looking at the shelf. She held her cup inside her palms as if reading her fortune in the tea.

"Not tonight," Popo finally said. "Soon. Popo will tell Grandson everything, soon."

"Really?" Gee's heart thudded slowly, heavily. His palms, sticky. He didn't know if what he felt was excitement or fear.

She smiled. A small, tired, sad smile. Gee had never seen such a look on her face before.

"But tonight Popo will go to sleep early. Popo still feels a stitch in her side from running." She shook her head. "To think Ming Wei used to win the running races on sports day," she muttered on the way to the washroom.

Gee watched her as she walked away, the slight curve in her back, her short iron-grey hair. The bathroom door clicked shut. He stacked the dishes and carried them to the sink. As he scraped the food he couldn't eat into the compost container, the skin on the right side of his neck prickled. A flash of white in the corner of his eye. Gee whipped his head around. But he could see nothing through the open kitchen doorway. Nothing but the table as he'd left it, the shelves of books behind it. He heard the toilet flushing, and his popo making her way to her bedroom. The creak of her bed.

It was only 8:25 P.M. Popo usually read or wrote until 11 P.M. Thoughtfully, Gee began filling the sink with warm water. Never mind, he told himself. She said she was tired, that's all. She would get a good sleep, and then tomorrow he would find out everything.

And what then? his darkness asked gleefully. *Once you know the truth about your past, what will you do?* Gee's heartbeat was slow and heavy; it never quickened when he was excited. Something remarkable, he thought. Something special. He wasn't like everyone else—he knew that very well, and he didn't lie to himself about it. That something awaited him he had no doubt. For he'd felt it his entire life, and maybe that was part of the disquiet.

Nervous excitement followed Gee to his room, and he could neither read a book nor go online. So he flopped back on his narrow bed, his hands clasped behind his head, his long limbs sprawling. He wondered how things would have been different if he looked more like his grandmother and sister.

He used to be filled with awe and wonder at his adventurous, enigmatic sister. The archaeological work she did during graduate school had her travelling to distant countries. She'd return on her annual visit with brown roughened skin and remarkable tales of ancient civilizations. She was a quiet and sober person. But when she smiled a light shone from her face, golden and warm. That she adored their grandmother was obvious. But if she loved their popo so much, why had she stopped visiting?

For a while Gee had imagined that Older Sister was actually his mother, and that she'd had him as a result of a teen pregnancy. But as he grew bigger and out of baby chubbiness, his features changed dramatically. He could very well see that Older Sister had no blood connection to him. Gee could also see that Older Sister and Popo were Asian, and that he was not. He didn't know what he was. Popo had never told him. Gee had never asked.

There were a lot of things that were left unspoken. When he was still little, when he was still called Baby G, he came to the realization that something had happened to Older Sister. Something bad. What that something was his popo had never shared, but Gee could feel the power of it, so enormous that he didn't want to know its name.

Because you know it has something to do with you, the little awful voice inside him sniggered. His faithful companion, his own little Mr. Hyde.

He'd never told Popo.... Because how could he ever tell her what it felt like? The nasty things he thought. Gee trembled. The edges of darkness were mysterious, tantalizing, delicious....

He covered his eyes with his thin forearm. "No," he whispered.

He did not know what he denied. But he could feel it lodged inside his chest, a foreign organ beside his heart.

Did you think your precious Popo would be there forever? the dark little voice jeered. *She's an old, old woman. Those kids did you a favour. Made you finally see!*

Gee yanked his arm away from his eyes and sat upright. If his grandmother died, what would happen to him?

She's not your real grandmother anyway. What does it matter?

"Stop it," Gee said. His heart began its loud slow thudding as the edges of a monstrous fear began to expand inside his chest. He rubbed his palm over his skinny ribs and took deep breaths. He swallowed his fear.

CRASH!

The sound shattered the night. Gee sat, stunned, for several seconds—and then leapt off the bed. He dashed past his grandmother's door just as she was opening it. Gee snatched up the field hockey stick that was propped in the corner by the entrance door and pounded down the creaky wooden steps to the store.

"Gee!" Popo called. "Come back!"

The store was dark. But the orange lights from the street glinted through the cracked window, the wet night air entering through the large hole in the glass. The revving of an engine. Gee watched coolly as the red taillights of a yellow Hummer screeched around the corner with the stink of burning rubber. A Hummer, he noted, was not an inconspicuous getaway vehicle.

The ceiling lights clicked on. A fragment of glass fell from the broken window and crashed on the floor. In the midst of the shards lay a large rock.

"Same old tricks," Popo muttered. Sighing, she sat down on the step where she'd been standing.

Gee glanced at her. She hadn't even reminded him to wear his shoes. He retrieved his runners that were in the stairway and slipped them on. His grandmother remained seated. Gee had to walk across broken glass, the shards crunching beneath him. The beautiful window was ruined, and it would be expensive to replace.

"Popo, will insurance pay to fix this?"

Popo was rubbing her palms over her face. "Only if it is reported."

"Then report it, Popo," Gee said.

"No."

"Why not?"

"No trouble."

"Look, Popo. Trouble came to us anyway. We can't just hide here, staying away from trouble!"

"Gee." Popo was almost pleading.

Gee was shocked.

"Gee is almost finished high school. Let Gee finish high school first, then...."

"What! What is it! We can't avoid things until I'm finished high school." Realization washed over him. "Wait a minute. You don't mean to say that you're not going to tell me about my past until I graduate from high school!"

"Gee," his grandmother begged. "Popo has thought about these things. She has! But sometimes if information comes too soon, if information is given before its time, it can distort. It can break. It can destroy. These things Popo has weighed, and that is why she has not told Grandson yet."

"It's that bad…." Gee whispered.

"No! Not—" Popo began.

"DON'T LIE, ON TOP OF EVERYTHING ELSE!" Gee screamed.

Popo recoiled as if she'd been slapped.

Gee clapped his hands over his mouth, his large dark eyes filling his face. Where had that rage come from? What was he *doing*? Self-loathing swept over him, but it wasn't strong enough to drown the dark voice inside.

She deserves it, the stupid lying bitch.

No, Gee thought. No. He could not bear it. What it was he couldn't say, but it felt as if his head would explode. He unlocked the door and ran into the wet night.

Popo did not call him back.

Chapter Three

Gee walked for hours, drenched, until the sun began to rise. He finally looked up and saw that he'd made an enormous rectangle and was close to an all-night diner near their neighbourhood. He was cold and wet, though these sensations didn't bother him so much. They stiffened his joints, but it wasn't painful. He moved slowly.

He realized his hand was clenched around something inside one of his pockets. He drew it out. A wet five-dollar bill. He would go to the diner and get a cup of tea until it was time for Rainbow Market to open. He didn't have his keys, and there was no point in waking Popo after such a night....

Gee stared at the crumpled bill. Would Popo be mad at him? Was he mad at Popo? He didn't know what he felt. It was all muddled and he didn't like it. He liked being able to control his feelings.

The door chimed as he entered the diner. He slumped into a booth and picked up the laminated menu. He should be hungry, but he didn't feel like eating. He'd never been a big eater, not like his popo. She used to chide him to eat more—*Fill up!*—until he asked her to stop saying it.

With a jangle of metal buckles and a stale waft of cigarette smoke, someone slumped into the cushioned seat opposite him.

"Hey!" The voice was overfriendly.

Gee flicked a look between the strands of his long hair.

It was the Neo Goth girl from yesterday.

Her eyes were overbright with lack of sleep revved up on coffee. She drummed her fingers on the table. "Never seen you come here before."

Gee frowned slightly behind the cover of his hair. Maybe if he ignored her she'd get the hint and go away.

She looked much smaller than she had yesterday, he noted. She was short. At least a foot shorter than he was. Her dyed black hair stood up in uneven hunks. Some of the tips were bright red, as if she'd dunked them in acrylic paint. Black vertical creases were all that remained of black lipstick; otherwise, her lips were pale. Her eyes were blackened underneath like a football player's. Gee didn't know if that was done on purpose, or if she'd just smeared them accidentally.

"You're a tea drinker, aren't you," she said decidedly.

"How do you know?" Gee asked.

The girl smirked. "I can tell. I'm good at things like that."

Gee wondered whether she was on drugs, and if that's why she didn't act like other people did around him. Anyway, it was time to get rid of her. He flipped his hair to the side and stared directly into her eyes.

Her eyes were pale, the same shade as honey.

Gee stared expressionlessly into her face. Waiting for the moment when discomfort transformed into fear. Fear into anger. All the negative responses his eyes, his person inspired.

The girl's eyes widened. Shock. A flash of fear. Then … curiosity.

Gee blinked, and sat back. This had never happened before.

The Neo Goth girl shook her head and a safety pin flew out from her messy hair and bounced off Gee's chest before falling onto the table.

The girl's laugh was a cross between a hiccup and a giggle.

Gee picked up the pin and held it toward her.

"You can keep it," she said. "Souvenir."

Gee didn't know what to do or say.

"I'm Cracker," she chirped. "Nice to meet a fellow night person." She extended her hand, and, after staring at it for a moment, Gee tucked the safety pin in his pocket.

The waitress stood beside the table. "Your order?"

"Do you have Earl Grey tea?" Gee asked.

"Figures," Cracker muttered.

The waitress rolled her eyes. "There's Red Rose, or Red Rose."

"That's fine," Gee said.

"Any food with that?" the waitress asked.

"Just the tea."

The waitress rolled her eyes again. She went into the kitchen instead of fixing his tea at the counter where all the supplies were laid out.

"You better leave a nice tip," Cracker advised. "She gets minimum wage for this crap job and the tips make all the difference."

"I know how it works," Gee said.

"Just saying!" Cracker said with exaggerated sensitivity. She leaned in close. "So, what happened? Did your gramma call the cops after all?"

Gee let his hair fall across his face once more. Who did she think she was, asking personal questions?

The waitress thumped the mug in front of Gee. The scent of bergamot rose in the air.

Gee glanced at the waitress's face. She was sheepish. "I like Earl Grey, too. I have my own stash for my breaks. You look like you had a shitty night, kid. Enjoy your tea." She walked away.

A smile broke across Gee's face.

"You should smile more often," Cracker advised. "Then you wouldn't look so scary. You're actually really good-looking," she added. "Not that I'm in any way hitting on you."

Gee turned to stare at her with incredulity. "Do you just say every little thing that pops into your head? Don't you filter any of it?"

"No!" Cracker scowled. "Don't be a moron! Of course I filter." When what she'd just said seeped in, she tipped back her head and laughed.

When she laughed, Gee noted, she was really good-looking too.

As if catching the edges of his thoughts, Cracker stopped laughing and glared. "Don't you dare hit on me! I'm not interested in you. I'm mostly into girls, okay?"

Gee shook his head. Her thoughts, her emotions, were dizzying. "Don't flatter yourself," he said, and sipped his tea. "You're the one who sat down with me."

"True," Cracker conceded amicably. She sank back against the booth and half-closed her eyes, as if tiredness had finally caught up with her.

"Don't you want to know what I'm doing out so late?" she asked Gee.

"No," he retorted. As soon as he finished his tea he would go home.

"I was going on a mission of revenge, for your and your gramma's sake, as well as for the greater good of queer justice," Cracker said sleepily. "But I'm already on probation, so I thought maybe I should save it for something really big. In case I get caught. It has to be worth it."

Gee couldn't help glancing up at her.

"Don't worry. I didn't maim anyone," Cracker murmured. "I'm not into physical violence. Just petty theft, vandalism.... Like Robin Hood." She yawned so widely Gee could see three fillings in the back of her mouth.

"What were you planning on doing?"

"Trash that fucking Hummer." Cracker shrugged. "He lives in a condo, a couple of blocks away from my place. I see him drive by all the time. It's hard to miss that fucking thing. He lives closer to school than you do, but he still drives. What a moron."

"We go to the same school?"

Cracker raised one eyebrow. "Just because you don't look at anybody doesn't mean people aren't looking at you. I'm in Mrs. Park's English class with you. Gee."

"Ms. Park, not Mrs.," Gee said. "And how do you know my name?"

"I love boys who've been raised by feminists." Cracker smiled. The smile fell from her face as she began to scowl. "Don't get any—"

"I know! I know! You're not into guys!" Gee shook his head. Cracker, she was … not boring. But that was enough. It was time to go home, apologize to his grandmother and see if she needed any help. He pulled the sodden five-dollar bill from his pocket, flattened it on the table and looked up for the waitress. Her back was to him, her arms crossed. Gee set his empty mug atop the bill. Began sliding out of the booth.

"Where you going?" Cracker asked.

"Home."

"Wait for me! Let me get my stuff."

Gee stared into Cracker's eyes. The girl did not look away. Her honey eyes shone bright.

"Why are you talking to me? No one else does. What do you want?" Gee's voice was flat.

Cracker turned slightly away, a small laugh escaping her lips.

Nervous? Gee wondered. Or self-conscious?

"You're really smooth, you know. Subtle." Cracker shook her head. "You don't fake stuff, do you?"

Gee frowned. "Fake what?"

Cracker sighed dramatically. "You know! Tell people what they want to hear. Pretend you don't notice their bullshit. Hide your true feelings. That kind of thing!"

Gee's heart lurched, but he kept his expression flat.

Your true feelings, the dark little voice crowed gleefully. *If she only knew!*

"Why would I bother saying things I don't believe?"

Cracker slapped the flat of her hand upon the tabletop. Gee's empty cup rattled. "That's why I like you!" she said.

Gee blinked. "You didn't know that about me before you began talking to me," he pointed out.

Cracker rolled her eyes. "You're relentless!" She looked down at her hands.

Gee followed her gaze.

Her hands were small, pale. Her fingernails were bitten so low her fingertips were malformed.

Feeling Gee's eyes, Cracker curled her fingers under into tight fists. When she spoke her voice was low. Quiet. "I saw something in you." She swallowed. "Something that feels familiar." She raised her head and smirked with bravado. "That good enough for ya?"

Gee stared into her eyes.

She held his gaze. Her honey-coloured eyes shone with a strength that Gee had only ever seen in his grandmother.

Gee looked away first, and slid out of the booth.

Cracker scissored her legs out of the seat, her unwieldy crinoline folds rucking upward. "Don't look up my skirt, you pervert! I'm wearing shorts anyway!"

Gee shook his head. "The whole world can see." She was unbelievable.

Cracker ran to her booth, tossed money on the table and ran back to Gee at the door, swinging her purse loosely in her hand.

"Don't follow me," Gee said as he began striding down the sidewalk.

The morning rush had already begun and buses whirred past, whipping cold air after them.

"I'm not following you!" Cracker said indignantly. "I'm going the same way, that's all!"

Gee shook his head. His long strides were too much for her, and she was panting for air, a little wheeze every time she inhaled. Her jangling buckles, her wheezy breath receded as she lagged farther and farther behind. "It's not good for me to run," Cracker panted. "I have a small hole in my heart."

Was she seeking his sympathy? Gee didn't care. He could feel her glares burning into his back but he didn't slow down. Cracker was interesting, but she was trouble. And, as his popo had always warned him, he must do everything to stay away from trouble.

Gee sighed. Even now.

"See you at school!" Cracker yelled from down the street.

Gee did not respond.

Popo, he thought. She was so stubborn. Not tell him about his past for another year and a half? She had to be kidding. He knew she loved him. But....

What was she hiding?

The skin prickled at the back of his neck. He didn't want to look again and encourage that Cracker. But he couldn't stop himself. She must be staring; the intensity of her gaze sizzled. Was she mad now? Gee glanced over his shoulder.

Cracker wasn't there. Aside from some people standing around at a bus stop, the sidewalk was empty. No one was looking at him. No one that he could see.

Gee stuffed his hands in his pockets and strode toward his home.

A HANDMADE SIGN, "Closed for Repair," was stuck to the shop door. The storefront window had been boarded up from the inside. It looked like sheets of plywood had been nailed into the frame. Had his grandmother done all that herself last night? A knot of guilt formed inside Gee's chest. He loped through the alley to the back of the building and ran up the rickety wooden stairs. He tried the doorknob.

The door opened.

Gee frowned. It wasn't like Popo to leave the door unlocked, especially after a night of vandalism. Their neighbourhood was prone to minor break-ins. Smash and grabs. A lot of car windows. His grandmother never left the doors unlocked.

"Popo?" Gee called out.

His words were too loud. And it was obvious the place was empty. It felt too hollow, too echoey. Without bothering to remove his shoes, Gee strode through the rooms. Nothing was in disarray. No one had come to terrorize the old woman. Gee's overloud heart began beating more gently.

Where on earth could she be?

She must have gone to look for a replacement window. At that used house-parts place where she went to find a bathroom sink. Yes, that would make the most sense. She was like that—handy and practical.

A piece of white paper, folded in half, was propped against an old leather-bound book on the large wooden table where they ate their meals. Someone had written *Gee* across the middle of the folded page. It was not in Popo's hand.

Gee plucked the letter from the table.

My dear young Gee,

I'm so sorry you have to find out this way. Early this morning, your grandmother had a fainting spell, then a terrible headache. She called me and I called the ambulance, just to be on the safe side. They took her to the Grace Women's Hospital for tests. They may have to keep her there depending on the results. Please phone me when you get this message. Try not to worry. It will all be fine—I have faith. Please let your older sister know what has happened. It might be best if she comes home for a while. If you don't want to be at home without your grandmother, you just come on over to the library and I'll give you my house key.

Sincerely,
Ms. Carlson

Gee went back to the top of the page and read through it once more. When he was finished he folded the paper in half once, twice, three times, and tucked it into his jeans pocket.

Popo was ill. Okay. It wasn't uncommon. Older people often fell ill. It sounded like a stroke. Popo had had a stroke. She was going to die….

No!

He had to get to the hospital. He didn't want to talk to Ms. Carlson. He would raid the petty cash tin and take a cab.

His chest felt tight. *Squeezed.* His breath was a little shallow. Rapid.

"I'm not scared," he whispered.

"You should be," a gritty voice growled.

Gee leapt. He grabbed the nearest thing his hand could clasp before dropping into a crouch. His eyes darted as he searched for the intruder.

The voice had come from somewhere low. Someone. Hiding inside their home, all along.

"Death by back-scratcher," the sarcastic voice continued. "Please, no. Anything but that."

Movement. Behind the crushed velvet chair. Behind the red velvet curtain. The cloth rippled as something sauntered along the length of the heavy material.

The pink nose came first, followed by a flat, wide head. Cold, yellow-green eyes surrounded by dense white fur, the pointed ears of an enormous cat.

Gee shook his head, took a step backward.

The creature sauntered out dramatically, placing his dainty paws as carefully as if the curtains were part of a stage and he the star of the show. He held his white tail vertically, although the tip flopped a little to the side. He gave it an annoyed little flick, but the tip wouldn't stay upright.

Gee stared at the red curtains, sweeping his gaze along the baseboards. He couldn't see the feet of the person hiding behind the thick cloth. Who had spoken? Because it certainly could not have been the oversized white cat....

Gee dragged his forearm across his eyes. He was groggy because he hadn't had any sleep. And the surprise of the news that Popo was in hospital. The cat hadn't spoken aloud. He was imagining things.

How had the cat entered the building? Maybe when Popo was ill the door had been left open.

The cat yawned enormously, exposing sharp little teeth and a pink tongue. "Are you quite finished thinking up pedestrian rationalizations for my ability to speak your common language?" it asked in a bored tone of voice.

Chapter Four

Gee leapt several feet backward, the bamboo back-scratcher raised like a flyswatter. He did not yell.

With a grunt, the cat heaved himself atop the red velvet chair and sat down. He wrapped his tail loosely around his hind-quarters, but the tip flicked up and down, almost of its own accord. The cat's yellow-green eyes stared, unblinking, at Gee's tight face.

"Trouble has come and you're unprepared," the cat said coolly.

"W-what are you talking about?" Gee's voice was hoarse.

"Trouble has caught up with you and more is coming. And you haven't begun learning how to control your darkness. I can smell it on you," the cat continued. "Like a flower, ready to bloom."

Gee's heart thudded, too slow, too hard, inside his bony chest. How did the cat *know*?

"I don't know what you're talking about," Gee whispered.

"Don't be a fool, on top of everything else!" the cat snapped. "Evil will come courting, and you are ill-prepared. I told the old woman to see to your education. 'Let him grow up innocent,' she said! 'For as long as possible.' Humans!" The cat shuddered.

Gee realized he still had a death grip on the back-scratcher. He loosened his hold and set it down on the table. He rubbed his palm against the outside of his jeans.

"You claim you know my grandmother," Gee said slowly. "Where is she now? What have you done?"

"Did you not read the note?" The cat narrowed his eyes into slits.

"You could have written it. Maybe you've done something to my popo!"

"Idiot!" the cat hissed. "I am your popo's guardian and companion, from long before you came into our lives!"

"I have never seen you before," Gee said flatly. "How do I know you're not lying? And, if you are my grandmother's guardian and companion, why aren't you with her, protecting her, at the hospital?"

The cat rose onto all fours and arched his back, his tail growing larger with his agitation. "Because she told me that if anything were to happen to her I must transfer my loyalty to you!"

Gee fell silent. It sounded very much like something Popo would do.... And the ill-tempered cat was behaving exactly as if he were being forced to do something he did not desire.

"I don't need your help," Gee said. "Protect my grandmother."

"Ignorant, arrogant, ungrateful git!" the cat snarled. "At least Melanie wasn't filled with such hubris! Your education is long overdue. Love and kindness are all very sweet and cozy, but ignorance is nobody's ally!"

A hard knot formed in Gee's throat. "What do you know about my sister?" Dark tendrils began to twist inside his chest and he clenched and unclenched his hands. Too much ... too many things were beginning to collapse.

"There is no point in talking to you when you know so little," the white cat scoffed. He padded in a circle and curled up on the cushion, turning his back to Gee. Annoyance emanated from the thick white fur of his hind end. He wrapped his tail around his body and extended a paw, protruding a single claw toward something on the large wooden table that served as the family gathering place and study area.

Gee approached the table. The old leather-bound book. Where Ms. Carlson had left the note. He didn't recognize the cover. He'd never seen his grandmother reading from it. No title or author name was written upon the cracked leather cover; he could, though, make out an embossed symbol. It looked like the yin-yang sign, but instead of a black and a white piece curling into each other there were three sections: black, white and grey.

"You want me to read this?" Gee asked.

"Unless you would prefer to eat it," the cat remarked.

Gee stood still, staring blankly at the cover of the ancient book. He shook his head. What was he doing, standing around arguing with a cat? His grandmother was in the hospital! For all he knew, he'd lost his wits and was talking to himself!

No, the cat was still there, its tail enormous with feline rage.

Gee ran to the tin of cash on the bookshelf. He grabbed all

the larger bills and crammed them into his pocket along with his keys.

"Where do you think you're going?" the cat hissed.

Gee ignored him. If he was hallucinating, he shouldn't encourage it by acknowledging it. And if he wasn't hallucinating, he had no reason to trust the cat.

"Come back here!" the cat yowled.

That didn't just happen, Gee decided. He tore out of the apartment and ran down the sidewalk toward the busy intersection. He spotted a yellow cab and raised his hand. Gee was inside before it had even come to a full stop. "Grace Women's Hospital," he said. "Please hurry."

The cab driver was silent, but he shot into traffic and wended between slower-moving cars.

Gee stared out the passenger window.

Now this is getting fun, his dark little voice snickered.

I did not just think that, Gee told himself. I would not think such a thing.

Who else could it be? the voice sniggered. *Just say it: me, myself and I!*

Gee began counting in prime numbers. 2, 3, 5, 7, 11, 13, 17.... The higher the number, the longer it took to figure out if it was prime. The numerical grinding occupied his thoughts and he kept at it, his lips moving as he divided in his head, until the cab pulled up in front of the hospital. Gee quickly paid the cabbie and ran through the main doors to the reception desk.

"She's not in a room yet. She's still in Emergency and will be held there until her first set of tests later on in the afternoon."

"I want to see her," Gee said. "I'm her grandson."

The receptionist's eyes skimmed over Gee's lanky hair, his wet clothing. "You're a minor, aren't you? You should wait until your mother gets here first."

"I don't have a mother," Gee said in a low voice. "My grandmother raised me. I'm her only family." He blinked. What if something happened to her . . . would he have to call her homophobic siblings? He had no idea what their phone numbers were. What would happen to the store? What would happen to him? Gee shook his head. "I really need to see her," he said. "Because— She doesn't understand English that well! I need to translate for her."

The receptionist raised her eyebrows, but the phone began to ring and a lineup of people was beginning to form behind him. "Go through those doors." She pointed with her pen. "Follow the blue line painted on the wall, all the way to Emergency."

Gee began to run.

"Walk!" the receptionist called after him.

The hallways in the hospital were busy. As he approached the Emergency ward, wheeled beds and stretchers began to line both sides of the corridor. The sound of people in pain, discomfort, someone's quiet weeping—was one of them his grandmother? Why weren't they put into proper rooms? Gee quickly glanced at each face through the lanky strands of his hair.

A teenage girl, vomit dried upon her clothing, stared blankly at the ceiling, her eyes dull. A middle-aged man, arms crossed atop his skull, groaned with pain. A woman stood at the foot of his stretcher, one hand clasped around his ankle. "He needs to see someone right away!" she cried out. "Can't someone give him something for the pain?"

A harried-looking nurse shushed her as she moved toward

them, and another stretcher was wheeled into the hallway to take up space along the corridor. It was so noisy. Busy and noisy.

Gee strode down the hall, searching for Popo's face.

A rough hand clamped around his skinny wrist.

Popo's eyes, the colour of chestnuts. Her eyes were tired, exhausted, but very much alive.

Gee hadn't known he'd been holding his breath until he began gasping.

Popo patted the back of his hand.

When he regained his control, Gee scanned Popo's face for some telltale sign of illness. She just looked old, tired, and very small inside the raised metal side-bars of the wheeled hospital bed.

"Ms. Carlson is to be blamed," she said decidedly, though her voice was quieter than when she spoke at home.

"What?" Gee asked.

Popo closed her eyes, but managed to smile. "Just a little dizziness. But the meddling librarian had to call the ambulance! *Che!* They can send her the bill. Popo will not pay for something she did not...." She dozed off before she could finish her sentence.

Gee stared impassively at her face. How could she be well, just yesterday, and then such an ill and old woman the next day?

You see, his inner darkness murmured. *You can rely upon no one. Not even your precious Popo. All is uncertainty. Everything you hold dear. Everything passes away. You're a fool if you think otherwise!*

Gee pulled his wrist out of his grandmother's lax hold. He turned to the nearest nurse. "Excuse me," he said.

The nurse, checking the pulse of a small child, ignored him.

Gee stepped closer and stared down upon her. "Excuse me," he whispered.

Something in his tone hit her hard. She jerked her face upward, blinking nervously.

Gee smiled without warmth. "Has anyone seen to my grandmother? What's wrong with her? And why isn't she in a proper room?"

The nurse glanced at the clipboard at the foot of Popo's bed. "The doctor has her scheduled for a series of tests. Her blood pressure was extremely low. Low enough that he wants to keep her overnight for observation. She's not in a room because there isn't a room to put her in." She pointedly looked up and down the crowded hallway. "If you have a problem with that, let the government know!" She moved to the next patient.

His grandmother's eyes were open again. "Popo might have overdone it last night," she rasped. "Popo forgets that she's seventy-five years old."

Seventy-five..., Gee thought wonderingly. They did not celebrate birthdays. He'd thought it was because Popo didn't know when his birthday was, but no one's birthday was celebrated. And Popo was seventy-five.

"I shouldn't have run off," he said. "I should have stayed to help you. Did you fix the window by yourself?"

"Not Grandson's fault." Popo flapped her hand. "Popo has been feeling a little dizzy for many months."

"What!"

"Che." Popo's eyes began closing again. "Thought it might be just an ear problem ... balance...." She fell asleep once more.

Gee glanced up and down the corridor. A few people had

dragged some chairs in from the waiting room so that they could sit beside their loved one. Gee leaned against the wall near Popo's head. He waited for word, more information, a move to a proper room, or for her tests, a doctor, but only nurses came and went, sometimes checking his grandmother's blood pressure and heart rate. Popo slipped in and out of sleep, like an invalid, and as the hours passed a small dark knot of emotion began to swell inside Gee's chest.

His face impassive, his feelings grew and seethed inside him.

It was all his fault. He shouldn't have left her last night with the broken window. He was such a fool. How could he not have seen that she was a frail old woman? He was so useless. So stupid. He—

No.... It wasn't his fault. It was Winston Chang's fault. If Winston hadn't harassed them, if he hadn't come back to smash the window, then his popo wouldn't have tipped into this bad medical emergency. She would have just rested, and got better, as she always did. It was Winston's fault, and Winston had to pay for what he'd done.

A touch upon Gee's upper arm. He whipped his face to catch the nurse's eyes. He stared, intently, and she recoiled, taking several steps backward.

"What is it?" Gee asked, letting his hair slide over his face once again.

It was the same nurse who had told him to complain to the government. "You've been here half the day. You should go home and rest, get something to eat. Even if she gets her tests today there won't be any results until tomorrow. You should rest and come back in the evening."

Gee thought it through. He glanced at his popo. She was sleeping, a small frown pinched between her white eyebrows.

"When she wakes up will you let her know I'll be back later?" Gee asked.

"Go on," Popo rasped, without opening her eyes. "Grandson only stayed so he could skip school!"

Gee smiled.

Popo reached up and patted him lightly on the cheek. "Grandson is a good boy. Stay at the house. Until you talk to Older Sister."

Gee shook his head. Melanie phoned on the third Sunday of every month. "Were you expecting a call?" he asked. But Popo had dozed off again.

"See," the nurse said. "Go on, now. It's nice to see a young man caring about his grandmother," she added before returning to the nurse's station.

It was almost two o'clock. Time enough to do what he needed to do.

"I'll be back later, Popo," Gee said.

"If something happens," Popo whispered. Her eyes were a little cloudy. Uncertain.

Gee swallowed hard. "Nothing will happen, Popo. You just rest for now."

"If something happens.... The cat...." She couldn't keep her eyes from closing, and breathed evenly, shallowly.

The cat! What about the cat? Gee's heart pounded slowly, loudly, inside his ears. What was going on? If Popo was talking about the same cat, then maybe he hadn't imagined a talking cat.

The cat might have really spoken. And if it did, what did his grandmother know about it? What did it mean about everything he thought was safe and real?

Gee shook his head. Too big, too many unknowns. What he knew for certain was that Winston Chang was going to pay for sending Popo to the hospital. He would deal with the cat later.

Chapter Five

He found her in the far corner of the almost-empty school parking lot with the other smokers. One leg bent at the knee, the treads of her heavy boot wedged into the chain-link fence, she held a cigarette in one hand, her purse dangling from the crook of her elbow. She was picking at the tips of her hair with the other hand, tugging off small clumps of red paint and dropping them on the ground.

"Cracker," he called.

The jeering, chattering voices quieted. A girl started giggling—Silence. Her friend had jabbed an elbow into her gut.

"Gee!" Cracker cried out happily. She dropped the cigarette and stubbed it out beneath her boot. "Told ya!" she shouted over her shoulder as she jogged toward him. When she reached him she was slightly breathless. Reeking of smoke.

"Where does Winston Chang live?" Gee asked.

"What? Who?" Cracker frowned.

"Winston Chang. The guy who drives the Hummer."

"Why? What happened? Did he come back today?"

Gee wondered how much he should tell her. He didn't want her thinking he wanted her company. "He vandalized our store last night."

"What!" Cracker asked incredulously. "Why didn't you tell me at the diner?"

Gee shrugged. "There was no point. And my grandmother didn't want more trouble. But now she's in the hospital." His voice had dropped to a low hiss. "And he's going to pay for that."

"He didn't hurt her, did he?" Cracker gasped.

"No," Gee said curtly. "But she spent the night fixing the window and she collapsed."

"Oh!" Cracker fumed. "What shall we do? Should we beat him up?"

"No." Gee shook his head. "My grandmother would really be upset if she found out. *We* are not going to do anything. *I* am going to trash his Hummer."

"Awwww, nice!" Cracker actually hopped with excitement. "I've always wanted to trash a Hummer!"

"You're not coming. Just tell me where he lives."

Cracker scowled. "You're not the boss of me! I'm not going to tell you unless I get to trash the Hummer too!"

Gee stared down at the dramatic black and white makeup on her face. He would have laughed at the childishness of her words if he didn't need the information so badly. Her black lipstick, her rumpled clothing from being out all night. Weren't her parents worried about her? Popo would never allow this kind of behaviour.

You can do anything you want now….

Gee shuddered.

Grandson is a good boy, Popo always said. And he was. He'd never gotten into trouble. Because if he did, he knew that it would disappoint her so very much. But if Popo wasn't there to remind him…. He wasn't slipping into trouble. Today was only an act of justice. He was righting a wrong, that was all. *They* were the victims. The victim had a right to fight back!

But Cracker—she was completely conspicuous and emotionally erratic. But … that might work in his favour; it was more difficult to catch two people at once. And if she had spoken the truth about being on probation…. "Okay, you're in," he said.

"Come on!" Cracker excitedly grabbed Gee's arm and began leading him toward the sidewalk.

GEE AND CRACKER were crouched behind a low concrete wall, waiting for a car to return and open the gate to the underground parking lot. The rain had pattered and dissipated into moody grey clouds, heavy and dark. The cold was beginning to stiffen Gee's arms and legs. He shifted his grip on the two-by-four he'd picked up at a nearby demolition site. There was a big nail embedded at one end that would add to the degree of damage.

Cracker pulled out a pack from her purse and lit her second cigarette.

"You have a hole in your heart," Gee stated. "And you smoke."

"Yes, Big Brother. And I also shoplift, kick small dogs and drink booze." Cracker glared.

Gee turned his gaze to the garage door. "No one is forcing you to stay," he said tonelessly.

Cracker didn't respond for several long seconds. She sighed, stubbed out the cigarette and stood up to stretch her knees.

A small sports car turned onto the sloping pavement toward the garage door.

Gee grabbed Cracker's arm to yank her down.

"We're in this together now," Cracker rasped, her breath heavy with cigarette smoke and coffee. "Whatever happens...."

A little shiver skated down Gee's spine.

The mechanical clanking of the garage door. The car whirred down the ramp and disappeared into the dimly lit parkade.

Gee and Cracker leapt over the little wall and followed it. Gee had to bend almost ninety degrees to make it under the lowering garage door. Cracker's breathing was heavy with effort, her boot buckles jangling loudly.

They ducked between an SUV and a Mini and waited as the driver parked her sports car and entered the elevator.

As soon as the door closed Gee and Cracker began trotting down the rows of parked cars. They kept hunched over at the waist in case there were security cameras.

With the two-by-four held tightly in his hand, Gee's heart pounded slow and heavy. His heart rate never seemed to quicken with exertion or excitement—it only grew louder.

Gee glanced at Cracker's face. Her eyes gleamed with excitement. He had his suspicions that Popo might not think very highly of Cracker. But he was doing this for his grandmother's sake.

Because the bigoted pig had taken power away from her—had brought doubt and fear into their home. Besides, it wasn't as if they were going to beat him up. Property damage hardly counted as vengeance.

A hint of a twisted smile curled along the edges of his lips.

"There it is!" Cracker pointed. She began to hiccup and giggle with glee.

"Shhhhhh!" Gee hissed.

Cracker clamped her hand over her mouth, but her eyes were wide and animated with feeling.

Gee gazed at her brilliant face. What must it be like, he wondered, to be so free with one's emotions? How vulnerable it made her. Such an open book.

And what would ever happen to him if he let himself go as she did?

Why don't you try? the little dark voice inside him giggled. *Just a little. It might feel really nice.*

Gee took a deep breath. He had always known he never should....

Cracker was yanking at his jacket sleeve. "See! See!" she whispered.

Gee concentrated on breathing. He was no longer angry. He was resolute. It was not his place to become personally involved with this act—he was only the messenger. He was sending a message to the pig dog that acts of ignorance and destruction would come back to him tenfold.

Gee tightened his fingers around his cudgel and straightened his shoulders. He let his hair fall over his face and began striding toward the vehicle.

Cracker hiccupped and clutched the sleeve of Gee's jacket with both hands.

He glanced down at her.

"I'm *not* hitting on you, I said!" Cracker whispered indignantly. "This is just nervousing!"

Gee did not respond. The Hummer seemed to almost glow, a moonlight halo that called to something deep inside him. His heart grew louder and louder inside his ears. He could feel the rush of artificially circulated air sliding down every strand of hair. A hyper-awareness of the *crunch, crunch* of some food debris beneath his sneakers. He slowly drew the two-by-four back, past his hip, then swung it side-arm, hard, *smash!* against the headlight.

The glass exploded. Glittering fragments flew, Cracker covering her eyes with her forearm, just as the car alarm began to honk and wail.

Cracker shrieked. Then began to laugh hysterically.

"Ten seconds," Gee said tersely. "Then run!"

Cracker raised her heavy boot and pounded her heel into the other headlight. Gee swung his cudgel again and again against the windshield. The glass cracked, a spiderweb of lines spreading outward.

Destroy the body, Gee thought. The windshield is easier to replace.

He alternated between kicking and pounding the yellow sides of the Hummer with his heel and the two-by-four. The doors dented inward with dull metallic thuds. Gee swung the cudgel in a vertical arc and pounded the nail through the roof. *Bang! Bang! Bang!* He punched holes into the metal, his mouth stretched into a wide loose grin.

Cracker, on the other side of the Hummer, was kicking in the metal. Gee could hear her panting and wheezing breathlessly with excitement. Gee yanked the embedded nail from the roof of the car and dragged its point along its body. *Screeeeeeeeeeeee,* metal against metal, a snaking line. Gee snapped his elbow backward to take out the side mirror. The glass popped and cracked simultaneously.

The sounds of destruction, Gee thought, were so sweet. So beautiful….

"No!" A voice. Enraged. Anguished.

Cracker peeped with fear.

Gee spun around.

The pig dog stood in the open stairwell, a dark silhouette in the framed doorway. His hands were clenched in tight fists. Gee ran around the Hummer, grabbed Cracker's arm and belted toward the fire exit, Cracker staggering behind him, scarcely able to keep up. "Faster," Gee said tersely.

He could feel the weight of her. Slowing him. He could hear the pig dog's heavy pounding steps.

He should let her go…. Gee hadn't asked for her help—she'd joined him of her own accord.

The weight of her lagging body fell from his grip. Cracker had dropped to her knees. Hands flat on the dirty pavement. The contents of her purse scattered on the ground. She was gasping, almost retching, for breath.

The pig dog a few metres behind her. His burls of fists.

Gee's eyes narrowed. He didn't owe her anything. He had no friends. A few more strides to the exit door and he was gone. He back to his life, and Cracker back on her own track, just as they'd been before she'd ever spoken to him. Gee's hand clasped the doorknob. He didn't need her, nor did he want her in his life.

Cracker screamed.

Unable to stop himself, Gee looked back.

Winston had grabbed Cracker by her hair. She raised her hands, trying to break his hold, but he continued yanking upward to draw her to her feet.

Gee stared. Winston wouldn't hurt her. He would just call the cops and Cracker would be charged with property damage.... She'd maybe have to do community service. Or spend some time in a juvenile home. Winston hadn't seen his face, so he couldn't be charged. Gee could just walk away from it all.

Cracker's gasping breath quickened. Short panting, desperate for air.

She couldn't take all the excitement. Her heart....

Gee's own heart thudded heavily inside his narrow chest. His palms felt sticky. He watched as Cracker flailed for her skirt pockets, attempting to plunge her hands into the messy folds of the crinkly material.

Winston grabbed her wrists.

The pavement blurred, stretched beneath Gee's steps. The parked vehicles loomed dark, silent. Cracker's eyes, wide, panicked.

Winston's eyes gleamed as he watched Gee running toward him. He released one of Cracker's wrists. She thrust her freed hand into her pocket just as Gee reached them.

Gee didn't know why he did it. His body took over. He smacked the flat of his palm into Winston's face, completely covering his nose and mouth.

Winston clamped his free hand around Gee's throat. Squeezed.

Gee could feel something in his larynx beginning to give. This is dangerous, he observed, coolly. You could very well die.

The small dark silent place deep inside him, the seed that had to be contained at all costs—the shell began to give. Minute cracks, spreading outward, finally weakening, a howling rage bursting through the seams. Roiling, swelling with sickening stench, sour, mildewed and noxious.

What was happening? Gee was choking, what was—

Elation swelled, bright, powerful. Awful. He could do anything.

Anything!

Gee could feel Winston twisting his face beneath his palm. His skin tingled. The boy's struggles were somehow so deeply gratifying.... The smell of curdled milk filled his nostrils and he closed his eyes. It reminded him of something he could not name. His palm growing moist, soft. *Spreading.*

"Ohmygod—" Cracker's voice broke.

Gee opened his eyes.

The pig dog no longer had his fist in the girl's hair.

Cracker was standing a metre away, her eyes wide, staring with horror. Something in her hand. She held it like a spray can.

Gee, following Cracker's line of sight, looked down. Winston was on his knees, his hands swiping weakly at Gee's bony wrist.

The skin from Gee's palm had spread, webbed, stretching thin between his fingers, white and elastic. Fingers, palm, elongated and pliant, his hand covered the boy's entire face, wrapping around half his skull to tenderly cover both ears. Gee could feel the loose skin flap in and out of the boy's open mouth as he desperately sucked for air.

Ticklish. Obscene. Monstrous.

Winston clawed weakly at Gee's arm, trying to tear away his suffocating hold.

Gee stared down at the struggling boy. On his knees. His gasps smothered, growing weaker and weaker. He was so very, very pathetic. Ugly. Ignoble. Disgusting.

"Stop it, Gee!" Cracker shouted. "That's enough!"

Just a little longer, the growing darkness inside him whispered. *In a few moments he'll be dead....*

Cracker raised her hand.

Gee almost smiled. Did she think a slap could stop him?

Zsssssssst.

Wet, cool. What—

Flames seared his skin. Eyes burning, tearing— Then the molecules hit his lungs and Gee began coughing, whooping for air.

The maddening pain. As if he were being stung by wasps. All over his face, the inside of his mouth, down his throat. His burning lungs. Gee released his hold on the boy's face to claw at his own eyes.

"Don't touch it!" Cracker shouted. She sounded far away. "You'll make it worse. It's pepper spray. Keep your eyes closed. I'm sorry! I had to stop you!"

Gee could scarcely hear her. Unable to stop himself, he tried to wipe the pain away. His fingertips *sank* into his face.

As if it were melting.

"Ohgaawwd." Cracker's voice was shaking. "Your *face*...."

Gee pulled his hands away. His skin— He could feel clots adhering to the tips of his fingers, stretching, like long strands of glue.

The pain. Receding. Growing numb.

His eyes. The tears were growing thicker. No longer liquid. Hardening. They were sealed shut. Gee swiped the back of his gooey hand over his sealed eyelids, and it was as if a sticky melted layer was sloughing from his entire face.

The sound of retching. Deep. Low. It was Winston. He hadn't died.

The jangling sound of boot buckles, pounding footsteps, receding. Gone. Cracker had run away. And Gee could finally see once more. In his hands, stretching in long white strands, were the remnants of his face....

His face.

He should be blind. He should be writhing with pain.

He felt nothing.

A soft *plat*, *plat*, *plat* of something moist hitting the dirty pavement. Gee looked down. Lumps of white melty skin dangled from his fingertips, stretching to the breaking point, dripping into a flat gluey pool. A wrinkly skin started forming on the surface as it began to harden.

The rage that had burst from his hidden place—it was gone. And what was left, Gee thought numbly.

What *am* I! the childish part of him screamed.

Noisy, he realized. So much noise. The Hummer was still honking and wailing and the wretched boy was crawling backward, away from Gee. Something in his eyes was broken and fearful.

Gee turned and walked away.

Chapter Six

Rain streamed down his face and his clothes were completely sodden, but Gee scarcely noticed the cold. Heavy wet clumps of hair stuck to his face and water dribbled down his neck. He did not shiver. He walked with his gaze locked to a point a metre ahead of him. If he kept on walking, looking straight ahead, he would not have to look upon the reflection of his own face.

His footsteps faltered and he came to a stop. Gee slowly raised his head to discover the familiar shape of Rainbow Market, their living space above it. All the windows were dark.

That's right, he thought dimly, Popo is in the hospital. So she couldn't help him. Popo didn't know that the world had changed today.

Don't go inside, the childish part of him entreated. Once you go in, the bad thing will happen. The bad thing that you've known has been there all along. Just keep on walking. Popo will worry, but you're old enough to quit school and find work. After a while you can send her a postcard, as Older Sister does, to say you're doing fine.... It's okay to have your own life, away from everybody. It doesn't mean you're a bad person. You're only a bad person if the people you love see you being bad....

A harsh sound burst free from his mouth. He clamped his arms around his middle, sealed tight his lips. If another sound broke out he wouldn't be able to stop it. His shoulders shook with the effort to hold it all inside. His eyes were dry.

Several minutes passed.

Gee's arms dropped to his sides. They hung, limp, his shoulders slumped. Exhausted. He slowly walked to the store entrance and unlocked the door.

The familiar odours of sweet fruit, musty herbs and dust filled his senses. Gee closed his eyes and inhaled deeply. He trudged up the narrow flight of steps that led to their upstairs home, the old boards alternately creaking and shrieking, a natural alarm system installed by time. Loud enough, Gee thought, to wake the dead.

If Popo were home, she would turn on the lights. She would pad to the kitchen and put on the kettle for tea. She'd tell him to sit and would look at him with her dark, penetrating eyes, and she would see that ugly thing inside him. If she were home he'd have to watch the love in her eyes ... turning. To fear and disgust. It was good that she wasn't home.

Gee stepped through the upstairs door and stood in the darkness. He was very much alone. A stillness hung in the air. Something was not right.

His heart began to thud, slowly, heavily. There had been a cat. A talking cat, Gee thought distantly.

"Here, kitty, kitty, kitty." A high giggle escaped his lips. Gee slapped his hand over his mouth, his dark eyes overlarge in his pale, pale face.

The lights. Hadn't he left them on when he'd run out? He flicked the switch and the glare blinded him for several seconds.

If emptiness was a presence it was heavy and oppressive. He glanced at the clock on the wall beside the large orange tree. What had happened to time? There was something he was supposed to do. He couldn't remember what it was.

Gee caught a flash of white in the corner of his eye. He spun around, only to realize that it was the blurry reflection of his face in the glass of the display cabinet. Gee spun away before he could focus on the details. He fought the compulsion to touch his cheeks with his fingertips. No! No! All of it, hallucinations. Please, he thought. Let it be hallucinations.... Because if it were real. If it were true.

His chest felt tight. *Squeezed.* His breath was a little shallow. Rapid. "It's okay," he whispered. "Everything is going to be okay."

"Actually, it's not," a gritty voice growled.

Gee twitched, but he did not cry out. He slowly turned around.

The fat white cat lay sprawled atop the old book on the dining room table. His tail slowly bobbed up and down as he stared disinterestedly across the room.

Gee dragged his forearm across his eyes. He was groggy from all the shocking things that had happened.

Look at you, the small dark voice deep inside him laughed. *You're a face-melting freak of nature, an orphan, a whacko who's talking to a cat. The only person who likes you is probably dying. And that dark and bad thing that you've felt all along—the one you could never escape? Your shadow companion.... It's finally caught up to you.*

"You're running out of time. Not that I care. But Ming Wei still cares, who knows why. There are things you need to do."

"I don't want to," Gee whispered.

"I don't want to!" the cat mimicked. "I'm scaaaaared!"

Something warm, wet, landed on Gee's slender wrist. It was white, a dab of something that hardened as it cooled. Like a bead of melted wax. Two droplets trailed down his cheek and Gee felt the slightest pinch of skin. He raised his hand to brush at the sensation.

Tears, Gee thought. I'm crying. He could not remember the last time he cried.

Did teardrops that turned solid count as real crying? Gee didn't know.

He was hollow. Empty. Emptiness was good. Emptiness meant there was nothing inside that would break and shatter.

"You're in danger, and you draw danger to the one you love the most!" The cat was standing, his tail vertical with displeasure. But the tip couldn't help but flop a little to the side.

Gee shook his head. He rubbed the back of his hand across his eyes. The hardened tears fell to the floor like more bits of wax. "No." His voice was harsh. "Not Popo."

"Then read this book!" The cat leapt off the table and landed on the red velvet cushion of the big chair by the window. He turned thrice before covering his face with his tail. "There you will find the answers to many of your questions."

Gee stared at the old tome. Was the cat speaking the truth? And if the book did contain answers to his questions, what if he didn't like what he read? A large knot was forming inside his chest. Sending tendrils up his esophagus, choking his breath. Because whatever was written inside that book had the power to destroy his world....

Gee took a long shuddering breath. He pushed the flop of dark hair back off his forehead and pulled the wooden chair away from the edge of the table. He sat down. His hand did not shake when he reached for the book. He let the cover fall open, and a musty, slightly cinnamon scent filled his nostrils. It was not unpleasant.

The first page was blank, opaque and brittle. Gee slowly turned it to reveal the next page. It was adorned with the same round symbol, the pieces curling together, entwined, in black, white and grey, but it was smaller than the one on the outside cover. Beneath it was a peculiar writing that undulated between cursive and ... something else.

Gee wondered if it was something like Sanskrit, or maybe Hebrew, a language whose letters he could not decipher. It was odd—the longer he stared at the flow of writing, the more he felt he could almost *see* it. Gee frowned and squinted. He could almost read it, the same feeling as a forgotten person's name, on the tip of the tongue.... Suddenly the illegible letters seem to shift—and then meaning followed.

The Book of the Realms

Gee shuddered.

No, the childish part of him pleaded. I don't want to. It's not fair. I didn't ask for any of this. It's not fair!

"Tick tock, tick tock," the cat muttered, his rounded hindquarters facing Gee, his droll voice muffled by the velvet back of the chair.

Gee could picture it clearly: he would snatch up the book and throw it, hard, at the awful cat. Hard enough to break bones. The cat would yowl with shock, his legs twitching spasmodically. Gee would knock the cat to the ground and kick him across the floor, repeatedly, until he was as loose and wretched as a dirty dishrag.

The fur on the cat's rump expanded as he turned one ear backward. As if he could hear what Gee was thinking.

And maybe he can, Gee thought. He stared at the title page of the book once more. He took a deep breath. Held. Then flipped the page.

He began to read.

THE *CHIRRUP CHIRRUP CHE-REE* of a robin seeped through Gee's stasis, and he slowly raised his head from the last page of *The Book of the Realms*. He did not know for how long he had been staring at it. His neck was sore.

Daylight shone through the crack between the two folds of curtain. The rain had stopped while he read through the darkest hours but he could not say when. He turned his head.

The cat was no longer on the red velvet chair. A few white hairs clung to the dense nap of the upholstery, and the seat was slightly indented.

Gee closed the book so that the back faced upward. In the centre was a small, embossed circular symbol. It was much smaller than the image on the front cover and the details were worn away with time. He bent a little closer.

It wasn't the three-pieced yin-yang symbol.

A spiral.... As he stared it began to swirl, turning inward and inward; he followed the lines, perpetually twining and twining and twining into the next dimension that spun around around around—

Gee tore his eyes away.

The light shining through the crack in the curtains was golden yellow. There was a dull, hollow pain in his stomach. Gee considered this sensation. Hunger, he realized. He was hungry. Popo was in the hospital and he had promised he'd go back yesterday evening.

And he, Gee, had once been a monster.

Gee stared at the empty red chair.

He did not believe in monsters. He believed in rationality. He believed in observation. The only monsters he could identify were human—the ones who'd been formed from cruelty and ignorance. The bigots, the bullies, the power-hungry. People with monstrous behaviour. Real monsters did not exist.

The small, tight dark voice inside him crowed with laughter. *Oh, you liar! You know they do,* the ugly thing whispered. *That's why no one loves you. Why your sister cannot bear being around you. Why there is nowhere for you to belong. Ohhhhh, you know all right. You've known all along. Once a monster, always a monster....*

"N-no!" Gee's voice, long unused, was hoarse. The sound rang through the empty room.

Something clicked, like claws tapping against metal. Gee twisted his head to look behind him.

No one was there.

The air *whooshed* as the furnace kicked in. Gee's heart thudded. He licked his dry lips. He folded his fear smaller and smaller, as he had folded the letter from Ms. Carlson. His rational mind took over.

The language of the book is vague, Gee thought. It's symbolic. Symbolism can be decoded in whatever way the reader chooses. And who knew who wrote the book? Books like this weren't meant to be taken literally—just like the Bible.

He whipt his white snake-like tongue and snatched
the wise woman.
Wrapt her up and inside his maw.
He engulfed her.

Gee shook his head as the stanza, unbidden, formed in his consciousness. It couldn't be real. None of it was real. He was a high school student. He would graduate next year and he would go to university like his older sister. There had been a stray cat in their home and he had imagined it had spoken to him because he was so very tired, and hungry, and his grandmother was ill.

Because he was scared....

Her mother cleaved him, cracking open like a
peach pit
split the tender centre mewling, a monster
turned a baby.

They snatched up the infant, innocent, beastly, from Half World they fled, they fled to the Realm of Flesh.

Gee could not stop the words in the terrible book from popping up in his mind. The images that formed filled him with fear and fascination. Confusion. A creeping sense of recognition. The déjà vu of dreams....

Half World. The words whispered, echoed inside him. Like something almost familiar. Something he'd forgotten—

How could Popo do this to him?

Gee pounded the heels of his fists on the thick table. He pounded and pounded until he could feel the physical pain. Maybe Popo had written this book herself.... Maybe it was an elaborate psychological experiment? Maybe she was a psychotic, abusive person.

Those irregularities in his adoption.... There were no papers. He had no birth certificate. His grandmother had found someone to forge documents. It had cost a lot of money.

Popo had kidnapped him from somewhere and his real parents were still looking for him, far far away. That made more sense than the gibberish book.

He wasn't a murderous monster from a different Realm! Ridiculous! Mad.

Popo! he raged. You did this to me! It's all *your* fault! That's why he didn't have a real name. Baby G. Like a foundling in a basket. Baby X. John Doe. Why hadn't she given him a proper name? The school had written his name as "Gee" when they saw Ms. Wei, saw that his papers identified him only as "G." They must have thought she was illiterate. Did the teachers think it would make him more Asian? Because it hadn't! When he'd finally asked his popo about his real name, she had been silent for a long time.

You must seek your own name, she finally said. When the time comes.

Her words had turned him to stone. And he asked her nothing more.

Popo hadn't given him a proper name. Because she felt guilty. She had no right to name him. She had kidnapped him during his infancy—*she* was the monster.

Gee thrust himself away from the table, the chair clattering loudly against the hardwood floor. He stood, staring down at the awful, awful book. "Not me!" he hissed. His hands knotted into fists.

What about your face, the dark little voice inside him crowed. *How do you explain what happened in the car park? Everyone's faces just dribble and melt off like that, don't they?*

He had to see. It was the only way.

Gee didn't know that his arms were clamped around his middle. With his flop of dark hair hanging halfway down his face, he stared at his feet as he approached the washroom. His pale slender hand floated above the doorknob. The stickiness of his palm against smooth metal. The door creaked. An errant, muted ray of sunlight shone through the frosted glass of the window. A faint odour of mildew lingered in the air. Gee shuddered.

He approached the mirror above the sink. His footsteps heavy. His arms clutched his middle so tightly it bordered on pain. Gee slowly raised his head and his dark hair slid to the sides, revealing his face.

He stared. His skin was not rucked, twisted, like a burn victim's. His skin was smooth, clear, as it was before everything had happened. His black irises, flat, expressionless, gazed back from his reflection. Everything was the same.

Everything was not the same.

"It's not the outside that counts," the cat singsonged in a preachy falsetto.

Gee twitched, but his expression did not change. The cat was crouched in the corner, almost perfectly camouflaged against the white walls. Only his cold yellow-green eyes stood out, distinct.

"What matters the most is what's on the *inside*," the cat concluded feelingly.

Gee left the room.

He was hungry. He would eat first. Everything was shifting, and he didn't know who or what to believe. He needed corroboration. From another human being. After he ate he'd go back to the hospital and ask his grandmother about the book. About the cat.

A roaring inside his head. Like a winter storm in a nightmare forest.

What if his grandmother couldn't be believed? What then? Who could he trust? Certainly not the cat. He couldn't rely on the words of a talking cat.

Something erupted from his lips. A hoarse croaking sound. For a moment Gee wondered if he was going to vomit. The sound burst out again.

Laughing. He was laughing—

The phone rang.

Gee leapt. His heart thudded ponderously inside his narrow

chest. The loud ringing filled up the hollow room. He did not want to answer it.

Make everything go away, the childishness inside him pleaded. Make it stop.... Gee shook his head. It was probably Ms. Carlson, calling to make sure he'd received the note, that he was okay. He picked up the phone. "Hello," he said, his throat dry.

A digital silence.

The sudden static was so loud that Gee had to pull the receiver away from his ear.

"What's happened?" The tinny voice on the other end of the line sounded very far away, but the strength and intensity still reached him.

For a moment Gee could not say who the familiar unfamiliar person was.

"Older Sister," he whispered.

The line crackled. His sister was speaking, but the sound was morphing in and out of meaning.

"I can't hear you!" Gee cried.

A mechanical static buzz.

Gee began shouting, in case his sister could hear him, even though he was unable to hear her. "Popo is in hospital. She fainted! Then had a bad headache. It might be a stroke!"

The receiver whined, high-pitched and awful.

"—in twenty-four hours!" the thin tinny voice reached him once more.

"What!" Gee shouted.

The line was dead.

Chapter Seven

Gee replaced the receiver in the cradle. Older Sister had phoned.... Twenty-four hours, she said. She must mean that she was on her way. From Peru.... Popo was right. Older Sister had realized something had happened. And she was coming back.

A wave of relief washed through him and Gee closed his eyes. Whatever was happening, whatever that cryptic book really meant, no matter if talking animals existed—he was not alone. Everything would be okay....

"It approaches." The cat's voice was small. Weary. He sat on his haunches by Gee's feet.

Iciness skittered down Gee's neck. "What...." He had meant to sound angry, but his voice wobbled and faded away.

The unpleasant cat was staring at his paws. His tail a flat dead thing upon the floorboards.

Silence.

Complete. Heavy, the very air was compressed with it. The inside of Gee's ears rang. A sourness rose from his maw, spreading across his tongue. He wanted to spit the foul taste out of his mouth.

The cat leapt.

Shocked, Gee was paralyzed. The cat's heavy body thudded against Gee's chest, but his claws did not sink into his flesh. The cat's claws were sheathed, and with nothing on which to snag, his round body began sliding downward.

Instinctively, Gee cradled his arms around the miserable creature.

The old cat's long sigh ended with a little purr.

Or, Gee thought, the heartless creature had indigestion.

"You must take me with you," the white cat hissed. His claws prickled against Gee's chest for a brief moment before they were retracted. "Whatever happens, you must take me with you. Darkness comes and you are not ready. But still, you must go." The cat shook his head. "Ming Wei! The things I do for you!"

The room was cold. The room was freezing. Yet the light that slipped through the cracks of the curtains was buttery yellow.

"What darkness? Take you where? Tell me!" Gee cried.

The cat did not respond. His head was tilted to one side, one ear sweeping for sounds Gee could not hear. The thudding of Gee's heart filled his head.

"Your past," the cat finally whispered. "It is your past ... in Half World. Remember...." The cat's voice was faint. Something was happening to his body; it was shifting, shimmering, from fur and flesh into a different kind of matter. "Your past does not have to be your future." The cat faded, almost completely transparent and weightless, before suddenly *contracting*. Something small and solid fell to the wooden floor with a dull *clunk*.

A small white stone sculpture, slightly larger than a walnut, lolled from side to side before lying still.

Gee crouched down to pick it up. The details were worn down with age, with time, and all that remained were hints of pointed ears, a sweeping tail curled around the hindquarters of a crouching cat.

Creaaaak.

It was the first step at the bottom of the stairway.

Gee's heart began to thud.

Slowly, steadily, each step screeched and squealed as someone began to climb the flight of stairs.

Gee stood, his fingers clenching the cat sculpture inside his fist. Someone had entered the store and was approaching their home.

They weren't his popo's footsteps. Popo stomped hard enough to frighten mice from entering the building. The person climbing the stairs took slow, measured steps. Careful. Implacable.

Gee's heart thudded with pain.

Then a light bloomed inside his chest. It was completely irrational—he knew that. But didn't the talking cat prove that irrational things were sometimes possible?

"Older Sister!" Gee cried out, his voice childish. Joyful. Melanie had magicked her way home somehow. She had special powers, too. Like the talking cat. Popo had been speaking the truth. Older Sister had known when there was trouble and she had phoned! And now she'd returned to make everything okay.

The creaking continued upward. Closer and closer.

"Older Sister...."

The person did not answer.

Cold, dankness began permeating the air. A deep-locked chill that sank into the bones. Aching. A waft of cold wintry brine.... It was the smell of the ocean. An icy, darkly, greenly ocean that claimed all who fell into its depths.

Swish. Swish. Swish.

The sound of the creaking boards, coming ever closer, could not drown out the other sound. Slightly liquid, moist. *Dripping.* The rich wet pungent odour of wet kelp.

Gee shuddered. It was not Older Sister. Not the older sister he knew.

What did he *know*? Maybe this *was* Older Sister. Her dark secret. Everything was coming undone.

The cat. He had said that it was his past, coming for him.

Half World.... Gee swallowed hard. He had wondered his whole life: Who was he? Where did he come from? What was his real name...? And now his past was coming up the stairs, smelling like death.

The ceiling spun a nauseatingly slow circle. Hungry. He was so intensely hungry. He wanted to vomit.

Squish. Slide. Squish. Slide.

The sound stopped.

It was on the other side of the door. Seeping beneath the door. It spread, slowly inward. The smell of cold wet salt. Staining the old wooden floor.

Gee watched it creep into the room from the other side of the closed door. The sound of breathing, like a distant tide, ebbing and flowing.

"Knock, knock?" a low playful voice said.

Gee clamped his empty hand over his mouth. He didn't know if he was holding back a guffaw or a scream.

"Knock, knock!" the voice repeated.

Maybe it was like vampire lore, Gee thought desperately. If you don't invite them in, you don't have to be the victim. If he said nothing maybe the creature would move on to the next victim down the street. It wouldn't have to be him. Not this time.

Gee squeezed hard on the stone sculpture inside his moist palm. Something stabbed his tender flesh. He twitched with pain, and opened his fist.

Protruding out of the stone, extending from one of the faintly defined paws, was a single live claw. Gee stared, mesmerized, as the living claw retracted inside the stone.

White Cat had said his past was coming for him. White Cat had said to take him with him....

Gee's shoulders sagged as he closed his fist. He didn't know what choices he had ... if any at all. And in the end, would it make any difference? And beneath the awful fear—

He was curious....

"Knock, knock," the low voice softly whispered once more.

The slow thud of his heart was so loud. Surely it could be heard from the other side of the door.

"W-who's there?" Gee's voice cracked.

Dank silence.

The low voice began to laugh. A rich sound, almost charming.

"Everything you want," the voice promised seductively. "All that was yours in the past will be yours once again." There was a pause. As if the person were taking a breath. Or swallowing. "Open the door."

Gee didn't know that his free hand was pressed against the

hollow of his throat until he felt the slow, heavy *thud, thud* of his heartbeat throbbing against his sticky palm.

You don't have to, the part of him that was still a small child pleaded. You can escape out the window, climb down the drain-pipe. You can dangle from the ledge and jump. It's not so far. You can run away and keep on running until all of this is so far behind it will never catch up again. It's okay. It doesn't mean you're a coward. Sometimes you have to run away to save your life.

Please.

Don't open the door.

Open it.

Don't open it.

Open it.

Yes.

No.

Maybe so.

Yes, no, maybe so!

Like the games the other children used to play in kindergarten....

Gee sighed wearily, his slender shoulders sagging beneath the weight of darkness.

He felt a thousand years old. And maybe he was, after all.

He released the death grip on his own throat. Skin pulled away from skin with a moist *squelch*. He stretched his hand, slowly, toward the doorknob. Only the tips of his fingers betrayed his fear, shaking almost imperceptibly. The coolness of the metal knob felt pleasant beneath his moist palm. Shivers skittered down the length of his entire body.

Good boy, the dark voice inside him praised.

Gee opened the door.

Chapter Eight

The woman reeked of the sea; the dark underside of a winter dock, of the earth's cold blood. Her wet, silky black hair was plastered to her head, clinging to the blue-white skin of her long neck like strands of seaweed. Her dark eyes were eloquent and liquid as a seal's....

Gee's heart clenched.

Her lips were grey in the pale, bloodless complexion of her face. And her dark, wet, patched dress clung to her body, the hem heavy, pooling behind her.

Drip. Drip. Drip.

Water fell from her odd black sleeves. They were of different lengths. The right sleeve, with its tapered end, hung almost to her ankle, her hand completely covered by the skin-tight material. The other sleeve ended by her waist. And the edge was ragged. Chunky.

The skin at the base of Gee's neck crawled. Something about her arms was *wrong.* Not because she was an amputee, but the sleeve, the torn place—

"Hasn't it been such a long time?" the woman sighed.

Gee took a step backward. A half-smile quivered upon her lips. A glimpse of something black inside her mouth.... He grimaced. What was she *eating*?

"Your hair is black," the woman murmured. "You're so *young*!" Tipping her head back, her mouth wide open, she began to laugh and Gee could see ... the black thing inside her mouth....

It was her tongue.

He backed away from her until the edge of the large table stopped him. The table leg dragged loudly against the floor.

The woman's eyes narrowed. Her black eyes gleamed. "Don't you remember me?"

Gee swallowed. He shook his head.

Popo! he begged. Help me! He sidled along the edge of the table, desperate to get to the other side.

The woman lowered her eyelids, tilting her head dramatically. "*Ohhhh*, he doesn't remember." She shook her head and water droplets flew from the tips of her hair, a spattering of wetness across Gee's cheek. "After all the trouble I had to go through!" she snarled, her face twisting with rage and madness. "Lilla had to pay the toll!"

Gee froze. The solid lump of the cat clenched inside his hand. He had no idea what she was talking about. And he was afraid.

As if a switch had been flicked the madness melted from the woman's face and she was lovely once more. "I'm *Ilanna*. Remember, stupid?" she teased, taking a step toward him. "We go *waaaaay* back, my darling."

She began to move her right arm, the one that was intact. The shorter limb remained hanging limp and ragged at her slender waist. Her right arm, sinuous and seductive, began weaving through the air....

So beautiful, thought Gee. So fluid. He shuddered, unable to distinguish between desire and horror.

Writhing, bending, twining, jointless and impossible. The arm rippled like a ribbon in water, a supple strand of kelp undulating in deep currents. Goosebumps swept over Gee's skin. His mouth dry. Disgusting.

So sensual....

The dark skin-tight material extended past the woman's wrist and completely encased her hand. Why was it hidden, Gee wondered. He could see how the tapered tip was pinned down with a shiny button with a black centre. Her arm was so very long....

The smaller dark circle in the button *contracted*.

Gee frowned. It must have been the angle of light, he thought. That's all.

The tip of the sleeve began to part. Splitting open, wider and wider. Gee couldn't help staring, entranced, waiting to see her mysterious hand revealed.... But there was no hand. Nothing but the open V of the sleeve—

Sharp needle teeth. The inside of her sleeve was lined with teeth.

Gee's heart thudded inside his hollow chest. Her arm wasn't covered with a long sleeve. It wasn't wet dark cloth.

Skin. Black, shiny, moist skin, slightly mottled with faint circles. Not a glinting button. It was an eye. The open sleeve was the gaping maw of a thick black eel....

The eel twisted, whipped toward Gee's face, snapping, a hair's breadth from his cheek. He choked, swinging his arms belatedly as he stumbled backward. But the eel had already retreated, posing S-shaped beside its mistress, ready to strike once more.

"Rilla," the woman chided. "Stop it! I'm still very cross with you. For what you did to Lilla." She gazed sadly upon the black stump of her partial left arm hanging dead beside her waist. "You should have waited until *I* had decided who would pay the toll. I only keep you now because you're the only eel I have left to serve as my arm!"

Gee swallowed. Not her *arm.*

Her left *eel.*

A sound erupted from between his lips. *"Ha, ha, ha, ha!"* Gee couldn't help himself. *"Hee, hee, hee, hee!"*

Ilanna threw back her head and laughed with him.

A needle of pain pierced the centre of Gee's palm. He yelped and opened his hand. The stone cat fell to the wooden floor with a loud *clunk.* Gee's heart stopped.

Rilla slowly lowered her tapered head toward the fallen object, Ilanna bending at the waist so that the eel could reach it. Rilla poked the stone with her snout and the figurine slid a few inches across the floor. The eel turned her head to stare up at the woman with her glittering eyes.

"Th-that's mine!" Gee's heartbeat thudded too loud inside his head.

Ilanna's eyes narrowed. Something passed between the woman and her eel— Rilla swung her head back to the stone cat and retrieved it in her jaws.

Fool, Gee thought. You're giving everything away. She says she knows you. If it's true that gives her the advantage. He observed the eel placing the cat in a patched pocket of Ilanna's dress. He had to hide his uncertainty from her.

"I'll keep it for you," she smiled. "Keep it safe."

Gee thought for a few seconds. "Thank you," he said. His right hand tightened into a fist. How strong was an eel? How strong, Ilanna? Had Rilla really ripped away the other eel arm? What did this monstrosity want?

Ilanna behaved as if she knew him.... He had never seen her before in his life. Where did they come from? Not his world. Not the world he shared with his popo.

The other place, the dark voice inside him whispered. *Deep inside, you know, you know, you know.... Half World.*

Gee's head sagged. He stared at the floor. Please, the childish part of him begged. Anyone. Help me.

"What am I going to do with you." Ilanna shook her head. "You're so pathetically *weak*. You're still such a *child*. Karu will destroy you and all this delightful travel would have been for nothing!"

Gee slowly raised his head. He stepped toward the corpse-white woman, close enough to feel the cold emanating from her core. The reek of kelp filled his nostrils. She was half a head shorter than he was and he stared into her eyes. Down, down, he looked his fill, and she did not break his gaze. Her eyes seemed to widen, eager, greedy. He reached for her darkness with his own.

"*Ohhhhhh*, yes," she smiled, "I knew it! I knew that horrid girl could not keep you from us. I knew it was only a matter of time for you to ripen and return to us in Half World."

Older Sister, he thought dimly. As the old book said. Melanie had carried him out and brought him to the Realm of Flesh.

It was all true.

The eel began nosing into the gap of his jacket sleeve.

"That *Melanie* stole you from your true inheritance," Ilanna whispered as Rilla's gelid, slimy body swirled around his slender arm, sliding upward, inside his clothing. "She took you away from what is rightfully yours."

Gee swallowed. "M-my real parents?"

Ilanna's eyes widened and she smiled, nodding encouragingly. "*Yesssss*. Your true father and mother are waiting for you," she breathed. "They've missed you so. As I have. We need you to come back...."

The eel slicked upward to the opening at his neck. Gee's skin crawled. Grotesque. Delicious.

"Everyone's waiting for you in Half World."

The little boy inside him almost cried aloud. His real parents—the parents he could not remember. A place where he might have belonged.

The eel squeezed its dense muscles around the length of Gee's arm. Slimy. His skin began to burn and itch. He was yanked close against Ilanna's icy body.

"You're very pretty right now," Ilanna whispered. "We can take the time to get reacquainted."

"Gee?"

The young voice, slightly muffled and uncertain, rose up from the store below.

Gee went still.

Rilla whipped out of Gee's sleeve and reared back toward her mistress. Ilanna's eyes narrowed, her thin nostrils quivering. Her little black tongue began peeking out from between her lips. "Is that what you're called now? *Gee?*" she whispered. "How quaint. How amusing."

"Gee, are you upstairs?" the voice called.

Something writhed inside Gee's chest. What was *she* doing here?

"I'm coming up," Cracker said. The wooden boards began shrieking as she climbed the stairs. "Okay?"

A little smile quivered on Ilanna's thin lips. Rilla flopped down to hang motionlessly at her side.

And Gee finally saw— The tattered edges at Ilanna's shoulder weren't messy seams of her dress, but ragged grey pieces of skin and flesh. The eel's tail was wedged inside the woman's empty shoulder socket. Where her human arm had once been brutally torn out.

The hairs on the back of his neck stood out. Was she even *alive*?

Are you? the darkness inside him tittered.

"I'm coming in…." Cracker was right outside the door.

If he warned her, would she listen? If he warned her would she be more at risk? What should he do? The cat was right, after all. Ignorance was no one's ally…. Gee's lips parted, his hand rising—

The door swung open.

Cracker stood, both arms outstretched, holding her canister of pepper spray like a gun.

Chapter Nine

Cracker pointed the nozzle directly at Gee's face. Her bright eyes were wide with caution, suspicion.

Gee glared. Go away! he emoted. Run while you can!

Cracker took in Ilanna, the dripping wet dress, the cold seeping from her body. She stared at Ilanna's mismatched black arms. Rilla, unable to stop herself, quivered with glee.

Cracker swung the spray can toward Ilanna's face instead.

"Is this your little friend?" Ilanna smiled. "What an absolute darling." Her black tongue peeked from between her lips. "She smells very nice...."

"I think you should leave," Gee stated. "Now."

"What's going on?" Cracker's voice was hoarse.

"Your friend can come with us. She looks like she likes parties.

Every day's a party in Half World." Ilanna slowly winked. She took a sliding step toward Cracker as Rilla began rising into an S-curve.

Cracker reacted. *Psssssssssssssssst.*

Gee clamped his forearm over his face.

Ilanna shrieked. When the particles of the spray hit Rilla's moist skin the eel began thrashing spasmodically.

"Come on!" Cracker shouted.

Both arms raised to protect his face, Gee stumbled blindly to the door. Cracker grabbed his sleeve and they thudded down the wooden steps.

Ilanna shrieked and shrieked. Rilla hissed with pain, thumping against the wall, thrashing against her mistress.

When the familiar odour of musty lemon grass and overripe fruit seeped into Gee's consciousness he finally lowered his hands. He stared down at the crooked part in Cracker's hair with anger and admiration and shook his head. The floorboards above them were thudding with uneven steps. They didn't have long. They burst out of the store. The air was cold, sweet. Wet.

Gee clenched his teeth. The cat! The cat had said to take him with him. And Ilanna had him in her pocket.

"What have you done!" a low voice rasped.

Cracker swallowed a shriek. Gee leapt backward. Cracker fumbled with her pepper spray but it was knocked from her hand. The can clattered on the pavement until it rolled to a stop.

The man—the bird. Bird man, Gee thought. Bird man. It's not funny.

Shirtless, his muscled torso was lean, gleaming with old white scars against his dark skin. His arms were ropey, his hands enormous. The grey feathers began at his neck and completely covered his avian head.

His curved beak. He moved so quickly Gee could only watch, stunned as a rabbit, as the gun-metal-grey beak bent down to tear out his throat.

A white blur flew through the air.

The bird man screeched with pain as a puff of feathers scattered from the top of his head. He swung his arms blindly as an enormous white cat thudded heavily to the ground.

"Karu!" Ilanna's muffled voice echoed from the second floor. "Karu!" she screamed.

The bird man hissed. He snapped his beak in the cat's direction before running into the store.

"Follow me," White Cat snapped. Cracker cast incredulous looks between Gee and the cat. "What the hell!" she choked. "What the *fuck*!"

The fat cat ran to the nearest alley and disappeared into the darkness, moving a lot faster than Gee would have thought possible. Cursing beneath his breath, he ran after the creature. After a few seconds he heard Cracker's pounding, jangling footsteps from behind. "Don't follow us!" Gee yelled without turning around. "Go home!"

Cracker did not answer.

The cat was gaining distance. Gee began to pant. He wasn't athletic and it was all he could do to keep the bounding spot of white fur in his sight. Cracker'll give up soon, he thought. She has a hole in her heart. She can't run forever.

Nor could he, Gee realized.

With White Cat in the lead, then Gee, and Cracker staggering behind him, they darted across double-lane roads to the honking of startled drivers. They sidled in the crevasse between close-standing buildings. They ran. They ran.

Gasping, Gee finally caught up to White Cat. The miserable creature was sitting on the sidewalk, staring at the dirty underside of one paw. "Look at that!" The soft pink nap of his pads was covered with filth. The cat shuddered. "Disgusting."

Gee took a deep breath. His shoulders slumped with exhaustion as he exhaled. The distant sound of jangling metal pieces—Gee shook his head. Cracker hadn't turned back.

White Cat was trying to rub his paws on damp grass. "Dirty, dirty," he muttered underneath his breath.

"I've only ever seen cats *lick* themselves clean," Gee murmured.

White Cat glared. "Thank you for sharing your remarkable observations. Why don't you lick the bottom of your shoes?"

"The cat—" Cracker wheezed. "Is really—" *Pant, pant.* "Talking!" The air whistled in her lungs.

White Cat's eyes widened with incredulity. "Are you *still* working with the one thought?" He turned back to Gee as if it were his fault. "Get rid of her."

"You are *so* rude!" Cracker gasped.

"No one asked you to follow us," Gee said. The cat *was* rude, but Cracker had no idea what kind of danger they were in. Gee swallowed. He didn't know either.

This is nothing, the dark voice inside him chortled. *We haven't gotten to the best part yet.*

Gee scanned the neighbourhood. A few people stood at a bus stop, but there was no sign of the monstrous eel woman, the bird man. Karu, she had called out. And her name was Ilanna. It sounded so pretty….

"I'm following the White Cat. Like the White Rabbit. Down the rabbit hole," Cracker said happily. "This is the best thing that's happened to me in years!"

The cat leapt. A blur of white fur. And before Gee could react, the awful creature had chomped on the back of his calf, then leapt away.

"Ow!" Gee yelped, and belatedly shook his leg. "What are you biting *me* for?"

"She's your problem. Not mine!" The cat narrowed his yellow-green eyes.

Gee pulled up his jeans and twisted around to look for puncture marks in the back of his leg. But his white skin was smooth.

Cracker crouched down. "Do you shave?" she asked, running her fingers across his hairless skin.

"Excuse me!" Gee dropped his pant leg.

Cracker's grin was crooked.

"This is serious," Gee said. "The cat and I are running from very bad people." He shook his head. She had no idea.

People? the dark voice inside him snickered. *They're as much "people" as you are. You mean monsters!*

Gee shuddered. "It's dangerous for you to follow us. I don't even know where we're going."

"Half World," White Cat growled. "I told you!"

Gee stared at the smooth skin of his palms. The heavy sound of his heart thudded inside his skull.

Half World.

That was where his real parents were. That was what that monstrous eel woman had said. The grotesque, sensual Ilanna....

"Come on!" Cracker's eyes gleamed. "A woman with a snake

arm? A bird-headed man? Like, are we going to Wonderland or ancient Egypt or a side show at a circus? This is *too* trippy, and I haven't even taken anything! No hangover. No withdrawal symptoms. It's all for free!"

"We are not going to a drug-induced Disneyland." White Cat was icy. "We will be entering Half World, a place of suffering, a place of pain. It is the Realm that all living things must enter after death. Do you understand what I'm saying?"

Cracker's eyes widened. "You mean Hell?" her voice was hoarse.

White Cat's tail quivered. "No, not Hell as you understand it. It is Half World. Everyone enters that Realm to return to the moment of the greatest suffering they experienced when they were alive. The source of their worst trauma. In Half World, the sufferers suffer this psychic pain, over and over again, until they pass through their suffering and attain Spirit."

A tiny frown rippled across Gee's smooth brow. Were his parents in pain? Did they suffer also?

Cracker blinked slowly. Her voice was small. "Even the good people?" she asked. "Do good people have to go to Half World too?"

White Cat made a noise like he was coughing up a fur ball. "You're still thinking of a model based on 'good' and 'evil'! Everyone suffers. Everyone goes to Half World."

Cracker took a step backward. She was shaking her head. "I've never heard about it before. I don't believe you."

White Cat mimicked a child's high-pitched voice. "And yesterday you didn't believe in talking cats."

Gee glanced at Cracker's face. Were there tears in her eyes?

"Go home," White Cat said curtly.

A single tear rolled down Cracker's pale cheek. She dragged the back of her hand angrily across her face, streaking her black eyeliner.

"No!" Her voice was low. "I'm going with you."

White Cat glared at Gee before turning to the girl who had suddenly become so grimly resolute. "You have no idea what kind of suffering you seek to enter!" the cat hissed.

"You have no idea what kind of suffering I live in now!" Cracker was fierce.

"You seek to enter a Realm before it's your time to do so. Mortals are meant to enter Half World only upon death. Even if you gain entry, there's no saying what will happen to your living body."

"I don't care!" Cracker shouted.

Something bulged in Gee's maw. It plugged his breath and he clamped both hands over his throat. What was it? He gasped.

Fear, the dark voice crowed. *Terror, anxiety—get used to it. That is what you breathe in Half World.*

He was choking. Not enough oxygen. Eyes bulging, he desperately wheezed for air.

Cracker's eyes narrowed. "Sit down," she ordered. She pulled, hard, on Gee's arm, and he was too panicked to resist. He crumpled to the cold sidewalk. Cracker pushed his head down toward his knees. "Breathe slower. Slower!"

Air caught in the back of Gee's throat in ragged fragments. He shuddered and rasped as he concentrated on inhaling, exhaling.

The monstrous fear in his throat receded. He began to shake. Popo.... He wanted to be in the same room with her. To see her face. That's all. Popo. Help me.

She's dead, the dark voice hissed.

Gee's arms hung lifelessly at his sides. His eyes were blank. "I don't want to go." His voice was flat.

"What!" White Cat shouted. "What did you say?"

"He doesn't want to go," Cracker repeated. She began rubbing Gee's back. Her touch was kind.

Gee's lip wobbled. He would not cry! He couldn't bear it if the freakish waxy tears fell once again.

"He doesn't want to *goooo*," White Cat mimicked, prancing up and down the sidewalk.

Gee stared at the cracks in the concrete. They had been patched with black pitch, but that was splitting apart as well. "No one can force me to," he whispered. "I can choose not to. Everyone has choices."

The fat cat whipped around and leapt. He landed with a heavy thud on Gee's chest, and he slowly toppled backward. The cold concrete seeped into his back. The weight of the cat was oppressive, his small paws digging into the thin flesh between his rib bones.

White Cat's eyes were enormous. "Nobody should enter before their time, but Half World has come for you nonetheless." The creature pressed his cold nose against Gee's, his yellow-green eyes glinting madly. "You have called creatures out of Half World for reasons you do not know. Should you remain here, you will endanger your grandmother, as the Half Worlders will seek to control you through the ones you love. You must lead them back into their Realm and face what ties you to Half World. The past will always try to catch up with you, no matter how far you flee. You cannot run away from yourself." The cat leapt off Gee's chest and, tail held aloft, started walking down the sidewalk. "The past is inside you already."

He did not look back to see if Gee followed. White Cat's words trickled behind him as he padded away. "Should you flee, you'll always be the one who is chased. Is it not better to be the one who seeks?" White Cat's tail lashed and then he held it aloft once more, the tip flopping a little to one side.

Chapter Ten

"Do you trust that cat?" Cracker's voice was low. "Do you believe everything he says?"

They'd been walking for over half an hour. In the distance, Gee could hear the roar of the freeway traffic beginning to grow. "I don't know," he muttered. "It might be true.... But there's no way to be sure."

The sound of their footsteps. Cracker's jangling buckles. Gee looked over his shoulder. He couldn't see Ilanna and Karu. Somewhere near or far away, he knew they still followed.

Gee returned his gaze to the awful cat's vertical tail. The cat made sure they didn't catch up, somehow keeping a consistent three metres between them, even when Gee picked up his pace. The horrid creature had said that *Gee* had called Ilanna and Karu out of Half World. But how could he call something he didn't even know existed? Why was it his responsibility to lead them back?

Your parents are there, the dark little voice whispered. *And your birthright.*

Where all the sufferers suffered, White Cat had said. Gee didn't want to go there. But a part of him.... What kind of birthright could there possibly be for a person in Half World?

Back in the parkade. When his palm had swallowed his classmate's face. Winston's life a frantic fluttering, like a panicked sparrow. And Gee the one to decide if the boy lived or died.... It had felt delicious....

Gee shuddered. No!

No. He wasn't like that. He glanced at Cracker. Whatever it was that tied him to Half World, it was no place for her. Cracker, passionate and so full of life. Half World would be filled with monstrosities like Ilanna and Karu.

Monstrosities like you, the dark little voice snickered.

He was not a monster! He cared what happened to Cracker. A monster wouldn't care.

"Please go home." Gee's voice cracked. "I have a bad feeling. You aren't meant to go to Half World. Please."

She didn't respond for several minutes. Gee glanced down at her profile. She dragged the back of her hand across her eyes, her smeared eye makeup beginning to spread thinner.

"My sister," she finally whispered. "Klara died in the summer. She— She killed herself. If Half World is real, if what that cat said is true.... What if she's there, still suffering? I have to see. I have to make sure she's okay."

A small frown flickered across Gee's face. "But she's already dead," he said slowly. "How can your going make a difference to her now?"

"What if it were your grandmother! What would you do? If you thought she might be suffering, even after death, you'd do the same as me!" Cracker's voice was harsh.

Gee stared at her jangling buckles. Popo could very well be in a coma, in the hospital. Was a part of her waiting for him to sit beside her? Wanting him to be there, to hold her hand and call her back to life?

Popo, he sent across the damp city sky. I'll be back as soon as I can....

"I'm sorry," Gee said softly to Cracker. "About your sister." He felt he should say something more, but he didn't know what it could be.

He glanced at her face again. Her profile was resolute, her expression unreadable. Cracker was the first person, apart from his grandmother, who wasn't repelled by him. And for that he was filled with a kind of gratitude he didn't want to examine too closely.

Maybe this was what it felt like to have a friend. But what kind of friend would he be if he led her into Half World? If it truly was like what *The Book of the Realms* had described, she would be in terrible danger.

But he didn't want to enter Half World alone, with only the company of the unpredictable cat. Still....

"Cracker." Gee swallowed the quaver in his throat. "What if going to Half World means you might not be able to come back?"

Cracker was silent for so long that Gee thought she was ignoring him.

"I couldn't do anything for Klara before," she finally said. "If

I get a second chance to help her, I accept the risk." She spun around, grabbing hold of his arms so that they came to an abrupt stop.

"Promise me. We'll see each other through this. Me, for my sister, you, for your birth parents. Promise we're partners in this. Whatever happens." She met his dark eyes with ferocity.

Gee swallowed hard. "I promise," he whispered. He didn't think he was promising only for his own sake.

Cracker smiled. Her golden eyes shone brighter than the light at sunset. But Gee couldn't smile in return. They resumed walking, in silence, for a long time. The jangle of the many buckles on Cracker's boots didn't sound jaunty. Her footsteps were heavy. And Gee was filled with a foreboding.

THEY FINALLY CAUGHT UP to the cat. He sat on the concrete ledge of an overpass, his whiskers bobbing intermittently with sudden gusts of wind. From below came the roaring of automobiles as they plunged in and out of two dark tunnels.

"Is that the Cassiar Connector?" Gee asked. He'd never stood above it before.

White Cat grunted. "There are doors lining the inside wall of the Connector. We enter the west-side tunnel. Door Four is the gateway to Half World."

Cracker peered over the handrail. A cement truck bellowed into the darkness beneath them.

A slight frown flickered across Gee's smooth forehead. "How do you know all this?" Just because the cat said it was Popo's companion didn't make it so. When Popo had mentioned it, maybe she'd been trying to warn him. Maybe the cat was another Half World creature sent to trick him.... "And why do you know?"

White Cat's eyes narrowed. "Melanie has been there and back, and she went through the Connector. Do you remember nothing of what you read in *The Book of the Realms*?"

A knot formed in Gee's chest. Melanie ... and now him. That book on the dining room table: it said that a young woman had carried a living baby out of Half World and taken it to the Realm of Flesh.

What was once taken, must be returned, the dark little voice inside him crowed.

Popo! Gee railed. Why didn't you tell me more.... He could feel a tightness in his chest, and his eyes burned.

"Come." White Cat was curt. "It grows dark. And the night will bring with it dark creatures." He sailed into a bank of twisting ivy that gradually sloped downward to reach the freeway below.

Gee thought he heard the cat muttering "Dirty, dirty" as he leapt from one spot to another. He wasn't certain if the cat meant the state of his paws or the dark creatures that were out to get them.

Gee took a deep breath. He folded his fear and his doubts smaller and smaller until he could scarcely feel their edges. His face blank, he picked his way down the ivy embankment as the twisting vines tried to tangle his feet.

"Ooooph!"

Gee spun around. Cracker had fallen. She began to curse.

He stretched out his hand to help her rise. Her palm felt warm against his own. "Are you hurt?" he asked.

"Uh uhhnn." She shook her head.

The cat's face glowed in the growing darkness. Cars roared past, their headlights blinding, a cold wind blowing gusts of stinking exhaust fumes.

"Quickly!" White Cat snarled, his fur standing on end. "They come!"

Cracker squeezed Gee's hand painfully. His heart began slow-pounding. They both looked back up the embankment.

Two silhouettes stood at the railing. The indigo sky was so beautiful behind them. One of the shadows turned, and they could see the profile of a sharp, curved beak.

The liquid sound of low laughter reached them. Her voice was so lovely, Gee thought.

"Come on!" Cracker pulled Gee toward the cat.

He shook his head, trying to free himself from the sound of Ilanna's laughter as they lurched and broke through the vines.

A massive delivery truck thundered past them with a blast of horn. White Cat's ears were pressed almost flat against his head.

Gee looked across the four lanes of freeway, the concrete divider that split them into eastbound and westbound. The vehicles hurtled in and out of the tunnel openings. He stared for a break in traffic. "We have to run across?" he shouted.

"Yes!" White Cat snarled. The whites of his eyes were showing and his fur stood on end. "The farther tunnel."

Cracker didn't even pause. She swooped up the cat in her arms and started dashing across the first two lanes of traffic. Gee stared, aghast, and then sprinted after her.

Trucks, cars, honked their horns as they swerved around them.

We will die, Gee thought. Die, don't die, we still have to enter Half World....

They made the divider. A brief island of safety. White Cat was shamelessly plastered against Cracker's midriff.

"What now?" she panted.

"Into the tunnel." White Cat's voice was muffled. "Inside wall."

Gee couldn't stop himself from glancing at the embankment again. The orange streetlights cast an eerie glow upon Ilanna's dress. The eel was writhing with frustration; her mistress's legs were caught in the mess of ivy. Karu bent down to help her untangle herself.

Grimly, Gee ran along the small ledge of concrete that protruded along the inside wall of the dark tunnel. He could scarcely hear Cracker's boot buckles over the overwhelming traffic noise.

The lights embedded in the ceiling were dim, their dirty glow casting an ugly pall. From the far end of the tunnel an awful roar began to grow as if a tornado were moving directly toward them. The air swirled with wet garbage, the sting of grit scoring their exposed skin, empty beer cans and dented hubcaps whipping around them like leaves. They ducked low and covered their eyes with one arm as they struggled deeper inside. White Cat began to yowl.

Silence.

Karakarakara. A tin can rolled along the rough concrete. It came to a stop. The after-roar of the wind lingered inside their ears.

The vehicles had vanished. The tunnel was completely empty. Cracker couldn't stop a small sound from escaping her lips. White Cat, for the first time, was speechless.

Gee looked over his shoulder.

The half-circle of the entrance was black. He had no way of knowing if Ilanna and Karu were there.

White Cat shook his head as if he were trying to dislodge something stuck inside his ears. "The same thing happened to Melanie. The tunnels became silent. Now is our chance to enter the portal." The cat twisted out of Cracker's arms and landed silently on the sticky concrete. He quickly padded deeper into the tunnel. Gee and Cracker hurried after him.

They passed the first door. Large, rectangular and framed with wooden beams, the emergency exit looked more like a barn door than an escape route.

Behind the door something enormous, something very far away, groaned. The sound was so deep, so low, it was barely audible. Their cells quivered with the vibrations.

Gee and Cracker shuddered. *What* was it? *Where* was it? Because shouldn't the exit hatch just open to the other tunnel that ran parallel to theirs?

Cracker slipped her small hand into Gee's sticky palm. Gee went still.

Her touch, so human. So fragile. Saturated with emotion. He folded his fingers around hers and gave a reassuring squeeze.

They raced after the cat, who was stretched out into a leaping run.

Door Two gave off a sickly sweet smell, like noxious flowers rotting. Gee held his breath, ran faster. Cracker was beginning to wheeze.

A liquid giggle echoed inside the concrete passage.

They were coming!

The staccato clacking of a great curved beak.

"Hurry!" Gee pulled Cracker's hand.

She was beginning to stagger.

Let her go, Gee's dark little voice snickered. *Ilanna and Karu will catch up with her first. And then they'll want to stop and play.*

Gee shook his head. He released Cracker's hand and grabbed her wrist instead. He pulled harder, and Cracker valiantly kept pace.

Ahead of them, White Cat suddenly veered off the ledge and onto the road, where he ran for several metres before returning to the ledge.

As Gee and Cracker came abreast of Door Three they caught sight of a heap of castaway clothes piled into the corner of the frame. The heap of clothing *shifted* and then slowly started to rise. A glimpse of cloven hooves, a rancid, oily odour, thick and confusing.

Cracker swore and kicked a warning with her heavy boot.

The heap resettled back into the corner. It began to wail. Like a mother mourning, like a flayed monkey, like a child dying.

The hairs on their arms, their necks, rose at the uncanny sound. Their footsteps faltered.... The wailing was so keen it tore at the heart.

"Make it stop!" Cracker screamed. She clamped her hands over her ears. "Save her!"

Set it afire, the cold, ugly voice inside Gee advised. *That will do nicely.*

"Beware!" White Cat snarled. "It's a trap!"

Cracker, unable to bear the sound, dropped to her haunches. Curled over, she bent her arms over her head and started rocking back and forth. "Save her," she wept. "She's suffering. We have to help her."

The cloth heap began to unfold once again. An inhuman limb began stretching toward Cracker as the thing continued keening, snuffling, sobbing.

Cracker staggered to her feet, her eyes glazed, her hands beginning to reach for the ruined thing. "I'll help you," she promised, her face frozen.

Gee didn't know what she was seeing. It couldn't be the heap of rotting cloth and twig limbs that he saw.

"She feels so much pain," Cracker crooned as the lurching thing drew nearer, its keening rising in pitch.

Its siren call, Gee thought. The sound of its suffering was the bait—to stun, to trap, the empathetic. To catch people like Cracker.

Not youuuuu, the dark voice gloated.

No, thought Gee. Not me.

He grabbed Cracker from behind, wrapping his arms around her skinny waist. "Come on!" he shouted, giving her a shake.

Her legs were wobbly, as if she were drunk. Gee began to drag her toward White Cat, who stood impatiently beside the fourth door.

The hooflike limb scraped against the concrete and the keening quieted. "Help?" The voice was childlike, sweet and tremulous. "Help me?"

"Klara?" Cracker's voice broke. "Ohmygod, Klara!"

"I'm thirsty," the childish voice quavered. "Please."

Cracker began to struggle. She was wiry and strong. Gee clung with all his might.

"Let me go!" Cracker screamed. "It's my sister! Let GO!"

Gee clung tighter. Gritting his teeth, he continued dragging her toward the fourth door.

The shambling cloven thing was drawing closer, the sound of its scraping loud against the concrete, its sweet little-girl voice grotesquely beguiling.

Cracker kicked wildly with her boots to break from Gee's hold. The thick treads landed on Gee's shin, his knee. The impact was stunning.

Cracker twisted, halfway free.

Something white sailed through the air.

White Cat, with a yowl, landed upon the misshapen monster. He scratched and swiped, a flurry of claws, and patches of rotting cloth flew through the rancid air.

"Oh." The thing's sweet little voice was lost. Ancient. The creature fell with a clatter of skeletal bones, desiccated hooves. The scattered remains were no more than litter strewn upon a dirty road.

"No!" Cracker cried, forlorn.

"Oh, *yesssss*," Ilanna sighed. "Darlings."

The Half Worlders were only twenty metres away. They weren't even running. Karu's eyes glinted, the feathers on his head upright. Ilanna's eel arm lashed violently.

"Rilla is very angry with you, Party Girl," Ilanna whispered. Her voice dripped in the dank, silent tunnel. "And so am I. When we catch you, we're going to eat you ever so slowly. Should we start with your fingers? Or should we begin with the toes?"

"Toessssssss," Rilla sighed.

"The Gate!" White Cat commanded as he twisted away.

Gee dragged Cracker with him, her legs regaining strength as they moved farther from the dregs of the empathy vampire.

There was no way he could leave Cracker behind, Gee realized. Now Ilanna and Rilla were after her as well.

As Cracker's senses returned, she began to run. Gee loosened his hold. Just as they reached the fourth door the keening began

to rise once more out of the tattered clothing, the skeletal limbs scraping their way back together again.

"No!" Ilanna shouted.

"Help me." The childish voice was heartbreaking.

Karu shrieked, the fierce cry of a raptor.

"No, Karu! What are you doing?" Ilanna screamed.

That thing wasn't on their side, Gee realized. The Half Worlders were just as much at risk as they were. And they had triggered its trap.

But it was an empathy monster … and how could those two feel empathy?

The cat scratched at the wooden slats of Door Four. He looked so much like a pet asking to be let out that Gee almost laughed aloud. Then he shook his head. He had to get a grip.

"The door must be opened once, closed, then opened a second time." White Cat's voice was urgent. "Open it only a little the first time."

"Why—" Gee began.

"Just do it!" White Cat hissed, glancing back at Ilanna and Karu.

Cracker, eyes stunned, had her hands clamped over her ears again so that she wouldn't be compelled by the siren voice once more.

Gee pried at the simple swing latch until it popped up. He grabbed the sticky handle. The door hung from a metal track; he just had to slide it sideways.

He pulled.

The door was stuck.

White Cat began to swear. Behind them, a din was rising. A

staccato of cloven hooves pounding the concrete. The raucous cries of a bird. The keening cry of the empathy monster. "Help me," the little-girl voice cried. "Don't leave me. I'm frightened!"

"Stop it!" Ilanna shouted at the bird man. "Leave that thing! They're getting away!"

Cracker, wide-eyed, placed her hands next to Gee's on the wooden slats of the door.

"Push!" Gee cried.

The door, shrieking on its pulleys, slid open about twenty centimetres.

They stood, staring stupidly at the strip of darkness.

A vast roar— A great vacuum yanked them toward the open space, White Cat screaming as he clung desperately to the rough surface of the concrete with his claws. His hindquarters were becoming airborne, and his yellow-green eyes bulged with terror.

The force of the vacuum sucked Gee's dark hair toward the opening, his clothes flapping. But his peril was not as great as that of the cat's. Maybe the wind had sucked away all his feelings, Gee thought, as he watched emotionlessly. How many more seconds could White Cat hold on? Would the tipping point come with the snapping of one claw, or two?

The sucking wind dragged the cat toward the open gap, his claws leaving eight ragged lines across the cement. Gee began counting: one one thousand, two one thousand....

Slam!

Cracker had kicked the door shut. She stood, panting, staring at the cat who had fallen flat atop the concrete ledge, his tail puffed with terror. Cracker glared at Gee. "*Do* something! What's wrong with you?"

He shook his head slowly. What had he been thinking? Why was he standing there? White Cat. He had told him what to do—

Gee grabbed the metal handle and wrenched it open for a second time.

Chapter Eleven

They stood, tensed, waiting for the great sucking wind to return.

The stillness was heavy. Unsettling. An odd grey light shone into the darkness of the tunnel.

"Go through." White Cat's voice was hoarse. He still lay weakly on the ground. His claws had retracted.

Cracker bent down, grunting as she raised him up. She stepped through the portal. Gee followed.

The dull grey light blinded for a moment. The air was silent, slightly metallic. Chill. The sound of grinding stone. They spun around. The portal was closing.

On the Half World side the door wasn't made of wooden slats. It was as if a great grey circular stone was being rolled back into place. Impossible to stop, they watched as their only exit shrank into an ever-thinning crescent.

Gee's flat dark eyes were expressionless as he watched the passageway disappear. All that remained was a smooth granite cliff face. As he shifted something crunched, disintegrated beneath his shoe. They were standing on a rock ledge, three metres wide, its surface littered with little white sticks. Mounds of the debris were heaped along the ledge where it met the granite wall.

Crump. Crump.

It sounded as if they were stepping on dried pretzel sticks.

Cracker raised one foot, disgust twisting her lips. "Gross," she muttered.

White Cat was strangely subdued. He didn't twist out of Cracker's arms. "Indeed." His voice was small. "You are standing upon the finger bones of those who came before you."

"Ugghhh!" Cracker exclaimed, hopping from one foot to the other, crushing ever more bones to powder beneath the heavy treads of her boots.

Gee fought the urge to titter. It wasn't funny. Wasn't funny at all. Why did he want to laugh?

Cracker's boot toppled a heaped mound of bones.

Something long and black erupted, flip-flopping wildly. The writhing, spasmodic movement drew it ever closer to Cracker's feet. She shrieked, leaping backward, one heel landing on the edge of the ledge, the sudden gaping pull of empty space.

Gee was too far away.

Cracker's eyes wide. One arm still clutching the cat. One arm reaching. Empty space. She slowly began to tip....

White elastic whipped faster than the eye could follow. Splattered around Cracker's wrist. And yanked her back with so much force that she was thrown to her knees, White Cat leaping aside at the last moment.

Gee stared numbly down the length of his white arm. It had elongated, easily two metres, and was almost as thin as a garden hose.

That is not me, he thought. That is someone else.

Cracker, shocked and relieved, was panting on her hands and knees. She didn't see Gee slowly unclasping her wrist and retracting his arm back to his side.

Gee didn't know how he did it. He could feel White Cat's eyes upon him. Gee could not meet his gaze.

"Thank you," Cracker croaked.

Gee said nothing. He opened and closed his hand. It didn't feel evil.... It was the same hand that had almost killed Winston Chang, but this time he'd used it to save his friend. He could control it. He would! He clenched his hand into a fist as he carefully made his way to the edge to peer into the abyss.

The bottom was so far he couldn't see it. The sky seemed to fall forever.

If you fall forever, Gee thought, would it stop feeling like falling?

Gosa, gosa, gosa.

The snakey black thing, almost a metre long, was trying to writhe itself under another mound of bones.

Gee's eyes narrowed. Something about it.... He moved closer.

Sensing his approach, the thing reared up into an S-shaped curve. *Hsssssssssss!*

Sharp needle teeth glinted in its wide jaws. The dark body, dusty from the desiccated bones, was taut. Readying for attack.

It was an eel. Missing the lower half of its body.

Gee stared at the ragged edge of flesh, the white jagged remnants of its spine where it had been ripped away.... Ilanna's amputated eel arm, the one who'd been sacrificed for the toll.

Rilla, she'd called the eel on her right. What had she called the left one?

"Lilla?" Gee whispered hoarsely.

The eel became still. It tipped its head to the side before slowly stretching upward to stare at Gee's face. Its jaws dropped open into a great eel grin, exposing its array of gleaming needle teeth. It began to weave slowly from side to side, like a cobra.

"Be careful!" Cracker, still on her hands and knees, cried out. "It might be poisonous."

The mountain ledge began to shake. Groaning beneath the colossal weight, the cliff face began raining bits of granite. Gee covered the back of his head with his arms while White Cat crawled beneath the shelter of Cracker's belly. A sudden lurch had Gee slamming against the rock wall, his back, his palms pressed against the flat surface. He closed his eyes as the mountain vibrated through his body.

The rock wall bulged outward, pushing against Gee's back. He stepped to the middle of the ledge, legs apart, as he rode out the heaving of the mountain. He stared up, up at the rock face as a stone giant creaked out of her prison wall.

Made entirely of the grey granite, she was easily over four metres tall. The creaking groan of her weight filled the air. "You must pay the toll," the Gatekeeper's deep, low voice intoned.

Gee stared. The toll. That's right, he thought. They had to pay a toll.

"I have money," Cracker quavered. She began stuffing her hands in her pockets. Her eyes lit up as she pulled out a twenty-dollar bill. "See!" she said happily. "We can pay!"

White Cat shook his head. He lifted his paw and stared sourly at his dirty pads.

"The toll," the Gatekeeper thundered, "is the smallest finger of your hand. The finger must be bitten off."

Cracker's mouth dropped open. When she finally *saw* the desiccated bones littering the cliff ledge she turned her head to the side and retched.

White Cat leapt away. Then calmly resettled his tail around his paws. He sighed and his tail lashed, only once. "I will pay the toll, Gatekeeper." He made it sound as if he were offering, slightly begrudgingly, to pay for everyone's lunch.

Gee's palms felt sticky. The terrible bulging feeling in his throat began to grow.

"The bridge draws near," the Gatekeeper intoned. She stared across the great abyss.

What had been emptiness was no longer. A hundred metres away was another mountain.

And what bridges the gap? Gee wondered.

The air was suddenly filled with the raucous cries of crows. Thousands, hundreds of thousands—the skies were splintered with their voices.

Gee raised his left hand to his mouth. He did it without thinking. He placed the base of his pinkie against the edge of his teeth. Eyes staring blankly, he bit down.

His teeth should have met the resistance of bone. But they did not.

They cut through his finger as if it were made of Plasticine. His mouth dropped open. The digit fell to his feet. Gee stared at his hand. No blood. No pain. His flesh was white all the way through—as though his matter was not flesh, was not human....

Before his very eyes, his skin, his flesh began to bulge and stretch, rippling his soft matter toward the missing place and pouring a new pinkie into existence.

Gee slowly opened and closed his hand. His new pinkie was no different from the one he'd bitten off. He stared at the white little lump on the rock ledge.

"Gee...?" Cracker's voice quavered.

The Gatekeeper swung out an enormous arm. The cawing of crows drowned the air and a torrent of black birds flew across the divide, so many that the sky was solid with them.

"The crows are the living bridge between the Realm of Flesh and Half World," the Gatekeeper intoned. "Speed is of the essence."

The black bridge wobbled and fluttered.

Gee glanced at Cracker's face. She closed her eyes. "I'm scared," she mouthed. Tears streamed down her cheeks.

"Run!" White Cat hissed. "There's no other way. Don't stop. Don't look down. Run!"

Cracker leapt off the ledge and began running across the backs of the crows with her eyes closed. White Cat bounded after, a ball of white fur leaping across a steady stream of glinting black feathers, overtaking the girl.

Gee cursed beneath his breath. That *Cracker*! She was beginning to list to one side.... What kind of idiot ran across a bridge with their eyes closed?

Gee sprinted onto the roaring blackness. It was as if they ran atop a swift dark river, their feet slipping on the sleek feathers, the crows dipping beneath their weight. Taking ever-longer strides, Gee's legs began stretching and he quickly caught up to Cracker. He clamped his sticky arm around her waist, propelling her faster, and they dashed the final metres in tandem.

White Cat reached the little plateau a few seconds before they did. Cracker was gasping, whooping for air. Her eyes were still squeezed shut.

Gee was utterly calm. He stared down at the girl—did she even know they were no longer on the bridge? He could see her racing pulse beneath the thin skin of her neck. The two spots of colour on her pale cheeks.

White Cat's eyes were no longer yellow-green. They were grey. His nose had turned grey as well. The cat, unblinking, looked him up and down. He opened his mouth to speak—stopped. He turned slightly around so that most of his back curved toward Gee.

They were on a craggy mountain. Little plants grew in crevasses, tiny pockets of soil. The wind smelled slightly bitter. Gee blinked. The plants were all in various shades of grey.

No colours, he realized. Half World looked like an old-fashioned black-and-white film.

Except for Cracker.

There was a wheezing rattle to her gasps. She sat down abruptly and forced herself to breathe more slowly. After several minutes colour returned to her face. Her skin glowed, almost obscenely, as if she were a piece of meat.

Gee stared down at his hands. The pale skin and dark eyes that made him stand out back home weren't remarkable here. Back home. What did that mean? Gee wasn't sure anymore.

Half World....

Cracker caught Gee's gaze. Her eyes, shining like amber in sunlight, widened with alarm. "You look different," she said. "Or it's me." She sounded dubious. She took in the cat, the mountain crag on which they stood. "No," she decided. "We're the same. Half World is colourless. And it's affected the cat."

A tiny frown marred Gee's brow. He shrugged carelessly and turned to White Cat, who was rubbing his front paw in a patch of small grey leaves. "What do we do now?"

The cat, finished with his front paws, found a new patch of foliage and began working on his back paws.

"I'm talking to you, White Cat!" Gee seethed.

The cat slowly looked up at him. "How should I know?"

Gee stared, incredulous. "You're joking! *You're* the one who said I had to come here. Well, I'm here. Now what?"

"All I said was that you needed to discover the nature of your connection to Half World. The Half Worlders who pursue us want you for a reason. They know more about you than you know yourself. I don't know what you're meant to discover here. That's for you to learn. What do *you* want to do?" White Cat asked. "I hope your wits didn't fall into the abyss when we ran across the bridge." His tail flicked erratically, as if he were dislodging fleas.

Gee's throat plugged with rage. He choked the mass down, his eyes bulging with the effort.

Cracker backed away.

"*I* didn't want to come here!" Gee hissed. "*You* told me that I had something to do. So what is it?"

Kill the cat, the dark voice inside him whispered. *He's not Popo's companion. He's something evil. Come to trick you. What do you know about him? What has he done for you?*

Gee's hands shook. "I don't want to be here. I just want everything to be back to normal...." His voice faded. Normal.... What was he that he could bite off his finger so painlessly? That his limbs stretched as easily as elastic. What about his bones!

Something hot burned in his eyes. A tightness in his chest. Gee spun around quickly, fearful that Cracker and White Cat would see beads of wax dripping down his face instead of normal tears. He swallowed and swallowed. The taste of something sour, bitter, in the back of his throat.

Popo, he beseeched. You should have told me more. Popo, are you still alive....

"Ughhh!" Cracker stumbled away from him, her voice filled with disgust.

A weary resignation filled his chest. So it has begun, he thought. Emotionlessly, he turned to face Cracker's loathing.

Her expressive eyes were directed at his feet.

A black, sinuous head poked out of the hem of his pant leg. The eel writhed outward, its body pressing close to the ground. The faintest glint of teeth in its upward curving jaw.... Lilla had hitched a ride back with him. And he hadn't even felt it.

"Kick it out!" Cracker screamed. "Kick it over the side!"

The eel reared up, hissing.

The distant sound of crows, the whirring rush of wings. The birds were regrouping across the divide for a second passage.

"Curious," White Cat muttered. His cool gaze was fixed on the eel. He looked up at Gee. "What now?"

Gee closed his eyes to think. He had no proof that White Cat was who he said he was, but he hadn't tried to harm them. Despite the creature's dubious traits, he'd saved Cracker from the empathy vampire in the tunnel, and also from Karu.... Gee could overpower the cat if it came to that. He could not overpower Ilanna and the bird man.

He looked around. There was a faint trail in the rough ground—it had to lead somewhere. There was no returning to the gate across the abyss from where they stood. And Ilanna and Karu were drawing ever closer. He couldn't face them. At least not yet.

You cannot flee from your past, White Cat had said. Discover your ties to Half World.

Knowledge is power, the dark voice whispered.

Power, Gee thought. Power would mean he wouldn't have to feel fear.... "I'm going to climb down this mountain," he said. Even if he could return to the Realm of Flesh, he'd only be leading danger toward his popo ... if she was even still alive.... He couldn't think about that! "I'm going to find my parents. And Cracker's going to find her sister."

The eel sidled back into his pant leg, curling several times around his ankle.

"That *thing* is not coming with us!" Cracker spat.

A faint frown whispered across Gee's pale brow. The hank of dark hair covered his eyes.

Sssssssssssssssssss, the eel sighed.

Gee crouched down and wrapped his fingers around the eel's body. The long hard muscles instinctively struggled against his grip, flapping wildly back and forth, but Gee clung fast.

"Gross," Cracker groaned.

Gee raised the torn creature up to his face and stared into the eel's bright, glinting eye. "Be good," he commanded.

Lilla dropped open her jaw and revealed her needle teeth in a great eel grin. She nodded her head with sincerity.

White Cat snorted. "Eels are good"—he began trotting on the faint path—"glazed with teriyaki sauce and served on hot rice."

Cracker, unable to help herself, giggled.

Gee glared after the cat. Tail raised, his puckered cat anus was his last word.

The eel slicked powerfully around Gee's wrist. A thick black bracelet.

"I'm keeping her for now," he told Cracker. "She might be useful. And we can dump her if she's trouble."

"I think you're making a mistake," Cracker said through gritted teeth.

The distant roar of wings grew louder as the bridge of crows flew toward them, the sound swelling, thunderous.

"Come on!" Gee shouted.

They ran.

Chapter Twelve

Down, down, they ran, losing track of minutes, hours, as if they were descending the tallest mountain in the world. The sharp switchbacks, the steep steps, the air rasping with the sound of Cracker's ragged breath—they ran for so long that they began to fear they hadn't gained any ground at all. But the grey foliage slowly began to change, tiny arid plants shivering in crevasses turning to clumps of small-petalled flowers, shrubby bushes, even stunted, malformed trees.

All around them, the continued grey of clouds or sky. Distance was flattened. And there was no sign of the bottom.

Gee and Cracker had passed White Cat. Not shaped for endless descent, he'd waved them along. "Right behind you," he groaned. "Not to worry."

They ran, down, down, ever downward.

Paff, paff.

So sudden, so complete, they didn't realize it until they felt the damp of the solid grey cloud bank envelop and obscure the lower half of their bodies. Only their upper torsos were visible above the line of cloud cover. As if they were cut in half.

Cracker yelped and ran back up so that she stood, panting, above the dividing line.

Gee remained. Half-buried. The sheet of cloud was almost the same colour as the sky, he thought. You didn't know it was there until you were in it....

Cracker's teeth were clattering. "It's freezing in there. Aren't you cold?"

Gee slowly turned a circle, his arms held above his head as if he were wading in water. "No," he said. "It doesn't feel cold to me." His joints, however, were beginning to grow stiff.

Cracker was biting her lower lip to keep it from quivering.

Sides heaving, White Cat finally caught up to them and flopped dramatically on his belly, three steps above the cloud bank. Annoyance and exhaustion rose off the cat in equal parts as he stared sourly at Gee. "That looks wet." White Cat's lip curled.

"It's damp." Gee shrugged.

"Don't stand in it." Cracker sounded worried. "We don't know what's underneath." Her arms crossed directly below her breasts, she cupped her elbows, her shoulders hunched forward. "I don't want to go in there," she whispered.

Gee looked down so that his flop of hair hid the annoyance flaring in his eyes. He needed people who would help him, not hold him back. What was the point of having a friend if she served no purpose?

Ditch her, the darkness inside him suggested. *Pitch her over the side before she causes you trouble.*

Gee shook his head. What was he thinking! How could he, of all people, imagine so horrific an act? If Popo had thought the same thing when Older Sister brought him out of Half World.... Popo didn't have to take him in. But she did.

Gee pulled his free arm out of his sleeve, transferring Lilla to his bared arm so that he could remove his jacket entirely. He held it up to Cracker.

Her lower lip was trembling and she dragged her arm across her eyes. She accepted Gee's offering and thrust her hands into the arms of the jacket, tugging the zipper to her throat. Rolling up the sleeves.

"We can't go back the way we came," Gee said gently.

"Yah, I *know.*" The edge in Cracker's voice had returned.

Obscured beneath his hair, relief bloomed across Gee's face. He almost smiled.

"Thanks, Gee," Cracker whispered. She grinned at him and the golden light from her eyes felt as warm as sunshine, sweeter than honey.

Gee blinked with surprise. "You should smile more often, too," he noted.

Cracker scowled. Before a smile broke through again.

Lilla, twined thrice around him, looked like a grotesque armband. She squeezed down, hard. *Ssssssssssssssss,* she hissed warningly.

Gee could almost understand what Lilla said. She will impede you....

Cracker made a groaning sound.

Gee whipped his gaze toward her. "What's wrong?"

"I would kill for a cigarette," she grimaced. "What a time to have to quit."

"Where's your stuff?" Gee asked. Cracker had had a purse. "Did you ditch it?"

Cracker looked away. "I dropped it at that underground garage. And I—I didn't want to go back." She shrugged. "If Winston reports us to the cops I'm done for."

Gee looked thoughtfully at the eel wrapped around his arm. An almost-smile at the corner of his lips. Winston wouldn't report them. He'd been much too frightened....

"What are you waiting for?" Cracker demanded. She began to descend.

"Carry me!" White Cat cried, holding up his front legs beseechingly, his paws flopping downward.

Cracker giggled at the cat's pathetic display. A tiny smile twitched in the corner of Gee's lips.

Cracker bent down to pick up the cat. "I'm getting too tired to carry you around. You're too heavy," she gasped as she clutched him around the middle. "You must weigh at least fifteen pounds!"

"I'm eighteen pounds," White Cat said proudly. "Ouch! Don't hold me like that!" He dangled, an inverted U, his whiskers horizontal with displeasure.

Gee glared. "Don't be stupid," he said. "Turn into stone again. You're smaller that way, and easier to carry."

White Cat's eyes narrowed. Gee could not decipher the creature's thoughts.

Wordlessly, the cat began to alter his matter, his solidity fluctuating between opaque and translucent as he seemed to expand and contract. As if he was breathing his change. The cat yanked his matter to his core, contracting faster than the eye could follow. A walnut-sized object fell to the ground, clattering on the stone step.

Cracker, her mouth an O of wonder, bent to pick it up. "He can change his shape *and* talk," she said. She cupped the stone statuette in her palms.

Gee shook his head. "I don't think that's going to be enough to make a difference in this place."

Lilla squeezed his wrist. Oddly, it felt reassuring. Gee glanced at his eel. The creature's jaw was curved into a wicked grin. He wondered if all eels grinned. Or just Lilla.

And Rilla.

"You should get rid of that thing," Cracker muttered. "I get a bad hit off it."

Lilla whipped her head toward Cracker's face and snapped a few inches from her nose. Cracker scrambled back. "Shit!" She glared at Gee. "See! I don't know why you keep it."

"She only did that because of what you said!" he retorted. Gee bit his lip. He didn't know why he was acting like such an ass toward Cracker. He couldn't even say why he wanted to hold on to the eel. But he did.

Because then you have a present to give to Ilanna when you see her again, the vile voice inside him snickered. *Because you want to see her again.*

Gee covered his face with his hands. His feelings. Too many mixed feelings. They had never plagued him so in the Realm of Flesh.

Because you didn't allow yourself to be who you really are. But you can, in Half World.

"What's wrong?" Cracker's voice was filled with concern. "Are you okay?"

"It's nothing," Gee said curtly. He lowered his hands. "We're wasting time."

Cracker's eyes flared with anger at his tone.

She looks tired, Gee realized. She's exhausted. "They're still coming," he said, more gently.

They both looked upward. The formation of the overhang prevented them from seeing what was above. The wind whistled, cold and sharp.

"I'm thirsty," Cracker whispered. "I need a smoke."

She's scared, the dark voice tittered.

"You shouldn't have come," Gee said. Bad things were going to happen. And it would be his fault. The corner of his lips twitched.

Had he been about to *smile*?

Gee spun away from Cracker. "We might find water when we reach the bottom," he said. His voice was flat. "Let's go." Jesus! he thought. There's something wrong with me. Only a loathsome person would think a friend's suffering is funny. A sick feeling spread in his gut, sour, reeking, acidic. A feeling at once repulsive and familiar.... Gee clamped his arm around his middle. His eyes wide with fear.

Hunger. A hunger so great he almost cried out. He held his breath, held it in, and the churning, writhing spasm receded.

Cracker, busy tucking the stone cat into her pocket, didn't witness Gee's struggle. She patted down her crinoline and began descending the stairs, stepping into the smothering mass of grey clouds. She brushed past Gee who still stood waist-deep in the cloud bank.

He watched her sinking lower and lower, as if she were descending into dirty water. The top of her head bobbed. Gone.

A curious emotion panged deep inside Gee's chest. A different kind of pain, one that was braided with admiration and affection. Was this what it felt like to have a friend? Troubled, he let his flop of hair slide over his face and plunged into the damp darkness after her.

Eyes open, he saw nothing but greyness. Cracker hadn't called out even once. She was very brave.

Or very dead.

"Cracker?" Gee's heart torqued again with the unfamiliar pain. "Cracker!" he shouted.

"Yes?" her voice sounded faint.

Relief washed over him. "Have you come out the other side?"

"Not yet. I can't even see my feet. I had to slow down."

Gee glanced at his feet. He could scarcely see his own chest.

"Oh!" Cracker cried with alarm.

"What! Just stop!" Gee commanded. "We'll get separated."

"It—it's nothing." Cracker laughed nervously. "The stairs went funny."

Gee continued down, one hand extended in front of him. He felt something. Cloth.

"Huh." Cracker sucked her breath.

"It's me," Gee said.

Something batted at his hand. Then Cracker's small cold fingers clasped his in a tight grip. He took one more step down to join her, yet when the ball of his foot touched the rock surface, he had the oddest sensation that he'd just climbed upward.

He wobbled with confusion.

"Did you feel like you went up instead of down?" Cracker whispered.

Gee nodded. Then shook his head. She couldn't see him. "Yes," he murmured.

"Maybe all of Half World is covered in fog. Everyone just wanders around, going up the down stairs. Falling off mountains. Getting lost. All alone." Cracker's teeth began to chatter.

"No," Gee said. "Half World is just underneath. We're almost there. We have to keep moving."

"How do you know?" Fear quavered in Cracker's voice.

"White Cat made me read a book. If what it described is true, then we're almost there." Gee was grim. If Half World was anything like the book described, even in symbolic language, it was going to be a nightmare.

Home sweet home, the dark voice crooned.

His parents were down there. Somewhere. His true family. The truth of the past. The answers.

Clattering high above them— The sound grew louder as it fell nearer, *clack, clack, crack!*

A chunk of rock disintegrated on the ledge overhead and the shards scattered.

"Come on," Gee urged, as he tugged Cracker's hand.

They pressed their backs against the side of the mountain and sidled down the disorienting steps, raising their knees too high for stairs that descended. Lilla, entwined around Gee's wrist, held herself horizontally in the air, six inches beyond Gee's hand. She led the way, snaking from side to side as if she were swimming against a river. Ever deeper she led them into the damp, impenetrable cloud bank.

The eel squealed. Gee jerked his arm backward. Stopped.

Cracker ran into him and Gee instinctively curved his arm around her waist to keep her pressed against the rock wall. His heart thudded, slow, loud.

Nothing.

Nothing leapt at them, howling, slavering. Nothing bit off their limbs, tore their faces from their skulls, nothing whispered evil words that drove them mad, that had them leaping off the side of the mountain to plunge to their death.... Gee extended his hand, his fingers groping. If anything snapped them off, he thought giddily, it wouldn't hurt him anyway.

Cold, wet ... metallic. His fingers tapped out something smooth, flat, the perfect size for his palm to rest on— A handrail, he realized, as his fingers curled around its edges. He pulled Cracker closer and placed her hand on it.

She gasped, and then sighed with relief.

Clinging awkwardly, with both hands, they used the railing as their point of reference as they continued descending-ascending.

A change. Gee didn't know what, how—

The quality of the stairs. They felt lighter than before. Without the density of stone. *Tack, tack, tack*, their footsteps rang.

They broke free from the cloud. A jubilant cry escaped Cracker's lips, only to fade away....

They were standing on the metal steps of a fire escape fixed to the side of a glossy high-rise, the ground far below them, glimpsed through the slats of the steps. Cracker teetered with sudden vertigo and Gee grabbed her elbow to steady her even as his gorge rose to the back of his throat.

Gee looked up. The stairs disappeared into the slate-grey ceiling of cloud. He shook his head. Where was the mountain?

Nonsensical. Illogical. Half World was a nightmare made material....

The city spread out around them in greyscale. In the distance darkness roiled against the grey horizon like the edge of a monstrous forest. A liminal light, pre-dawn, or dusk, the land dark and the skies completely clouded.

Pagodas, castle turrets, skyscrapers and minarets, huts, cabins, tents and freeways.... An odd system of canals and bridges— Was there a moat around the outer edges of the city? Gee thought he could see the glint of water. Creaking wagons being drawn by oxen as a bullet train sped above them on raised tracks with a rushing wind, a staccato clatter, a strobe of brightly lit windows. Gone.

Pale grey lights flickered in windows and turrets. White neon signs clamoured and flickered and dark shadows huddled around open fires. The stink of singed fur, exhaust, was noxious and sweet.

Dogs howled.

Gee shivered. A frisson of something shimmered down his back. Lilla squeezed his forearm encouragingly.

A feeling—not unpleasant, it tingled in his nape and pimpled his skin with emotion. Like a name on the tip of the tongue. Like the dream that fades upon waking. He clutched at the elusive strands of the unmemory, willing it to rise to the surface.

Welcome home, the dark voice inside him crooned.

Chapter Thirteen

Someone, somewhere, was dying slowly. He moaned and screamed, begged and wept.

"*Jesus*...," Cracker whispered.

A zeppelin slowly drifted by, so close that Gee could see the glint from the forks and knives of its guests who were seated at small tables, drinking from slender flutes filled with champagne.

"How will I *find* her?" Cracker's voice was lost.

Gee swallowed the excitement fluttering inside his throat. Of course! He hadn't forgotten why they'd come to Half World! It was only that everything was so unusual and intriguing....

They stared at the nightmare vista in silence. Cracker, despairing, and Gee, with emotions he could not name. In the distance thunder rumbled. Or the echoes of bombs. A crackling, screaming laughter rose up from the sidewalk far, far below them, the crazed hilarity continuing on and on and on.

Gee shuddered. No. He did not know this monstrous place. This was not his home. His home was with Popo, above the store. Their table, where they ate their meals and read their books in easy silence. Where he had grown up, inside the safety of her unwavering love.

The sooner he found his parents, and understood his ties to Half World, the sooner those ties could be severed. And he and Cracker could go home.

Gee cleared his throat. "Maybe your sister's already passed through. She's probably already in the Realm of Spirit. That's what the book said: after people have worked through their troubles, their suffering, they pass into Spirit."

A flare of hope brightened her eyes before it faded. Cracker's head dropped. She started descending once more, the sound of her boots on the metal steps heavy and listless. "I hope you're right. But Klara suffered a lot before she died," she whispered. "I just have to make sure she's not still here. Suffering. I have to know."

Lilla stared at Cracker's back before twisting around to meet Gee's eyes.

"Sssss, sssss, sssss, sssss," Lilla snickered, her head bobbing up and down.

Gee smiled—

He recoiled. He hadn't been laughing at Cracker's pain. No—he'd just been delighted with the idea that an eel could laugh. Gee wasn't the kind of person who laughed at people's pain. He wasn't....

He glanced down at his pale hands. His new little pinkie. An arm that extended like an elastic band. His stomach clenched. Writhing, painful, a twist of muscle so severe he felt faint. As the sensation slowly ebbed, Gee realized what it was.

That hunger.... So hungry he felt sick with it. He'd never felt so famished before. When was the last time he ate? He couldn't remember. His soft supper with Popo? It felt like years ago....

Popo.... Gee's eyes were dry. Have they finished running the tests? Did they send her home?

She's dead, the dark, cruel voice spat. *Like Cracker's sister. Cycling through her pitiful pain in this Realm. As all mortals do upon death.*

"No!" Gee hissed.

Cracker stopped and looked back. "What?" Though her face was etched with exhaustion, her eyes still shone golden in the grey light. She'd rubbed her kohl too many times and the fading black smears around her eyelids and cheeks made her resemble a ghoul. She looked ready to crumple on the ground with weariness.

Gee had no idea how much time had passed. It could easily be the morning of the next day, he thought. Cracker needed to sleep. But Gee, he didn't feel sleepy. His thoughts jerked away from examining too closely the difference between their body's responses to Half World. Only the after-ache of hunger clenched his belly. There had to be someplace where Cracker could rest for a little while.

"You better pull the hood of my jacket over your head," Gee advised. "Your eyes stand out. And we don't want to draw attention."

"What do you mean?" Cracker asked.

Gee swept his hand through the air. "Everything is black and white here. Except your eyes. Your eyes still have colour. The same thing happened to M-Melanie, my older sister. It's black and white in Half World because it isn't a living place. But you've come from the living, so your eyes are still alive."

Cracker's amber eyes widened. She took a step closer to peer at Gee's face, and then bit her lip and looked away.

"Mine have no colour," Gee said flatly. "They never have."

They never have....

Gee's vision blurred, and he blinked rapidly. I'm okay, he told himself. I'm okay!

"We need to reach the bottom and find a place to hide and rest. And eat," Gee added. A sour flood of saliva filled the back of his mouth at the thought of food. He swallowed. "Then we can look for my parents, and your sister."

Cracker looked troubled. She opened her mouth to say something, but stopped. Closed her lips and forced a tired smile. She gazed into his black eyes and did not look away. "I'm not hungry. I feel sick to my stomach." She pulled the hood over her head. "But I'm thirsty. I hope we can drink their water."

Hunger squeezed Gee's middle once again, twisting with shocking intensity before slowly fading. "We need to hurry," he whispered.

What did people eat in Half World? What did he used to eat, in his past life, before he was adopted by Popo? Please, he begged, though he did not know to whom he prayed. Let us complete our journey and return home before the hunger grows too strong.

THE METAL FIRE-ESCAPE STAIRS zigzagged down the side of the building. Every other floor had a small emergency exit door in the wall, but there were no external door handles. Cracker's pace was failing, her breathing growing more and more ragged. She no longer mentioned craving cigarettes. And the ground seemed very far away.

Gee stared at Cracker's back. His jacket made her look even smaller.

Tack. Tack. Tack. Her footsteps were slow, her buckles scarcely jangled.

The eel stirred on Gee's forearm. Startled, he looked down. He'd almost forgotten that Lilla was there.

The eel slid along his skin, extending her head beyond his fingertips as if divining. Lilla arched her head upward.

Gee's breath stopped. He slowly tipped back his head.

Shhhhhhrrrrrrrr! Lilla's hissing was filled with rage, frothing with slime.

Through the stair slats, high, high above them, small shadows. The lingering echo of a liquid laughter.

Gee's heart thudded, slow. Loud. Fear so deeply entwined with curiosity he could not separate the two. Ilanna....

Lilla, her lower body firmly wrapped around Gee's skinny wrist, whipped her head downward, yanking hard on his arm. The eel writhed from side to side as if trying to pull him *away* from her mistress.

They had to hurry. He had to tell Cracker—

Crash!

Cracker cried out. The fire escape door. Open.

Gee's heart thudded inside his throat. How—

It was a middle-aged man. Skin sagging from his cheeks, his thick neck. Dressed in a white shirt, the cuffs unbuttoned, his lower half in boxer shorts. Bare feet. His eyes stared, vacant.

"What?" Cracker cried.

Gazing beyond them, the man walked calmly to the handrail of the fire escape. He bent over it at his waist, kicked with his feet and plummeted, head first, as fast as a stone.

Cracker screamed.

A shriek of delight drifted down from high above them. "I *heaar* you," Ilanna called, her voice tinged with triumph and malice. "We're right behind *youuuu*!"

Choking with horror, Gee squeezed past Cracker, who was frozen in place, and grabbed the edge of the door just before it clicked shut.

"Stop him!" Cracker cried, her face white with shock as she stared at the place where the older man had plunged to his death. "Stop him! Stop him!"

Gee grabbed her wrist and pulled her through the door. Slammed it shut behind them.

"Help him!" Cracker struggled for the door handle, desperately trying to yank her wrist out of Gee's clasp. "We have to help him!"

"He's dead!" Gee shouted. "He's already dead! He died a long time ago!"

Cracker began sobbing.

Gee, still holding on to his friend, began running down the densely carpeted hallway. "They're coming," he panted.

They whipped past identical doors as if they were trapped in a nightmare cartoon. Door after door after door. The same framed photo. The same side table with dried grey flowers. They ran and ran down the longest hallway in the world. Spilled into an open area. Two elevator doors.

Gee came to a stop so suddenly that Cracker thudded into his back. Her gasps mixed with her sobs. Gee stared at the two elevator buttons. Up or down?

Ilanna would think they'd go down. Because that made the most sense. So should they go up, instead? To throw them off?

Cracker, sobbing quietly, was no help.

You don't need to choose, his dark voice soothed. *Let inevitability decide for you. Your choices won't make any difference in the end....*

White Cat's furred head popped out of Cracker's skirt pocket. The rest of his body must still be stone, Gee thought wonderingly, because at eighteen pounds he'd rip right out.

"Quickly!" White Cat hissed.

Far down the long hallway, a scraping at the metal door. *Thud! Thud! Thud!* The pounding at the door overlaid the loud beating of his heart.

Ting.

Gee whipped around just as the doors of one of the elevators slid open. A waft of wet fur, moist blood, billowed outward. It smelled like a dog freshly struck down in the rain. Gee's lower lip quivered.

A room service boy held aloft a large tray of food covered in plastic wrap.

"Are you going up, sir?" the young attendant asked cheerfully.

"Eyes," Gee hissed at Cracker as he pulled her into the open car. He placed himself between her and the boy. Cracker tucked her chin to her chest and turned her face away.

White Cat had disappeared back into her pocket.

Thud! Thud! Thud! The noise echoed down the long hallway. The sound of something breaking loose. Cracking. The distance that had felt so far when they were running now felt hopelessly inconsequential.

"Shall we wait for your friends?" the room service boy asked coyly. His white-gloved finger hovered above the "Open" button.

Gee brushed the boy's hand aside to tap the "Close" button. He glanced at the attendant's face and offered a semblance of a smile.

The attendant's eyes widened and he staggered backward, the tray wobbling in the flat of his raised palm even as the doors slid shut. "Mr. Glueskin!" he gasped as he fumbled with the master keycard. He swiped it through the magnetic reader and the elevator resumed its upward journey. "I'm so sorry, sir. I didn't recognize your hair. You've been away for so long. You look much younger.... You look wonderful!" the boy fawned, lowering his eyes.

Roaring filled Gee's head and his heart thudded slower, louder. "Mr. Glueskin...," he mouthed. The name like a face, glimpsed in a crowd. A flash of recognition.

Gone.

Oh, god, Gee thought. Glueskin.... The smothering palm of his hand. His melting face. His elastic limbs.... No. Oh, no.

Ohhhhh, yesssssss, the nastiness inside giggled gleefully.

The attendant cleared his throat. "I see you have one of Miss Ilanna's eels. I hope she's well."

Gee thought rapidly. "Very well," he said. He glanced at the boy from beneath his hank of hair.

The boy raised his chin. He sniffed the air curiously, then closed his eyes and inhaled deeply, a dreamy expression on his face. "That smell," he murmured. "I haven't smelled anything like that in ages...."

Gee glanced at the top of Cracker's head. Caught sight of the items of food the attendant held up beside his ear. Movement. Little legs quivered and squirmed. Limbs pressed flat beneath the plastic wrap. Tails twitching, the shudder of panicked muscles beneath matted fur. The appetizers were *alive*.

Juices filled the back of Gee's throat, hunger squeezed his belly. Only to be rocked by a wave of disgust.

Cracker glanced his way, her eyes flaring gold.

Gee jerked his head. Look away, he emoted. "Those appetizers are so fresh." He smiled at the attendant. "They smell great."

"Noooo." The boy's nostrils were waffling with delight. "Something much better. Fresher. Sweeter. Ohhhhhh." Saliva hung from his lip, sagging lower and lower. His mouth dropped open to reveal a dark pit, a distant roar rising from his belly. The attendant slowly turned toward Cracker, his black eyes growing larger and larger. "It's overwhelming...."

Cracker, chin pressed into her chest, had stopped breathing. She had plastered herself into the back corner of the elevator car. There was no escape.

Ting!

The doors shushed open to the penthouse floor.

The room service boy shook his head as if rousing himself from a daydream and sucked the long bead of saliva back into his mouth. "Of course, I know it's yours," he said to Gee deferentially. He held the tray of food higher above his head, straightened his posture and reached out with his free hand to hold open the door. "After you, sir," he said, bowing his head. "If I may speak on behalf of Mirages Hotel, we're so pleased you've returned. Would you like to have me send someone to your suite with refreshments? Make sure you have everything you need?"

Gee's eyes flickered. He had a suite here. On the penthouse floor. He made a show of patting his front and back pockets and then held out his empty hand. "I seem to have misplaced my keycard." He shook his head and laughed apologetically. "Maybe you can open my door for me." Gee leaned in close and winked.

A small frown formed on the attendant's brow.

Gee could feel Cracker yank repeatedly on his back pocket, but he ignored her.

"Very good, sir," the boy responded, his voice slightly doubtful.

Gee held the door open with his hand and swept his Lilla-wrapped arm dramatically. "After you," he insisted.

The eel hissed warningly at the attendant, and he hurriedly stepped forward. Glancing once to see if they followed, the boy strode down the luxurious hallway.

"There've been a few changes while you've been gone," he murmured. "Some of your neighbours have moved on. New guests have moved in."

"But my suite remains the same?" Gee asked sternly, though his heart thudded loudly. He turned around to glance at Cracker. To see if White Cat was sticking his head out of her pocket.

"What the fuck?" Cracker mouthed silently. She held her palms upward and shrugged incredulously. The cat remained out of sight.

Gee jerked his chin as if to say, Never mind!

"Of course, Mr. Glueskin," the attendant simpered. "We would never give up your room. It will always be here for you. Forever."

Forever.... Gee gulped.

The boy stopped before Door Four. He retrieved his keycard and swiped it through the magnetic reader. A light clicked. The attendant turned the handle awkwardly and held the door ajar.

"I'm sorry I can't come in to help you settle in, sir, but I need to get these canapés to your neighbour before they perish." He giggled.

Gee almost sighed with relief. "Not at all," he said gruffly. "Carry on with your work." He yanked Cracker's wrist, forcing her into the foyer of the suite. He stood in the doorway to block the attendant's view of her, even as the boy craned for a good look.

The attendant's eyes narrowed. "If I may be so bold, sir," he whispered. "Your new guest smells intoxicatingly delicious. If you don't eat her quickly, I'm afraid you'll be forced to share with others who are like us!" His eyes widened, as large as saucers, and his mouth turned into an O of roaring wind, the force of the sudden vacuum ten times the strength of the open gate in the Cassiar Connector.

Gee raised his hand instinctively, simultaneously stretching his palm thin and splatting it over the boy's mouth.

The boy staggered.

Gee shed the skin from his palm, leaving the large white patch on the attendant's face.

In his alarm, the attendant lost hold of the platter. It fell to the dense carpet, the living canapés tearing out of the plastic and darting wildly about.

Farther down the long hallway, a door opened.

A small person, with an oversized, rotten pumpkin for a head, wobbled into view. Instead of a jack-o-lantern face she had only two small holes for eyes, as if someone had plunged a pencil into the sagging pumpkin flesh. "Yew idjit!" she screamed. "Ketch thim, or ill eetchyu insted!"

"Mmmhrrmmm." Gee choked back his giggling. How could

the pumpkin head speak? How could she eat? She didn't have a mouth....

Lilla rose up to Gee's face. She dropped open her jaws, her head bobbing with silent eel laughter.

Still smiling, he slammed the door shut and spun around.

Cracker stood with her hands on her hips. "What the HELL are you doing?"

Chapter Fourteen

"We have to get out of the building!" she shouted. "They're coming after us!"

Gee's lips turned downward. "I used to live here. Before … before I was adopted by Popo. There might be clues here that will help us. Because *I* don't know where my parents are. And *you* have no clue where you sister is. There's no point just running around lost. We need to learn more about how Half World works. Maybe—maybe there's a map, in—in my office!" Yes! A faint almost-memory flickered like an elusive minnow. He used to have an office….

Gee brushed past Cracker and strode into the living room.

Stopped.

Even in the darkness he could feel the room's size. The high ceiling. The window-wall across the room that revealed the flash and dazzle of the city so far below. Gee patted the wall for the light switch.

Click.

Gee's mouth fell open. So rich. So gorgeous. Even in black and white ... the pale grey fern pattern unfurling upon the walls. Lush carpet, dense and soft beneath his feet, antique furniture whose well-polished legs and armrests gleamed. In front of the heart-stopping window was a grand piano. It looked like a child's toy in the expanse of the room. Mine, Gee thought. All mine. A frisson of pleasure whispered up his spine.

"Don't be stupid," Cracker snapped. "We're like sitting ducks. Those monsters are right behind us. We have to leave! Now!"

Gee could not stop from scowling. "Look," he hissed. "Did you see how that room service attendant treated me? He was *afraid* of me. I have *power* here." He opened and closed his hands, enjoying the squeeze of his supple flesh. Lilla clenched encouragingly around his forearm. "They've kept my suite for me because they're afraid not to. So we don't necessarily have to run. Right? Get it? And you're missing an important detail. That attendant knew you're alive because of the way you smell. If you leave here there's no saying who or what else would be after you! We could stay for a little while," he smiled, cajoling. "We need to rest. We can order some food. You don't look well."

Cracker's face grew still, her voice cool. "You're changing. Have you noticed? You're being irrational. Like you've lost sight of why we've come here."

"NO ONE FORCED YOU HERE! SO JUST LEAVE ME THE FUCK ALONE!" Gee screamed, white spittle flying.

Cracker flinched, raising her arms to protect her face.

The monstrous rage faded as quickly as it had surged. Gee's trembling fingers covered his mouth. Oh, god….

"I'm sorry," he whispered. "I'm sorry. I-I don't know what's wrong. I didn't mean—"

The front door snicked shut.

Cracker was gone.

The silence of the room was made worse by the dull thud of his heart. He'd never felt more alone in his life.

Lilla swirled up his arm and over his shoulder, settling familiarly around his neck as if to say, See, you still have me. Her cool, moist body felt slightly sticky against his sensitive skin. Itchy.

Good riddance! the dark place inside him spat. *She was useless. Getting in the way. Now we can do what we want!*

Gee uneasily approached the vast window. It was sort of true. She *was* a difficult person. She didn't understand that he needed to explore this place. To understand who he was, to discover his legacy….

His study. He knew in his gut that he had one. Where he'd kept important things. There would be clues. Gee strode down a hallway and angrily began opening doors. Extravagant bedrooms, enormous washrooms. He left their lights on before striding on to the next room.

A study! Tall wooden shelves filled with leather-bound books of all sizes. Ohhhh, he'd been a learned man! He knew it! He'd been rich and intelligent as well as powerful.

Like you've lost track of why we've come here! Cracker's accusation rang inside Gee's mind.

He squeezed his eyes shut as a high-pitched whine pierced his ears. Gee shook his head and reached for one of the tomes on a shelf. The leather cover was unadorned. No title. Without an author's name. Gee opened the cover. No title page. He began flipping pages.

Blank. Blank. Blank. Something.

It was a crude drawing. Scrawled with black crayon. A stick figure of a man with a long stick tongue pulling a stick child into his open mouth. Beside the struggling girl was a dead stick dog, its eyes drawn x x. A knife sticking out of its back.

A picture drawn by a psychotic child.... The book fell from Gee's nerveless hands.

He grabbed another book. Frantically leafed through the pages. No words. No text. Empty pages. Violent stick drawings. Book after book after book. Scattered on the rich carpet.

Gee backed out of the study.

He hadn't been a scholar.... The books were in the shelves for show. That couldn't have been him. Gee gritted his teeth. Those weren't his books! He loved reading. Loved it! Taught to read by his popo by the time he was four years old. Popo who taught him....

The reason why he'd entered Half World. He had come here to discover his ties to the past—so that he could sever them. So that he could go back home, to Popo.

So he wouldn't have to be a monster....

What had he done?

Cracker, out there, alone, reeking of Life, in such danger. He'd promised her they would see each other through, together.

No! She wasn't alone. She still carried White Cat! And he needed him. He needed them both. To stay human. To find the way home.

A harsh sound escaped Gee's lips. He grabbed at Lilla's looping length around his throat with both hands and pulled frantically. "Get off!" he cried. "You're not my friend!"

Lilla desperately clung tighter. In her fear she began exuding a thick gooey slime, and Gee's fingers kept slipping.

"Let go!" he cried, trying to reach the rough edges of bone where she'd been torn away.

Knock. Knock.

Gee froze.

Elation ballooned inside him, as sweet as lilac. She'd come back!

"Cracker!" Gee laughed, a part-sob. He ran to the front door and eagerly turned the handle. "I was so stupid! I'm so s—"

Cold air sank into the foyer, heavy as guilt.

"Darling," Ilanna breathed. "What a merry chase you've led. I didn't have time to eat, and now I'm so very hungry." Her dewy eyes lowering, she stared at the rings of black curved around Gee's neck. She gasped. "Lilla!" she shrieked. "Is that you?"

Gee backed into his suite, his head sluggish with fear. He'd been caught.

Karu, taut and muscled, strode inside after Ilanna, his bright raptor eyes sweeping around the room. He ground his sharp, curved beak, a sound that sent shivers down Gee's spine.

"Where is she?" Karu rasped. "The girl?"

"Yes, darling," Ilanna cooed. "Where is that delicious thing?"

Rilla stretched toward Lilla's coils, but Lilla whipped around, snapping. Rilla jerked backward and began to hiss.

Ilanna torqued her body at the waist, the force of the momentum batting Rilla's head against the wall. "Of course she's still mad at you, idiot!" she snarled. Ever mercurial, sweetness dripped from her words as she switched to Lilla. "Don't be mad at Mummy, Lilla. It wasn't Mummy's idea to leave you as toll!"

She turned her intensity toward Gee. "Well? Where is she, our little treat? We can start by feasting upon her. So fresh from Life, just think how strong she'll make us!"

Unwillingly, saliva pooled in the back of Gee's mouth. Ohhh, yes. To eat. To tear, to gulp and swallow—

Stop it! he told himself. What are you *thinking*? Gee cleared his throat, lowering his chin so that his hair covered his eyes. Jesus! What was wrong with him?

Something fluttered in his esophagus. It trembled and quivered, distracting and urgent. He had to focus. He had to trick Ilanna and Karu. And get away. Find Cracker, before she was torn apart. So they could find what they came for. So they could go home. He had to hurry!

"She fell," Gee said slowly. "Off the stairs. A man was committing suicide and he didn't see us. He knocked Cracker down, the cat with her," he added.

Lilla was very still around his neck. Would the eel betray him?

Her innermost coil, hidden by an outer layer, began squeezing, stopping Gee's breath. He remained expressionless, but pressure began building behind his eyes, inside his eardrums. Lilla gradually loosed her grip.

It was a warning.

Gee raised his hand to stroke her side. Yes, he emoted. I understand. I'll keep you with me.

Ilanna's eyes narrowed with suspicion. "Karu!" she barked. "Go down to the ground level and search for her body."

Karu ruffled his feathers, slightly put out, but turned to obey.

"And eat something while you're out there!" Ilanna demanded. "You haven't eaten for too long. Do you hear? You'll be pulled back to the start of your Half World cycle, idiot bird! Don't come back until you've eaten! And don't think I won't be able to tell."

"I know when I need to eat. I eat enough to keep me from returning. I don't eat to gorge like you!" He stalked out, the door slamming behind him.

"What do you mean," Gee asked carefully, his tone even, cool, "about eating and the Half World cycles?"

Ilanna swayed toward him, the sea-salt wet perpetually streaming down her dress, the moist *squish, squish* as her bare feet soaked the thick carpet. Her dark seal eyes glinted as she moved closer. The reek of the icy seas filled Gee's senses.

"Haven't you eaten since you've returned, my darling Glueskin?"

Gee shuddered to hear her say the awful name.

Rilla began slowly twirling up his arm, snaking toward Lilla. Ilanna pressed her wet torso against Gee's body.

Gee, shocked, did not move away. She was so very cold.... As cold, as muscular as an eel.

"See how clever I was, getting rid of Karu," Ilanna whispered. "Aren't you pleased?"

Gee shuddered. She was so frightening. So exciting. No one had ever been attracted to him before. He liked how it felt....

This is not good for me, the boy who'd been raised by Popo thought frantically. This is not the time, nor the place!

Your popo is dead. You can do what you like in Half World! the nastiness inside him hissed.

Gee caught his hand rising, reaching to touch Ilanna's wet

kelpy hair. He forced his hand to fall. Focus. On what you need to do. He cleared his throat. "Tell me, first. About how eating works in Half World."

Ilanna sighed impatiently and pressed her forehead in the dip beneath his collarbones. "You've forgotten too much," she whispered. "*You* were the one who first woke from your Half World trance. When everyone else was still stuck in their stupor of suffering, you tore free from yours. You discovered that eating other sufferers extended your Half Life—the energy from their disrupted Half Life becoming yours even as they were flung back to the start of their stupid cycle, and you to do as you please. And during your years of eating and growing, you saw me and you fell in love." Her giggle sounded like a trickle of water as she nuzzled her face against his thin chest. "You set me free from *my* suffering. And that's why I'll love you forever. No matter what you do. No matter where you go. I'll always find you."

Was she nibbling through the cloth of his T-shirt? The hairs on the back of his neck tingled.

"You are the most powerful of Half World. You have the capacity to alter patterns." Her voice was filled with admiration and longing.

To be desired now…. Gee's head swirled wildly with his thoughts, his strange feelings. Popo would not approve. That was certain. But maybe just one kiss—

He had what? *Eaten* other Half Worlders? Had he eaten *people*?

He pushed Ilanna from him as he gagged, dry-retching, nausea splashing sour in the back of his throat.

Ilanna leapt away, causing Rilla to flip-flop off Gee's arm. Revulsion twisted Ilanna's eloquent face as she stared at his weakness.

And even as the nausea began to fade, a tide of hunger roared, twisting Gee's gut with a need so great he couldn't stop himself from groaning. He wrapped his skinny arms around his middle, bending at the waist to ease the ache in his muscles.

A long white bead of saliva dropped from his lips. It landed on the thick grey carpet. Without soaking into the strands, it began to harden.

"Fool!" Ilanna spat. "You've not eaten either! What is wrong with you! You, the visionary who broke the cycle of perpetual suffering! We have pleasures, now, in Half World. We thrive. And we are immortal! Do you understand? If we eat and eat and eat, we can continue with our Half Lives, never to revert to cyclical suffering. We are free!"

To feel such hunger, Gee thought numbly. To sate it. He dragged the back of his hand across his trembling lips and stood up. At what cost?

God, was it true? That book. On Popo's table. The one that the cat had forced him to read. It said that the monster had eaten and eaten when none was meant to.... But he'd thought it was symbolic.

He could not be that monster. He wasn't!

Ilanna strode to the window and stared out at the dark city. Rilla lashed from side to side as if channelling her mistress's emotions.

"You must eat," Ilanna said decidedly. "Now. It's the surest way to deal with the peculiar aversion you seem to have developed during your time in the weaker Realm of Flesh. You will gorge, and when you've built up strength I'll take you to your parents so that your transformation back into your true form will be complete. We can undo the harm that disgusting Melanie has wrought upon Half

World. And we can, once more, begin to erode the bindings that keep the Three Realms apart. Let Half World flood the boundaries to the other Realms. Let all turn into Half World!"

Ilanna turned to a small panel set into the wall and had Rilla press one of its square buttons. Several seconds passed before a static-filled bleating began sounding in regular intervals.

An intercom, Gee realized. So old-fashioned. He almost giggled.

"Yes, sir. How may I be of service?" The tinny voice was brimming with enthusiasm.

"We need fresh canapés. A dozen of your best. With a bottle of blood wine," Ilanna snapped. "And be quick about it."

"Very good, madam," the tinny voice said.

Ilanna slowly spun around.

She was so graceful, Gee couldn't help thinking. The sensuality of kelp flowing under water. She swayed back and forth as she approached him once again. Her eyes gleamed, wet, full of desire and power. She pressed against him and her icy chill sank into his flesh, a cold that throbbed between pain and desire.

Gee's teeth began to chatter.

Ilanna giggled. Rilla began to thread through his hair, even as Lilla hissed warningly from Gee's neck. Ilanna slid one foot up the back of Gee's calf.

Something sharp stabbed through his jeans, abrading his skin. Gee glanced down. Ilanna's toenails were covered with barnacles. Was that a small oyster? He shuddered with revulsion. Longing.

Soft cold kisses. Along his jawbone, approaching his neck.

Lilla, disgusted, slid down his back and dropped to the floor.

She propelled herself awkwardly, like a snake, to nestle peevishly around a piano leg.

His neck bare, Ilanna began biting, stinging his sensitive skin.

Oh god, Gee thought. Her eel tongue. But his disgust wasn't strong enough for him to push her away. Goosebumps rippled across his skin. Gee, uncertain, lips slightly parted.

She kissed him, cold, long, tasting of the winter sea.

Was this what it was like to kiss a mermaid? Gee wondered. Salty, so intensely cold, and full of drowning....

Let me drown like this forever, he thought. Give me more. Give me all of it. Never let it stop.

Chapter Fifteen

He didn't realize she'd stopped kissing him until he opened his eyes.

Her eyes were gleaming and a little sneer twisted the corner of her lips.

Gee pulled away. His muscles were stiff and his joints wouldn't bend. He tottered, on the verge of falling straight backward. He swung out his arms for balance, but they were almost locked motionless.

Ilanna broke into trickling laughter. "Ohhhh, my Glueskin," she sighed fondly. "This always happens with you! I guess I'll have to take a hot bath so I won't be so cold."

Gee stared at his smooth palms. He opened and closed his fingers. The joints were sluggish and stiff with cold. He could scarcely close his fingers into fists. "What's wrong with me?"

"Nothing that won't wear off, darling." Ilanna rolled her eyes.

"Your glueskin doesn't fare well with cold temperature, *stupid.* Don't you remember!" she snarled in a sudden fit of rage. Her distorted face softened and she shook her head compassionately. "Poor baby. Can't remember anything. Don't worry. Ilanna will take care of you."

"But this didn't happen to me in the Realm of Flesh. I was like everyone else...," Gee whispered.

No, you weren't. Don't lie to yourself. Don't be pathetic!

Ilanna shrugged. "Half World isn't like the feeble Realm of Flesh. The sooner you understand that with your body, the better." She strolled toward the hallway. "I'm taking a hot bath so my cold doesn't make you, well, frigid." She tittered. "I'll show you what we can do with our bodies in Half World." She opened her eyes wide, looking as helpless as a baby seal. "Then we'll feast on crunchy little Half Lives to build up our strength, hmmmmm? Don't eat the room service boy, darling. Save him for later." She disappeared down the hallway.

Gee's heart thudded painfully. Ilanna's cold wetness had seeped through his clothing. His knees ached. He shuddered. Once she started filling the bathtub he could flee.

"By the way," Ilanna said.

Gee twitched.

She leaned against the frame of the hall entrance. "I'll leave Rilla here to keep you company. She doesn't like hot water. And maybe she and Lilla can make up." She made a moue with her lips toward Lilla.

Lilla turned her head away.

Ilanna clicked her tongue. She glared at Rilla. "Well, you know the drill!"

Rilla turned toward the beautifully carved hallway frame. She opened her jaws wide and clamped down on the wood, her sharp teeth sinking in.

Ilanna gritted her teeth. She yanked herself away from her eel, screaming as more than half a metre of Rilla's tail end was wrenched from her shoulder socket with a wet squelching sound. She staggered against the opposite wall, panting, eyes squeezed shut.

Gee hadn't had enough time to look away. He stared, aghast, at the incredible pain she suffered. What horror had she gone through that she'd ended up with eels instead of arms?

Ilanna caught Gee's look. "Don't pity me!" she snarled. Her rage melted and she smiled with such selkie sweetness that he almost smiled in return.

"I don't want your pity. I want you to be who you were before: Mr. Glueskin, hero of Half World. Powerful. Cruel. Monstrous. And you will," she smiled. "It's what you were born to be."

Rilla, her teeth embedded in the wood, could not release herself. She bit down harder, thrashing wildly from side to side until the wood began to squeak and grind. With a great crunch she bit right through and fell to the thick carpet.

She was close to two metres long. And her bite.... Rilla could bite right through Gee's arms, his legs. She turned toward him, her jaws open in a great eel grin. Slivers of shredded wood were caught between her glinting teeth.

"You have a nice visit and wait for room service while I warm up." Ilanna's voice faded as she disappeared down the hallway once more. The roar of water filling the tub.

Gee eyed Rilla. Could he outrun the eel to the door? He glanced at the walls for a clock. He had no idea how much time had passed since Cracker left. Time seemed odd, stretching and contracting. It felt as if he'd arrived in Half World a week ago. But surely he'd been at home, above Popo's store, only yesterday?

He had to catch up to Cracker. Fast. Before she was lost. Before he lost himself. Because the longer he stayed with Ilanna, the longer he stayed in Half World.... Gee stared at his stiff hands, opening and closing his fingers. He was changing. His body, his thoughts. The edges of his rage. His longings.... Cracker was right. He had to hurry. If he ever wanted to return home. Before—

Damn that White Cat! He needed him now! All he had was half an eel, with no way of knowing if he could trust it.

Lilla, as if sensing his thoughts, began raising her head, her small glinting eye utterly unreadable.

The ache in Gee's joints began to subside as his body returned to room temperature. He stared at the backs of his hands and forearms. Did he have bones? Did he *ever* have bones? The pinkie that had reformed after he'd bitten off the toll—it looked no different from the original. Even if Rilla bit off an arm or a leg, maybe he'd be able to shape himself another. Because he had to get away, now, before Ilanna and Karu came back. Surely he could outrun an eel on land. He glanced dubiously at Rilla.

The eel slowly raised her head upright, twelve inches above the floor, like a cobra. She snaked toward him, weaving from side to side, hissing softly.

Lilla hissed her own warning and began gliding out from the shelter of the piano.

A bell chimed. Both eels turned toward the entranceway.

Room service, Gee realized. He fought an urge to giggle. It wasn't funny. None of it was funny.

The bell chimed again. Gee moved toward the door, and Rilla followed.

"Room service!" a cheerful voice announced.

Gee slid his hands through his dark hair before letting the strands slide back to obscure his face. He opened the door.

It wasn't the young attendant from before. It was a chimpanzee, wearing the hotel uniform and holding aloft a plastic-wrapped tray of writhing canapés, a bottle of wine.

Gee wished a cap was part of its uniform … so that he wouldn't have to see the hole in the ape's head, the exposed glistening brain, the mess of wires that were embedded in the vulnerable folds, the colour of soft tofu.

"Room service!" the chimpanzee repeated, the right half of his face grimacing while the left side smiled.

Gee stepped back so that he could bring in the tray.

The ape lurched from side to side on his bent legs, somehow managing to keep the tray from falling. He placed it on a side table and bowed extravagantly.

"Thank you," Gee said, his voice scarcely audible.

"Thank *you*, sir," the attendant enthused.

A tip. He should give him a tip. Gee patted his pockets, heard a faint jangle. He slipped his hand into his pocket, but it was only his house keys. He'd spent all his cash on the taxi back home from the hospital. It felt like months ago….

Gee blinked. "I'm sorry," he said. "I don't seem to have any change."

"Thank you, sir!" The room service attendant saluted. "It's the thought that counts! Thank *you*, sir, for not eating me!" In his excitement he forgot all decorum, dropping from his upright posture and loping down the hallway on all fours.

The plastic wrapping crinkled, crackled. The *slap, slap, slap* of something struggling.

Gee stared at the tray of "the freshest" canapés.

Tightly encased by several layers of plastic, the dozen rats had room to move only their pale, naked tails. Some of them, caught in a panic, twitched spasmodically against the transparent binding. They shuddered and convulsed before flopping back weakly, spent.

Liquid pooled inside Gee's mouth. Raging hunger and disgust roiled inside him like worms. He swallowed.

Rilla and Lilla had drawn closer. Long strands of gooey slime hung from their open mouths. *"Eeeaaaaatsss,"* Rilla hissed, bobbing back and forth. As if she'd been hypnotized by the sight of the quivering rats.

The distant roar from the bathroom stopped. The tub must have filled.

Gee reached for the tray and tore off the wrap. Two seconds of stillness.

The rats erupted. Silently, instinctively, they darted for the walls, seeking vents and openings. The scrabbling of tiny claws. The eels whipped after them, unable to control their predator drive.

A bulging in the back of Gee's throat. As if a limb were trying to grow out of his maw. The compulsion to catch a plump, quivering rat was so great he could scarcely bear it. He slapped himself. The sound, more than the pain, jolted him out of his instincts.

Gee ran for the door. Faltered.

Damn it! he thought. He didn't owe her! He had no reason to feel responsible! But he couldn't stop himself from looking back.

Rilla was by the piano, her mouth plugged with half a rat. Lilla, too slow-moving without her bottom half and tail, hadn't caught any prey.

"Lilla!" Gee hissed.

Both eels whipped their head toward him, the pale rat tail dangling from Rilla's jaws, swinging wildly.

Ilanna sauntered into the room, steam rising from her naked body. The ragged grey edges of skin circled her empty shoulder sockets like decayed lace.

Lilla began thrashing toward Gee. But Rilla, intact, reached him first, the squirming rat still caught in her teeth.

"Stop him, Rilla!" Ilanna cried, her voice thick with rage.

Rilla clamped down with her jaws to snap the rat in two just as Gee swung back his leg and kicked the eel's side. Her heavy, muscular body sailed through the air.

"No!" Ilanna cried as she rushed toward her eel.

Gee darted for Lilla and gripped her around her middle, slime squeezing out from between his fingers. He ran. Out the door. Down the hallway, even as Lilla curled up his forearm, running so hard that he crashed into the elevator. He banged at the down button.

Please, he begged. Please, please, please let the car be empty. He looked over his shoulder, heart thudding loud and slow inside his head.

Ting.

He whipped his head around as the doors slid open. A small sound escaped his lips, his relief so great.

No one. No Karu. Gee staggered inside and *click, click, clicked* the button to close the door. He started breathing once the doors slid shut.

Gee stared at all the different buttons on the panel—he had to flee in the direction Cracker was most likely to take. He dragged his hand across his face. Think! Think!

His stomach squeezed and rippled, acute hunger a stabbing pain, forcing him to double over. He dropped to his hands and knees. He'd never been so hungry before, ever in his life—why did he hunger so, now? He was so hungry he could eat.... His eyes fell upon Lilla clenched around his forearm.

He could eat a live eel....

Lilla, as if feeling his thoughts, squeezed more tightly.

Gee shook his head. He forced himself upright and pressed the button for the lobby. The hotel workers knew him only as Mr. Glueskin, the horrific monster. That meant they were unlikely to attack him.

The elevator wasn't moving.

Gee pressed the lobby button more firmly. The car did not move. What—

He needed a key. He had to swipe the keycard through the magnetic reader in order to leave the penthouse level. He was trapped, suspended in a box, until someone with a keycard swiped first.

Did Ilanna realize this? She wouldn't have a card either, would she?

But she could push the elevator call button and the doors would open, revealing him, as easy as opening a birthday present....

He should make a dash for the fire escape route, down the length of the hall. Or should he wait for a random guest or hotel worker to call the elevator back down?

Yes, no, maybe so! the nasty voice inside him tittered. *Yes, no, maybe so!*

Chapter Sixteen

The elevator lurched, and began descending.

Gee almost wept.

The numbers lighting up above the door didn't stop at the lobby. Gee tucked himself against the side of the car as it continued descending.

The car halted at sub-basement level 2. The doors slid open.

A moist waft of cooked meat, wet fur and dirty laundry rolled inside the enclosed space. Gee's gut churned. He didn't know if it was hunger or nausea.

A room service attendant, holding a tray with champagne on ice, stepped into the car. He did a double-take when he caught sight of Gee. "Mr. Glueskin, sir!" he exclaimed.

It was the boy who'd been taking canapés to the pumpkin head, Gee realized.

"Are you looking for that delicious guest you had with you?" The attendant leaned toward him and winked. "I saw her down here with a cat! Of course I didn't try to catch her myself—I know she's your special treat. Are you playing hide 'n' seek to make it all the more exciting?"

Gee cleared his throat. Phlegm rattled, and he swallowed it down. "Yes, as a matter of fact." He smiled with what he hoped looked like malicious anticipation. "I thought raising the stakes would make the *capture* so much more *satisfying*."

"Very good, sir!" The boy nodded enthusiastically.

"But she seems to be a clever little mouse," Gee complained. "I don't suppose you could provide me with a little *hint*."

"Oh, it would be so unsporting, sir, if I mentioned that I might have seen a mouse entering the Archives." The attendant opened his eyes wide, affecting innocence, as he pointed down the long hallway.

"Ahhh," Gee sighed. "One must be sporting, at all costs, in order to be a gentleman." He punched the attendant's free arm, hard enough to hurt. The bottle in the ice bucket clattered. "I do admire your integrity." He winked. "I'll be sure to reward you later."

The attendant took a step back, his expression fearful and confused. "Thank you, sir?"

Gee strode confidently out of the elevator, when an idea flared inside him. He spun around to catch the edge of the closing door, forcing it to open once more. "One other thing," he whispered.

"Yes?" The attendant instinctively tried to push himself deeper into the farthest corner.

Gee could see that the boy struggled to stop himself from

raising his arm to protect his head. As if he expected Gee to strike him.

That someone could be so frightened of him. It was awful.

It was heady....

Gee cleared his throat. "Ilanna has become tedious. She has her charms, but I've grown tired of her antics. Have security escort her out of my suite. She is to have no further access to my quarters. See that this is dealt with, and you shall be...." Gee paused.

The room service boy held the tray with both hands in front of his chest so that the champagne partly blocked his face.

"Appreciated," Gee said slowly.

"Of course, sir! Right away, sir!" the boy cried over-enthusiastically.

Gee released his hand and stepped back. The elevator doors slid shut.

A wide grin spread across his face. He was getting better at this! A small flame of hope flared inside him, and he raised Lilla jubilantly into the air and shook his closed fist. "I can do this!" he exulted.

Lilla hissed warningly and Gee sheepishly lowered his arm. He dropped his head so that his long hair fell across his face, tucked his hands into his jeans pockets and sauntered casually down the hallway, glancing at the doors from the corner of his eyes, looking for a sign.

His fingers brushed against something small and cool in his left pocket. Gee frowned and pulled it out.

It was a safety pin. The one that had flown out of Cracker's hair and landed on the table. She'd said he could keep it for a souvenir.... Gee squeezed it tight and then returned it to his pocket. He picked up his pace, swiftly passing doors marked with signs. "Laundry," he read, "Kitchen," "Supplies."

A muffled little giggle.

Gee flicked a glance over his shoulder, half-expecting to see a child on a tricycle....

The hallway was empty. Silent.

The hairs slowly began rising on the back of his neck. All those rooms.... They should have been noisy with the sounds of cooking, the thrum of washers and dryers, the raised voices of the workers.

Why do you think Half World functions in ways you find familiar? the nasty little voice inside him tittered. *Half World is governed by memory and pain! Suffering and despair.*

The little giggle rippled again. Gee whipped his head forward.

The long hallway was empty.

In his peripheral vision he could see a small, unmarked wooden door slowly swing open. Unlike the other doors in the passageway it was unlit on the other side, and the light from the hallway didn't penetrate the darkness. A little gust of air blew outward and brought with it the odour of slightly mildewed books. Old paper. Age.

"This must be it," Gee whispered.

Lilla extended her length a few inches past Gee's hand. She opened her jaws as if tasting the air inside her mouth.

A barely audible giggle wafted toward him.

Gee swallowed. "Cracker?" he whispered. He stepped through the little doorway and, slightly hunched over, began walking down the dark passage. Little bits crackled and crunched unpleasantly beneath his sneakers. "Cracker," he called again, a little louder.

Scrabbling of nails, claws, along the walls. Gee shuddered. Must be rats, he thought. Only rats.

The darkness intensified. Dim shadows, black against grey. He couldn't see where the passage led. The sound of his slow heart was loud inside his ears. He walked carefully, his hand outstretched. Lilla, ever cautious, spiralled up his arm to curl around his neck.

Behind them, the small door to the hallway slammed shut. Utter blackness.

The sound of his own breathing. Too loud. Like the breath of an Other.

His outstretched fingers felt something rough. Slightly damp. He jerked his hand away. Tentatively reached out once more.

Wood. Pieces of wood. The heads of heavy metal nails, large and rough. A metal ring, embedded. Gee curved his fingers around it and took a breath. He pulled.

The door screeched on old hinges. The musty, complex odour of ancient books and dust washed over them like a slow-moving wave. If at all possible, the Archives behind the small door was even darker.

"Are you there?" Gee's voice was no more than a rasping whisper.

It was as if the entire room was holding its breath.

Gee swallowed. He could feel the size of the room through the open doorway. He should just turn around and feel his way back to the main hallway. It was too dark to see or do anything. He could find a flashlight and come back. He turned away.

Two small hands slammed into his stomach. Gee staggered backward, only for his calves to hit something solid. He crumpled at the knees, tripping over something huddled on the floor. Gee fell through the doorway and into the Archives. Landing hard on his back, his breath was knocked from his lungs.

Childish giggles. From either side of him. The patter of little feet. The door slammed, the iron ring clanking from the other side.

Something *whisked* past him, the cool air of it whipping the bottom edge of his T-shirt, skating against his skin. Gee yanked his arms and legs toward his torso, standing up, twisting his neck from side to side, trying futilely to see in the utter darkness.

A trail of giggles behind him. Too close.

Lilla hissed warningly.

"Who are you?" a sweet childish voice asked.

Gee slowly turned around.

From some distance away came a loud *clack*, as if a large switch had been flipped. Light blazed from the enormous ceiling. Blinded, Gee covered his eyes with his forearm.

Childish whispery voices. Their voices breaking into laughter.

Gee's skin prickled. Lilla seemed to press herself flat against his collarbones. He had no idea how many of them there were. Their voices moved about like gusts of errant wind. And where was Cracker?

Four little girls in a row; they were no older than five or six years old.... Dressed in identical frocks and white buckled shoes, they stood silently before him with their hands clasped behind their backs. Their faces were exceedingly white, their skin overblown. Soft-looking. As if they were bloated with water and rotting from within. Children who were, each in a different way, terribly maimed. Quadruplets. Or clones. An uncanny duplication made horrific with their maiming.

"Where did you come from?" A child who was covered with gaping, bloodless cuts stared at him. The girl's eyes were as dark as an abyss.

Something tightened inside Gee's gut. Her eyes, he thought, are just like mine.

"He's funny," a girl with empty eye sockets chortled.

Lilla squeezed Gee's torso from beneath his shirt. It felt like a warning.

"I want to play with Older Brother," the girl with the slashed face said. "That girl is no fun. Let's play with Older Brother!"

"Wait!" Gee cried. "What girl? I need to see her. She's my friend, Cracker."

"Do you have crackers?" The eyeless girl's mouth fell open. Black saliva began to dribble from her lips.

A fifth little girl in a wet smock stepped out from a row of books. She beamed up at Gee, almost every inch of her exposed skin covered in shiny black leeches.

Quintuplets, not quadruplets.... They were horrible to look at, repulsive ... but they were still little children, who had died some horrible death. Gee swallowed. So young. He crouched down on his haunches. "My friend's name is Cracker," he explained gently. "We're here to do something really important, and then we have to go back home. In time for supper." Gee smiled. The back of his eyes felt hot.

If only it were that simple. He and Cracker, visiting old family members and then rushing back home for supper. Popo, cross, would tell him it had been his turn to make the evening meal. But she would ask him if he was hungry. Whip up an omelette, maybe, and mushroom soup. Sautéed spinach and hot steamed rice.

Gee's stomach squeezed so hard he almost bent in half. He panted through the pain that seized like a cramp.

A small, cold wet hand touched his shoulder. The girl with

the leeches, her face much too close. Her eyes were unbearable. "Is Older Brother hungry too?" she asked, her childish voice so sweet, her breath reeking of rot. She patted his shoulder sympathetically, and the *thwap, thwap*, of her sagging flesh sounded as if it was ready to fall off her bones.

Gee pulled away—he couldn't help himself. He quickly scanned the enormous room: the ceiling easily eight metres high, rows of shelves filled with dusty books of various sizes and shapes. There were cubbies brimming with rolled parchments, pieces of broken pottery, dolls missing legs and arms, stuffed animals with no heads. Gee's eyes narrowed. The book that cat had made him read: it had mentioned the Archives of Unfinished Books.

There must be an archivist. Surely not these little girls? "What are you girls doing here?" Gee asked. "Are you supposed to be here?"

"We *live* here, stupid!" the girl without eyes hissed, her small teeth rotten and broken.

Gee stood up slowly.

The girls moved around him so that he was encircled.

"I want to speak with the archivist in charge," Gee said sternly. "My name is Mr. Glueskin. She would have heard of me."

The children began chanting in low whispery voices. And as the volume rose, the words came faster and faster.

"Fudge, fudge,
Call the judge
Mr. Glueskin's gonna have a ba-by!
What's it gonna be?
Girl? Boy? Slavering monster?
Girl? Boy? Slavering monster?"

These girls didn't know the previous Mr. Glueskin, not like the room service boy did. Frustration roiled inside Gee's head. The little brats were wasting his time. And why wouldn't they answer any of his questions about Cracker? He'd felt sorry for them for having died early, and died horribly. But maybe that was his mistake. To treat them kindly. Maybe they understood only cruelty and pain. An odd little grin began spreading across his face.

The girls, standing in a loose circle, ceased chanting. They simultaneously turned their faces to stare impassively at Gee.

Empty eye sockets, torn bloodless faces, pale overblown flesh, pouchy and sagging—

A low moan. Beyond a row of bookshelves.

Gee's heart thudded loud in his ears. "What have you done to her!" he shouted.

The little girls simultaneously took one step closer. "Did you yell at us?" the eyeless child asked. "Did you?"

"We don't like to be yelled at," the leeched girl said coldly. "We hate it."

The girls encircled Gee, holding hands as if they were playing a game. "We hate it," they chanted. "We hate it."

They turned circles around him, faster and faster, until they were a blur of white dresses. "We hate it, we hate it," they chanted. "We hate you. We hate you!"

They're little children, Gee told himself. He could overpower them. He didn't want to hurt them. But they were already dead, weren't they? They spun around him so fast he was growing dizzy. So difficult to think. Something *bulged* in the back of his throat. Eyes wide, Gee clamped his hands over his mouth. He convulsed to keep it in.

26

He couldn't. He mustn't.

The horrible little creatures. They were children....

No different from rats. The lively rat canapés they served at the Mirages.

Twirling around him. Like targets in a carnival. Tasty, squirmy and so nourishing—

No! Gee pressed his palms desperately against his mouth. *Popo,* he cried. *Please. Help me. White Cat....*

His jaws. Loosening. Unhinging. Eyes wide, Gee cast about the room. Something. To make them stop. Spinning and spinning. His mouth opening, inexorably....

Make it stop before it was too late.

Chapter Seventeen

There was no one. No one to stop him.

Gee crammed his forearm into his widening mouth. Plugged the tickling bulge, the compulsive muscle in the back of his throat. He bowled through the spinning girls as if they were playing a game of Red Rover.

The girls scattered like bocce balls, whisking away in five different directions, the *patter patter patter* of their footsteps echoing between rows of books. Into the depths of the massive Archives.

Gee ran toward the centre of the room where he'd heard the groan coming from.

The compulsion from the back of his throat slowly receded. He could finally loosen his jaw's grip, let his forearm drop from his mouth. He didn't even notice that his teeth had broken through his white flesh....

Gee careened around a set of shelves and came to an open space furnished with a long wooden table. Pieces of parchment, folded sheets of paper, were strewn all over the floor.

The table looked like the one back home, at his grandmother's place....

On the table, taped flat to the surface, completely immobile, was Cracker.

"Jeeesus!" Gee hissed.

The edges of the table were set with mismatched plates, bowls and teacups. Broken dolls and maimed stuffed animals sat in the twelve wooden chairs that circled the table. Cracker, catching sight of Gee in the corner of her eye, began fighting at the bonds. Her mouth was stopped with tape, but he could see she was furious. Terrified.

"Mmmm mm mmmph!"

Gee ran to her side, knocking several chairs out of the way. They clattered loudly against the stone floor. He began babbling as he tore off the tape. "I'm sorry! This is going to hurt. I'm sorry I yelled at you. I didn't mean it. I'm better now. Are you okay? Did they hurt you?"

"Ahhhh!" Cracker cried, as Gee tried to gently pull the tape away from her mouth.

Thank you, Gee thought, as he stared at her. Thank you for being alive. He ripped the tape off her arms, from her shoulders. They'd looped the strips around the entire table, and Gee had to duck up and down to unwind it.

"I hate kids," Cracker rasped.

Gee, ripping tape away beneath the table, broke into a grin.

"I'm never going to be a mother," she muttered.

Gee brought the length of tape back up, tore the freed portion off, tossed it to the side and began ripping off what remained.

Arms and torso free, Cracker, groaning, sat up. She had looked weary before, but now she looked as if she'd gone through a round of chemotherapy. Her complexion was grey and her golden eyes were so dim Gee could scarcely discern their colour.

Not good, he thought. What was happening to her Life Spirit?

What a waste, the nasty voice inside him whispered. *Don't let it go to waste.*

Gee shook his head, as if shaking would drive the evil voice out of him. "Where's White Cat?" he demanded. He felt a wisp of cold air whipping past him. The echo of childish little feet. "Why didn't he help you?" Those little kids. What did they want? Gee tried ripping at the overlapping tape around Cracker's knees.

The cat's head popped out of Cracker's skirt pocket, a disgusted look in his eyes. "You might have noticed, but I was trapped? Beneath tape? There *is* the matter of, well, *materiality* and *space*, you know." Suddenly the cat hissed, the pupils of his eyes flooding the irises. "Those terrors are back!" He ducked back inside.

"What was that?" a child voice breathed.

Gee twitched.

The girl with the leeches was standing right beside him. He could see the top of her head. Leeches squirmed inside her wet strands of hair, glinting and writhing.

"Was that a kitty?" she asked wonderingly.

"Kitty! Kitty!" the girls' voices cried from throughout the cavernous room. They pattered toward the table, smiling so sweetly it almost broke Gee's heart.

He had to be careful. The girls weren't powerless. They had

overcome Cracker. He could trick them, Gee thought. They're still little.... "Simon says STOP!" he cried. The four girls lurched to a stop, but not before they teetered, staggered.

"I saw you all move," Gee said decidedly. He pointed. "Go back to that bookshelf."

"Awwwww!" the girls moaned as they stomped farther back.

Gee could hear Cracker ripping at the rest of the tape.

The girl with the leeches was staring at the pocket where White Cat had disappeared.

"You have to go back too," Gee said, "to make the game fair. Simon Says go join your sisters."

"I don't feel like playing fair. I don't feel like playing. I'm so *hungry*...."

Plat. Plat. Plat. Drool was actually falling from her lips, splattering on the floor.

"Yes," her sisters whispered. "We finished eating all the rats and mice and bugs a long time ago."

"Hungry, hungry," the girls chanted, drawing closer toward them.

The hair rose on the back of Gee's neck. The girls were little cannibals.... Just as he used to be ... in the past. When he used to be Mr. Glueskin—

Just like you are now! the ugly voice snarled, filling Gee's head with rage and fear. Swamping him. Overwhelming. And on the tail of those emotions roared his own unbearable hunger. It clenched his muscles like a cramp, twisting so intensely it took his breath away. He would have fallen to his knees. He caught the edge of the long table with both hands, his knuckles turning white with the effort to remain standing.

A leech-covered hand patted one of Gee's rigid claws as he panted through the horrible spasms. "You're hungry, too." The little girl's voice was tender.

Gee stared at her awful hand. It was so messed up. The sufferers who suffered. Who went on to create new suffering. It wasn't right. He didn't want to be a part of it. He wouldn't! If only he could control his own feelings....

Gee widened his eyes with exaggerated outrage and turned to sweep his gaze over the little girls. "You've all been very bad children," he accused.

The girls came to a standstill. They glanced nervously at each other.

The leech-covered girl boldly inched closer. "No, we haven't!"

Three of her sisters gasped in admiration. The eyeless girl was silent.

"You caught my friend. You taped her up. And you were going to eat her!" Gee admonished.

A small voice whimpered. It was working!

"We're sorry," the eyeless girl beseeched.

Gee looked down at the child's face. Black tears ran from her empty sockets. "We didn't mean to. We'll fix it better. Don't get mad at us. We don't mean to be bad." Her tone wasn't playful. The maimed child's lips were twisted, quivering with terror.

Gee wondered if he'd stumbled upon their horrible cycle....

"I'm not sorry!" the leech-child said defiantly.

"Stop it, Sherylyne!" the sister with the slashed face pleaded. "You always get us into worse trouble!" Another child started weeping.

"We're trapped here. And she hurts us and she hurts us,"

Sherylyne spat. "If we eat things it makes us stronger! It takes longer before she comes back. To kill us again. So we got to keep on eating because *it's not our fault*! We're going to eat your friend. Then we're going to eat you!"

Yesssssss. His body remembered.... A different kind of eating, before those days of meals with Popo, of humble greens and stir-fried tofu.... A different kind of hunger—aching, overwhelming, and the pitiful weakness that came with the need, always, until the first *snap* of his incredible tongue, the delicious fullness in his gullet, how everything became more solid, more real. Sweet energy, exploding through his body—

Gee's stomach twisted, writhed. He gasped, clamping his arms around his middle, folding over with the intensity. The hunger attacks were growing more frequent ... and his will, growing weaker.

If you eat just one of the little girls, the bad voice inside of him cajoled, *you'll have strength enough to survive. To do what you must so that you can go back home.*

Gee clamped his hands over his ears, unaware that a low moan escaped his lips. What kind of logic was that! After doing such a horrendous thing, how could he possibly go home? It was the Other's voice. Not his own. It couldn't be. It mustn't.... Because that's not the child Popo had raised. Popo could never love that other child.

Cracker rolled off the side of the table. She sagged beneath her weight, sucking her breath in with pain, but she managed not to crumple. "Gee," she cried. "Gee!"

White Cat leapt out of Cracker's pocket, landing lightly on the cold floor. "You must fight it!" the cat snarled. "Hold fast. Do not succumb to the feeling!"

"Kitty!" the leech-girl cried. She ran toward the cat, her arms outstretched.

White Cat sprang atop a set of shelves housing square cubbies, knocking scrolls and old newspapers onto the floor.

"Kitty cat! Kitty cat!" the girls screamed, laughing as they ran after him.

White Cat leapt onto a set of higher bookshelves and loped along the top, away from Gee and Cracker.

"Kill the cat! Kill the cat!" the chasing children screeched with joy.

"Come on," Cracker said. "Let's get out of here."

Gee couldn't stop tracking the leaping, darting movements of the little children. How easy it would be to catch one. Just a matter of whipping out his tongue. His arm. Wonderfully elastic. And, *smack*! His palm would stick to the back of the child's head and he'd yank her back. What he would do....

"Gee!" Cracker shouted. She grabbed a fistful of his T-shirt and shook hard.

Lilla stuck her head out of Gee's collar and hissed.

"Ugh!" Cracker instinctively backed away—right into the child with no eyes.

"Got you!" the little girl crowed, wrapping both arms around Cracker's skinny waist.

In the far recesses of the Archives White Cat yowled and yowled and the roar of little girl voices rose up, triumphant.

"Get off of me you little creep!" Cracker cried, pulling at the little girl's arms. But the child clung tighter than a tick, giggling madly.

Her four sisters marched back, holding White Cat aloft in their small hands. They seemed to feel no pain as White Cat slashed his claws along their hands and forearms, rending their soggy flesh.

"Do something!" Cracker shouted at Gee.

Gee stared helplessly. He could use his Half World powers, but if he started down that path he'd put himself at terrible risk of not being able to control them. What if he ended up doing the unconscionable?

The image of Popo's crinkled face, her keen bright eyes—the only person who'd always met his gaze—formed, unbidden, in his mind. She looked so real, so close, that his heart spasmed with emotion.

You're a good boy.

The sound of her voice filled him up with a warm, wondrous light. A good boy....

Was he hearing her voice because she'd died?

No.

He didn't believe it. He wouldn't! Gee took a step toward the eyeless girl.

A great *clang* resounded in the Archives. Someone had slammed shut the small entrance door.

"I'm *back*," an adult voice rang.

The girls froze. Mid-stride. As if they were playing Simon Says. Their faces stiff with terror.

"What are you naughty girls up to now?" a kindly voice asked. A slender woman wearing a smart skirt and jacket and a small pillbox hat pinned pertly to her head *click-clacked* down the rows of books toward the great table.

The quintuplets screamed and screamed. The four girls dropped White Cat and the eyeless one pushed Cracker out of her arms.

They began running about in different directions, skittering atop the bookshelves, scuttling across the ceiling like terrified lizards. They darted and fled like panicked prey.

But they did not run toward the door.

The stylish woman chased after the terrified children. She dashed about the great room, her fury terrible in her impassive face, whisking past Gee and Cracker as if they were pieces of furniture. She grabbed one girl by the arm, then another by the leg, shoving them into a sack.

Gee was numb. The finely dressed woman didn't seem to see them; her compulsion to capture the children was all that existed.

"Jesus," Cracker whispered.

"Gather your wits!" White Cat snarled as he bolted for the door.

Gee shook his head. He grabbed Cracker's arm and began running after the cat.

A small white hand clutched Gee's wrist.

Most of the child's fingernails were ripped away and the bloodless flesh was soft and spongy. Gee looked at the child's face. Looked past the squirming black leeches and saw the terror and hope in the little girl's eyes.

Gee swallowed. "Come with us," he finally offered.

Black tears swelled in the corner of her eyes. Sorrowfully, she shook her head.

"This is the part when we die," she said tearfully. "Then it will start all over again."

Chapter Eighteen

"What are you saying?" Gee whispered.

"Who's there?" the beautiful woman called out. She blinked nearsightedly in their direction but seemed to see only the child. "To whom are you talking, Sherylyne?"

The little girl gulped her sob.

Gee didn't think. He wrapped his arms around the girl, lifted her up and draped her over his shoulder. She flopped, a dead weight, as they ran toward the door.

Lilla slid out of his T-shirt and twirled down Gee's arm once more. She clung, tightly looped, around his wrist. Gee extended his hand behind him so that Cracker could hold on. After a moment's hesitation, she clasped his fingers. They stepped out into the black passageway that led back to the hotel hall.

Gee could see a faint glow around White Cat. Or was it an

afterglow? Whatever it was it kept Gee from walking into the walls.

From behind them the little girls' shrieks were punctuated by the icily enunciated words of the beautiful woman. "Never keep the door unlocked," she declared. "How many times must you be told? Never let the moths inside. Never play until your chores are completed. Never cry. Never try to run away from me. Must I tell you every day? Every goddamn day and you never listen! Never! Never!"

One by one the girls' voices became silent. All that was left was Cracker's rasping breath. The jangle of her boot buckles.

The little girl flopped too loosely against Gee's shoulder, growing heavier with each step.

"Sherylyne!" the woman's cheery voice called from the doorway. "Where have you gone, you naughty little girl?"

Would she start chasing them, too? With her hideous sack?

Gee and Cracker caught up to White Cat, who was scratching at the door to the hotel hallway. Gee pushed it open and the cat dashed through, Cracker and Gee following right behind. They spilled into the light, blinking blindly.

Cracker pulled the door shut. Spun toward White Cat. "That was the worst idea ever!" she cried. "What were you thinking?"

White Cat's tail lashed, once, and he turned his head slightly to the side. "It's not like I *recruited* the new archivist," he said drolly. His ears briefly flattened.

Gee wondered if that was a non-verbal apology or an insult.

"We're no closer to finding my sister," Cracker whispered. "And now we've got an extra kid, to top it off...." She shook her head wearily. "I still haven't had a drink of water." She grimaced, an expression twisting between a smile and a sob. Her adrenalin burnt up, she looked ready to drop.

"I thought the archivist could help us," White Cat muttered. "An archivist helped Melanie. At the very least, I thought there'd be a map, not homicidal cannibal children. Sorry if I overlooked that possibility. How short-sighted of me."

"Those maps were useless!" Cracker said. "Every single one of them! They were all maps of Half World, but none of them were the same. Even the directions were different! Every single map was entirely different!"

"Well, now we can surmise that everyone has created their own version of Half World," White Cat sniffed. "We've learned something important."

"But how do I find my sister?" Cracker cried.

A twinge of resentment needled inside Gee's chest. All Cracker ever talked about was her sister. As if she didn't have any thoughts about *his* reasons for being there. And here he was, spending time and energy to save her life, when he could be that much closer to finding his own parents. Her presence meant more work for him. If he didn't have to worry about her, he'd be that much closer to going home.

Gee shifted the child to cradle her in his arms. He stared at her slack face, repulsed by the clinging leeches. Cracker was right about one thing: he'd added another burden. He could just leave the child in the hallway. It wasn't his concern, anyway.... It wasn't as though *he'd* killed the girls. The archivist had.

She was heavy. Her weight seemed to be growing. Like the Japanese youkai that feigned at being a baby. Crying for aid until some fool picked it up. And then it latched on, growing heavier and heavier, until it killed the nosy do-gooder dead....

Gee awkwardly repositioned the girl in his arms. Eyes rolled completely white, the girl's head flopped loosely on her neck. Her mouth slack.

She was dead.

Gee sank to his knees and lowered the little girl to the floor.

"Jesus," Cracker muttered.

The girl's edges slowly began to fade, her solidity growing transparent. The leeches faded from sight, one after the other.

The child suddenly opened her eyes. Gee's heart plugged his throat.

White Cat hissed.

Sherylyne eyed her new environment eagerly. "Where is this place?" she asked. "I've never come so far before. We're not allowed to leave." The girl's voice was hoarse. "We're trapped in the Archives. We're murdered every day."

Cracker gasped. Gee glanced up at his friend.

Her face was contorted with awful realization.

The little girl's voice was growing thinner. "We heard that a long time ago, someone called Melanie had come to set everyone free. But not us. We weren't set free. So we began to eat. Little things. The rats and mice. The spiders and things. And it helps us. It does. We can stretch out time before she kills us again. But all the little things aren't enough. We needed to eat something bigger."

Gee grasped the child's arms, but his fingers passed through her flesh as if she were made of mist. She was growing fainter and fainter.

"You should have let us eat you." The child was barely audible.

And then she was gone.

"Fool child," White Cat muttered, his voice full of censure.

Gee stared at the ground where the girl had lain. His empty hands slowly curled into fists. "She's just a little kid. She's murdered *every day*! If eating makes things better for them what's the harm in it? Everyone's dead, anyway. What difference does it make?" He was standing now, looming over the cat.

White Cat's eyes narrowed into thin slits. "Can you not see? They've discovered that if they eat other Half World creatures, they gain more energy. It delays their being yanked back to their worst suffering. But they're just prolonging their time in Half World. However awful the trauma, they need to work through it in order to pass into Spirit. They need to suffer and suffer and finally surpass the suffering. Only then are they free."

"It's not fair!" Cracker's eyes shone like topaz. "They were abused and killed, and they end up here to suffer more? It's not their fault! The victims have to suffer with their murderers? That's just sick!"

White Cat padded circles around the outraged girl, his tail twitching. "Your value-based thinking is well-intentioned, but naive. The universe does not place value upon the workings of individual components. The universe only seeks balance."

"Then what's the point," Gee whispered. "If everyone ends up here anyway, what's the point in trying to be good when we're alive?"

White Cat stopped. "That is a very good question. And all individuals come up with their own answer." The cat's thick white tail flicked from side to side. "What is yours?"

Gee didn't have an answer. He felt so tired. So awfully hungry.... What was the point of anything if you ended up a demented monster in Half World? Who cared, anyway?

Popo did, he thought wearily. Popo cares.

Cracker tucked her arm through the crook of Gee's elbow. "Why are you doing this?" she asked the cat. "It's hard enough without your making it worse. Why can't you help us instead of confusing us with questions we have no answers for?"

"Just because you haven't thought of the questions doesn't mean they don't concern you," White Cat stated. He stared at them accusingly. Then he sighed, half-closed his eyelids and turned his back. His tail lashed from side to side. "They're scarcely more than large children themselves," he muttered beneath his breath. "Fool."

Gee wasn't certain who the cat was calling a fool. Maybe they were all fools.

"Yet it remains," White Cat shrugged, "for everyone, no matter their age." He extended his two front paws and stretched dramatically, exposing and retracting each individual claw, one by one, as he arched his back to a series of alarming cracks. *"Yowch!"* the cat exclaimed.

"Are you okay?" Gee asked begrudgingly. He looked at the cat more carefully. The snarky beast's whiskers were drooping and his fluffy white fur was duller than before. Alarm fluttered inside Gee's chest. White Cat wasn't vulnerable somehow, was he?

"Don't mind me," White Cat sighed dramatically. "I'll be fine. As long as you two are still alive, that's all that really matters. What's the life of one cat? I've lived a long time already anyway. Don't worry about me. As long as you're well and happy my life will not have been in vain."

"You're awful," Cracker breathed. "Is your popo like this?" she asked Gee. "Is that why the cat's like this?"

Gee scowled at White Cat. "Popo is nothing like him!"

White Cat clutched his fat furry middle with his two front paws and tipped backward, rolling a little from side to side. His laughter sounded like an attack of hairball and an ill-played bagpipe combined.

A laughing cat, Gee thought, was a very strange thing to behold. "Just ignore him," he said. They turned their backs to the snickering cat.

Cracker looked worse than White Cat. She'd lost Gee's jacket somewhere in the Archives and the application and removal of the tape from her stockings had left them completely ripped. They sagged around the tops of her black boots like elasticless socks, exposing her bare white legs. Her face was ashy with exhaustion. She looked as if she'd aged ten years since her arrival in Half World.

Gee wondered if he looked as bad. His hunger had turned into a persistent ache, like a rotten tooth. It wore at him, draining his strength. Weakening his resolve.

"You look like shit," Cracker muttered.

"You look worse than shit," Gee retorted.

Cracker's grin was as warm as summer honey. It faded quickly. "What's worse than shit?" she asked.

"Diarrhea," Gee decided.

"Ha, ha," Cracker said. "Yuck."

Gee sighed. He gazed at Lilla ringed around his wrist. Even the eel was growing more listless. He gently unwound her from his arm and slung her about his ankle instead.

Cracker's lips pursed with disapproval, but she kept her thoughts to herself.

Maybe she was too tired to argue about the eel any longer, Gee thought. He bit his lip. His hunger kept on growing, and Cracker was getting weaker. At what point would they run out of the energy, the will, to make the long journey home?

"I wonder. . . ." Gee's voice was small. "Maybe we can just go b-back. . . ."

"What!" White Cat cried.

Cracker remained silent.

"I-I don't need to see my parents. There's nothing good in Half World—I've seen more than enough of it. If my birth parents are still here, it can only be bad, anyway. I. . . ." Gee could scarcely speak. "I don't even know them. I never did. I just want to go back."

"You still think you can deny your past? You still think you can outrun it?" White Cat's voice was cold.

"Why not?" Gee begged. "Lots of people do! Tons of people are adopted as babies and never find out who their parents were. They turn out okay. Why can't it be the same for me? It's not fair! I didn't ask for this! I don't want it!" He realized how he sounded. But he couldn't stop himself. If he were capable of it, he would have wept.

White Cat's tail was fluffed enormous. He minced up and down, his nose up in the air. *"Ooooh, it's not faaaiiir!"* he mimicked. "He didn't ask for this. He doesn't want it!"

Anger flared inside of Gee, but it guttered quickly. Too hungry. It was making him weak and pathetic. He could feel Cracker's eyes staring. "Don't you think?" Gee pleaded. "Let's go back now. Before it's too late. . . ."

Cracker's eyes were troubled. She slowly shook her head. "I

can't, Gee. I'll keep going by myself if I have to. But I can't go home before I've seen my sister. What if she's stuck, suffering, like those awful little girls? I have to help her if she is. I couldn't help her before. I have a second chance now, and I won't give it up!"

"Don't you get it?" Gee cried. "There *are* no second chances here! It's just a loop of suffering until you turn to Spirit. Half World is the state of suffering. Until you become Spirit. It can take years. Some of the sufferers turn into monsters because they can't bear suffering anymore. Just as those little girls did.

"And what if *I* turn into a monster!" Gee shouted. He'd said it. He felt as though he'd vomited a tumour. It was a relief. To have it out. To have voiced it aloud.

But Gee could feel a new little tumour of fear starting to grow. Malignant.

You'll always feel fear until you accept the monster! his dark voice snarled.

Gee winced as if he'd been slapped.

Cracker placed her thin arm around Gee's vulnerable back. "You won't turn into a monster," she scoffed. "Why would you? You're not like them. We're human beings. We'll do what we have to and go back to our lives where we belong. I promise." She spoke as if she believed the things she said. She still met his eyes, without looking away.

Gee shook his head. Didn't Cracker understand? All the Half World monsters they'd encountered had started out as humans....

Chapter Nineteen

Cracker suddenly swung away. Half-crouching, she tottered several steps off as a thin stream of vomit gushed from her mouth.

White Cat, fur standing upright, bounded in the opposite direction. He shook his front paw as if flicking off water. "Disgusting," he shuddered. "I can't bear vomit! It's not personal," he added pompously.

Cracker retched again. Gee hurried over to her and rubbed her back. "What's wrong?"

Cracker began to shiver. She spat, and spat, before slowly standing. Her cheeks were paler than Gee's own, and her eyes were sunken. "Ever since we came down through the clouds," she said, "I haven't felt right. But it's getting worse."

Gee stared intently at his friend. Her golden eyes were dim, and long creases were forming in the hollows of her cheeks. As if she were growing old....

"Come over here, away from that mess," White Cat ordered.

Gee curled his arm around Cracker's back to support her.

"Don't get any ideas about me." Her voice was hoarse, her breath reeking of bile.

Gee almost smiled. "I know. You're into girls." He led her toward the cat.

White Cat clicked his tongue. A large white blur ... then a heavy weight thudded against Gee's chest and he staggered. Immediately the weight began sliding downward. Instinctively, Gee cupped his arms around the cat's furry mass. "Why can't you just ask me to pick you up?" he asked.

"Raise me to her face," White Cat demanded.

Gee held the cat up, grunting slightly with the effort.

The cat placed one paw upon Cracker's collarbone and sniffed at her cheeks, peered into her eyes. Cracker tried to smile, but her lips twisted.

White Cat opened his mouth, his tongue protruding a few millimetres as he crinkled his nose with a cat's grimace. His ears lay flat. "Her Life is beginning to diminish," he said. "You're right about one thing. She must return as soon as possible. Half World is no place for the living."

"What about me?" Gee whispered.

"Half World is leaching her very Life. There's no saying how long she can stay here before she's lost so much she won't be able to return to the Realm of Flesh."

"What about me?" Gee repeated.

"What!" White Cat snapped.

"What about *my* life?" Gee was almost certain that his voice hadn't wobbled.

White Cat looked away. He ruffled his fur before it settled once more. "Put me down," he said. Gee began gently lowering him to the ground. The cat leapt out of his arms as if he were in a hurry to escape Gee's hold. He stood with his tail held vertically, except for the tip that flopped to one side. "You were born of Half World," White Cat said. "You are not the same as Cracker."

Gee was frozen.

He'd read that in *The Book of the Realms;* it shouldn't have been a surprise. But it hadn't seemed real in Popo's home. Now the cat's words were like a punch to the gut.

A small hand slipped into his icy palm. Cracker gave a little squeeze. "You're wrong," she told the cat. "Anyway, I don't care if I can't go back. It's already like Half World there for me since my sister died." Her voice was soft. Fierce. "And Gee is just like me. We're both *human*. Not like you, I'd like to point out. And I'm *not* going back until I've saved Klara."

The feel of Cracker's hand meant more to Gee than he could ever say. His eyes burned. To have someone to believe in him....

"Do what you like!" White Cat snapped, his tail twitching angrily. "I don't care what happens to you anyway. You weren't part of the plan. For that matter, I couldn't care less what happens to you!" he scoffed at Gee. "I only came to offer my unappreciated advice, because I care the tiniest bit about that stupid woman, Ming Wei, who sent me on this pathetic journey! Do what you please," White Cat seethed. "But don't you dare forget that if you return to the Realm of Flesh without having resolved your past, you'll always lead Half Worlders back to the ones you love. You will bring evil after you and danger to Popo!" The cat pounced, clamping his paws around Gee's knees, his claws digging into his calf. White Cat chomped through the thick jeans, piercing the meat of his thigh.

Gee kicked and kicked, trying to shake the animal off his leg, but the cat clung like a burr.

"Stop it!" Cracker cried.

"Ming Wei!" White Cat yowled. "The things I do for you!" He flared, a white incandescence, before the rays of light contracted, solid, to drop onto the carpet. Ill temper seemed to seep out of the small cat figurine.

"Are you all right?" Cracker rasped. Though weak from vomiting, she slowly began to crouch down to check Gee's leg.

He grabbed her elbow. "It's okay," he said. He didn't want her to see; there wouldn't be any blood. Just like his little finger when he'd bitten it off for the toll. For all his denial, he could not explain his inhuman body.

Cracker, straightening up, didn't argue. Suddenly, she grabbed his T-shirt, right below his neckline, and yanked his face down to her height.

"Wh—" Gee staggered.

Cracker kissed him on the cheek.

Her Life.... Life wasn't only the golden light in her eyes. It was also an intoxicating perfume that seeped from her scalp. Her pores. Her breath. She smelled sweet with it. Why had he not noticed it before?

She smelled so very delicious....

"Ugh!" Gee cried with revulsion. No! No! He hadn't thought of her as food! He hadn't!

Cracker crinkled her nose. "I told you, I'm into girls!" she said indignantly. "I'm not hitting on you. You just looked like you needed a kiss. But it wasn't a *kiss* kiss, stupid."

"It's not that," Gee said weakly. "I'm sorry." He turned his head away. He couldn't tell her about the unbearable hunger. He bent down to pick up the little stone cat, and, after a moment's hesitation, slipped it into his jeans pocket. "It's something else." He couldn't tell Cracker about the dark voice inside him that told him to do heinous things. If she stopped believing in him, how much easier it would be to slide toward evil....

You know you want it, the nasty voice inside him purred. *Be true to yourself. Imagine your relief in letting go of all those pathetic inhibitions. Such glorious, delicious freedom....*

Behind Gee's long hank of hair his eyes were wide with fear. His fingers trembled. If they hurried, maybe he could make it. Please! he begged. Before it all fell apart. Because there was no way he could convince Cracker to turn back before seeing her sister. And, despite the awful fear, Gee would not knowingly lead harm back to Popo.

For Popo, for her safety....

He would walk farther into darkness. He would try to be brave.

THEY LEFT THE HOTEL through the deliveries access next to the kitchen. From the laneway behind the hotel, they scurried to a nearby plaza.

The people and creatures who wandered about were ghost inhabitants. They didn't see Gee and Cracker, and went about their ghost business unaware of their presence, just as the archivist had. Gee sighed with a small measure of relief.

They sat on the edge of the large stone fountain, naked stone statues set throughout the pool. Water flowed with a low roar. Gee's stomach writhed. He clamped his arm over his middle and gazed up at the high-rise hotel. The top of the building was obscured by a low sheet of grey clouds. The mountain's still there, he told himself. It has to be.

"I'm drinking that water," Cracker rasped. She stared at the water flowing from an urn, poured perpetually by a naked woman hewn out of stone.

Gee looked dubious. "How can we tell if it's safe?"

"There's nothing floating in it." Cracker's voice was a dry whisper. "It smells like chlorine. That would have killed germs."

The hairs on the back of Gee's neck prickled. He froze. Slowly, casually, he looked around the plaza as if he were admiring its design.

There were too many dark passageways between the walls of the buildings. Shivers rippled down Gee's spine. He whipped his head around. From the corner of his eye he saw a shadow dissolve into a narrow space between a domed church and a concrete wall.

Lilla, still wrapped around his ankle, hissed softly. She was looking in the same direction.

Gee's heart thudded. "Is it Ilanna?" he asked the eel in a whisper. So stupid! He should have had hotel security hold her in the hotel. Asked police to charge her with trespassing. So she could be taken away. Now she could be anywhere, plotting her revenge. And Karu— Karu was still out there....

The sound of slurping. Gulping. Cracker was kneeling by the side of the fountain. She sucked water from the cup of her hand, her eyes blissfully closed.

"Wait!" Gee cried, belatedly.

"It tastes fine." Cracker continued gulping.

Something was wrong. Gee could feel it, heavy, in the air. "Let's go," he said urgently. "This area is too open. I have a bad feel—"

It plummeted so fast. A blur of motion. *Splat-thud.* Splashing. Into the fountain. Dark droplets pattering on his bare arm.

A body. The skull exploded. A mass of splintered bones. Black blood spreading. Cracker screamed several seconds too late.

"Don't look," Gee said hoarsely. He wrapped his arm around Cracker's head and covered her eyes with his hand. Virtually holding her in a headlock, he pulled her away from the fountain. They could have been struck. It was so close. Gee's heart thudded slow and loud inside his head. What happened if the living died in Half World? He didn't want to find out....

"It's him, isn't it?" Cracker's voice was high-pitched. "The jumper. The one who jumped off the fire escape!"

Oh, god, Gee thought. She was right. Unable to stop himself, he looked back.

The man's white shirt was black with blood. It spread like paint beneath the ruins of his body. Gee's nostrils flared. Two dabs of black blood on his upper arm. It smelled rich, like melted chocolate, slightly bitter, and sweet.

His tongue whipped out, a chameleon flick. The soft white tip soaked up the blood. Back in his mouth before he could think, before he could stop. His eyes widened and his lips trembled.

What have I done?

Disgust and horror, twin snakes, twined with a growing giddiness. The blood tasted so delicious. A harsh sound escaped from his mouth. Oh god. They had to hurry. He was starting to lose it.

He couldn't even control his thoughts. His actions. It was starting to slide away.

"It's okay." Cracker tried calming him between rasping gasps for air. "We couldn't stop him. Don't look back, Gee. I won't look either. You can let go now."

Gee realized he was practically dragging Cracker along a narrow passage. His breath snagging in his throat. A panic of air and pain. He slowed to a stop and released her. He sank onto his haunches. He covered his nose and mouth with both hands and rocked back and forth.

Mmmmmm, mmmmm, good, the voice inside him crowed. *Eat. Eat like you want to. Eat to make you big and strong. Ohhhhh, so powerful. Beyond anything you've ever imagined. Power is delicious tooooooo.*

"What is it? What's wrong?" Cracker croaked.

Hands still covering his mouth, Gee shook his head.

Cracker's worried face remained etched with exhaustion. Lines were beginning to form alongside her mouth, and she had double bags beneath her pale gold eyes. She looked as if she was close to forty. Not a sixteen-year-old.

"Maybe," Cracker's voice was hoarse, "you should wait here. By the hotel. I can go look for my sister by myself, and come back later."

"No!" Gee cried, his hands falling from his face. "No. We made a promise, remember? That we'll see each other through. We have to stick together. Or something bad will happen." Unable to help himself, he began to giggle. He sounded like he was five years old.... Stop it! he told himself. Get a hold of your emotions. They were all over the place. Uncontrolled. Irrational. When his entire life he'd been able to control them.

It's my turn now, the nasty voice crowed. *MY TURN!*

"This place is bad for you," Cracker said gently. "You're changing, Gee. Sometimes ... sometimes your eyes go funny. Your energy changes." She hadn't said she was afraid of him.

The carefulness of her words touched him more than he could say.

Gee dragged his palms down his face. "We need to stay together," he whispered. *He* needed to stay near her. Her goodness was all he could hold on to. There was good still left inside him. But without her, it would run out more quickly. He could be good, longer, for her than he could for himself.

Grandson....

Gee could almost hear his grandmother's strong, kind voice. And for you, Popo, his little child heart cried. "We have to hurry," he said.

Cracker nodded grimly. "The water's no good here."

"What!" Gee cried. "Are you okay? Are you sick? I told you not to drink it!"

Cracker shook her head. "No, not like that." She swallowed hard. "It didn't take away my thirst. It's like I haven't drunk at all."

Gee stared at her face. "Maybe because it's Half World. And everything here is only here after death.... Maybe the water's dead, too."

He would not think about his own lack of thirst. Why he only felt hunger, and she did not.

"I'm okay, still," Cracker said. "We can survive. Humans can survive at least three days without water." A weary sound escaped her determined lips. "I'm so tired, too," she admitted. "I wish I could get some sleep."

Gee stared at his pale hands. He felt no need for sleep. Had he ever felt sleepy? He couldn't say. Maybe he'd only ever had the habit of sleep, but without the actual need....

Seventy-two hours.

That's not very much time, Gee thought. But are we even *in* time? If Half World is timeless, then why did she even *need* water? He squeezed his eyes shut. Half World was illogical. It was irrational. So it was stupid to use measures from home as a way to understand it. If Cracker was thirsty, she was thirsty.

If you're hungry, you're hungry.

"Three days is enough time to find my sister and your birth parents," Cracker said. "If we knew which way to go."

"No maps," Gee whispered. "Not the laws of space and time that we know...." There was something just at the edges of his memory. A piece of information. Was it something White Cat had said?

Gee drew the stone figurine out of his pocket. He glared at the inert cat sitting on his palm. "Help us!" he hissed. "Tell us where! Tell us how!" But the cat remained stone.

Who had said it? Something about the workings of Half World.... Was it Ilanna? What was wrong with his memory? It used to be so good. Why couldn't—

"Memory and pain!" Gee cried out.

"What?" Cracker rasped. She was leaning against the dark brick wall. Her eyes partly closed.

"Half World is made out of memory and pain. Everyone's memory and pain creates a part of it, for themselves. That would explain why all the maps you saw in the Archives were completely different. But if the sufferers make their own little Half World, if the pain they feel is shared, then they must share that moment."

"What are you saying, Gee?" Cracker's voice was thin.

"I'm saying you have the memory of where your sister is inside you. You just have to sink into the pain. And you'll go there. You can find her." Gee was almost smiling. He was right. The truth of it rang like a bell inside him.

"Oh, Gee." Cracker was shaking her head. "That's a terrible place. I've worked so hard not to be stuck there." Tears filled her eyes.

"Look," Gee said, torn between compassion and frustration. "No one is forcing you to go to Klara. We can just search for my birth parents instead. You don't have to see her."

Cracker dragged the back of her hand across her eyes. "I'm *conflicted*, Gee. That's the human *condition*. It doesn't mean I won't do it." She grabbed hold of his hand. A small warmth remained.

Warm, the way bread dough swelled, sweet, yeasty and delicious....

Gee took shallow breaths through his mouth as they began walking.

Cracker didn't notice. She closed her eyes even as they continued. She walked blindly into pain, reliving memory.

"Gee?" Her voice was small.

"Yes." Gee was curt. Their footsteps rang loudly. The buckles on Cracker's boots sounded like chains.

"If I fall too deep.... If I sink too low, please don't let go."

Gee's heart clenched. She trusted him. She was counting on him.

"I promise," he whispered.

Chapter Twenty

They seemed to be walking in a city, but a city without system or design. Devoid of colour, everything fell within the shades between black and white. Grey buildings seemed to grow out of the ground like deformed plants. The streets and passageways meandered and spiralled, pedestrian bridges that went nowhere. Cars and buses sometimes sailed pass, sirens wailing, the clattering clamour of horse-drawn carriages careening on cobblestone. Neon signs flashing in white and greys, Hotel! Girls! Girls! Girls! Pizza! Early Payday!

Sometimes explosions shook the air.

They walked on and on, concrete morphing into worn cobblestones fading into dirt paths that solidified to pale grey concrete. Piles of garbage lay in rotting mounds and narrow unlit passageways sometimes glinted with eyes, the scurry of claws. The air was heavy with the reek of raw sewage, decaying meat and smoky fires, a distant droning and roaring like an enormous factory.

Shadows sometimes called out to them, asking for spare change, a hand, a piece of bread, their voices cagey and pleading. But most people were trapped in their Half World cycles and didn't seem to see them. Most of them looked human....

Gee and Cracker ignored them, not daring to meet anyone's eyes. They walked as quickly as they were able, though sometimes Cracker clung to Gee's arm as her strength faltered.

The echo of their footsteps chased their heels. The faint jangle of Cracker's boot buckles. As time, as space, seemed to stretch, elastic and ungoverned, uncertainty gnawed inside Gee's chest. "Are you sure this is the right way?" he asked.

Cracker did not answer.

Gee glanced at her face, worried.

Cracker's eyes were glazed. She stared straight ahead, but she didn't seem to see anything at all. Had she even heard him?

"Soon," she finally whispered. "Close."

Gee tried to pick up their pace.

The jangle of her boot buckles grew louder. The cobblestones beneath their feet were uneven and exhausting. Gee looked over his shoulder.

A shift ... perception slipping, between physical and emotional.... The air was thick. The air was thin. And though they stepped forward, Gee felt like they were sinking. It took all he had not to let go of Cracker's small hand, to grab hold of anything solid, the lamp post, the walls, to break the nightmarish fall.

We are not falling, Gee told himself. *It only feels that way.* He closed his eyes so that his senses wouldn't confuse him.

"Klara," Cracker whispered. "Klara, I'm coming."

They didn't notice the shadow that followed in their wake.

"Oh!" Cracker gasped.

Gee opened his eyes just as he was placing his foot.

The ground wasn't there. The sense of falling, slow and dreamy, down the flight of stairs into a dark unfinished basement....

Cracker jerked him back.

Gee sat down, heart thudding slow and loud. Willing the vertigo to fade.

"Oh, god," Cracker whispered. She yanked her hand free of Gee's grasp and staggered up the stairs.

Gee heard her thudding across the floorboards, the wheeze of her breath. "Wait!" he called too late. He climbed the stairs to the main floor. Into a big shiny kitchen.... Large pots gleamed, hanging from hooks above an island stove. All the countertops were made of thick slabs of marble. Even the faucets on the sink looked expensive.

Lilla's coils flopped heavily around his ankle. Gee glanced down at the eel. She was losing her lustre, her muscles growing slack. *"Eaaaaaaats,"* she hissed sadly.

Gee's gut writhed in agreement.

The sound of Cracker's footsteps running up a second flight of stairs.

Gee gently unwound the eel from his leg. "Wait here," he said, setting her atop a high stool at a long marble counter. "I'll come back."

The eel rested her head on her topmost coil, her eyes dull. She was silent as Gee ran after his friend.

He hurried through the house, looking for the second staircase, self-conscious about his grubby shoes stepping all over the polished hardwood floor. The house was uncanny with silence. Heavy, and awful. The stairs to the second floor were carpeted, and his footsteps were swallowed. He caught up to Cracker, who stood, frozen, just inside an open doorway.

"Cracker?" Gee rasped.

She did not respond.

Gee stepped around her into a large messy bedroom. A vanity covered with hairbrushes, blow dryer, makeup, perfume, rubbish and empty mugs. The musty smell of weed. Clothes strewn over a desk and chair, a small two-person couch. Cracker's sister wasn't in her empty bed, the blankets and bedcovers slumping toward the floor.

Cracker wasn't looking about the room. She was staring at a tall wooden wardrobe set against the opposite wall.

"What is it?" Gee asked gently.

Her eyes were wide with terror. Gee moved toward the wardrobe.

"Stop!" Cracker screamed.

Gee froze.

Cracker began panting, as if she were running, about to collapse.

"Is your sister in the wardrobe?" Gee's voice was low, soft.

A small moan escaped Cracker's lips. Tears were streaming down her face, her hands clenched into tight fists.

"You don't have to look," Gee said. His eyes moved back and forth between Cracker's suffering and the two closed doors of the wardrobe. "You don't have to do this. We can leave."

Cracker swallowed a harsh sob. She shook her head furiously. "I—" She swallowed hard once more. "How can I go back without having tried? I can't. To fail, twice. I can't."

Gee strode to the wardrobe and pulled the doors open.

Cracker gasped.

Klara hung from a belt cinched around her blackened neck. Her grey tongue protruded; the reek of faeces and urine rolled out of the enclosed space.

"Oh. . . ." Cracker's voice broke. "Oh no, oh no!" She began to scream.

Gee slammed the two doors shut. Swallowed back a surge of nausea. He grabbed Cracker and dragged her out of the room.

"Get her down!" Cracker sobbed. "She might still be alive! It takes twenty minutes to die! I looked it up! I read about it. We might get her down in time!" She fought against Gee's hold, twisting, kicking, to get back to her sister.

"She's dead," Gee said. "I'm sorry, but she's dead! She wouldn't be in Half World if she weren't!"

Cracker, beyond reasoning, twisted free from his hold and ran back to her sister's room. Gee wearily followed.

Cracker flung open the wardrobe once again. Klara remained, motionless. Dead.

Cracker stepped half-inside the wardrobe and wrapped her arms around her sister's middle to lift her up. Her weight was too great; Cracker couldn't hold her aloft. Klara's body just swung from side to side as Cracker grew more desperate. "Help me," she begged Gee. "Please!"

"You're too short," he said. "Get out of there." Cracker stepped out and Gee wrapped his arms around her sister's middle. Her cold, lifeless weight felt awful, and the stench of her soiled clothing filled his nostrils. Gee's stomach heaved and he had to turn his head to the side.

"Hurry!" Cracker cried.

Grimly, Gee lifted Klara's body. He raised her a few inches, but it wasn't high enough to create the slack needed to undo the buckle digging deep into her bruised flesh. Klara's weight began listing to the side.

"I'll find something to cut the belt!" Cracker said. "Just keep on holding her!" She ran out of the room.

Gee tried to gain a little more slack. Klara's dead weight spun to the opposite side.

So futile, he thought. To die like this. What did Klara suffer in life that she would rather end it all? What was the point in living, he wondered, if we all die just to end up in Half World, only to die and die again?

White Cat's head popped out of his jeans pocket.

"Uhh!" Gee exclaimed, almost dropping Cracker's sister. "Don't do that!" he cried. "What's taken you so long? Come out and help us!"

White Cat wrinkled back his mouth to expose his sharp teeth in a cat grimace. "Release that dead person," he snapped. "She is cycling through her Half Life as she is meant to. You do her no greater service by interfering in this way, for Spirit's sake!"

Tight bands of pressure squeezed Gee's temples. He could feel his heavy heartbeat throbbing inside his head. He spoke slowly. Carefully. So his rage would not spill out again. As it had in the hotel, with Cracker. "If there's no *point* in trying to help Cracker's sister, why is there any *point* in my meeting my parents?" Gee whispered. "Why must *I* go see my Half World family when Cracker doesn't have to?"

"Idiot!" White Cat yowled with frustration. "Because you were born of them in Half World! You are not truly alive, as Cracker is! Can you not accept this? And the longer you waste your time with her sister, the more you're frittering your idiot friend's Life away! Ohhhhhh!" the cat hissed. "Ming Wei! It's all your fault!"

Gee's heart lurched. "What do you mean? Does Popo have something to do with all of this...?" Not Popo. It couldn't be.

White Cat completely ignored him. "If you had told him the truth years ago, he wouldn't be blundering around now, an idiot in fool's clothing!"

Relief washed over Gee, and with it his arms' strength gave out. Klara's body flopped horribly once more. Gee closed his eyes. Popo wasn't a betrayer. His lower lip trembled.

The cat's words filtered in. "Hey!" Gee exclaimed. "Who are you calling an idiot?"

"And you!" White Cat accused. "You grow ever weaker, you reek of it. You must meet your parents before you have too little strength remaining to do that which must be done."

"What must I do?" Gee asked. "Tell me. Please."

The cat's large fluffy head began pulsating with a weak glow. "Leave your friend if you must, but go quickly to find your birth parents. Someone has followed you here, and you cannot waste your strength fighting them. You must go!"

White Cat's head surged like light before contracting, tight, back to stone. He disappeared into Gee's pocket.

Gee's arms fell to his sides.

"What are you doing?" Cracker cried, as she ran into the room with a pair of scissors. "Raise her! She's choking!"

"White Cat said that someone's followed us. We have to leave!"

Cracker's eyes were fixed upon her dead sister. She cut at

the thick leather of the belt with the scissors. She scarcely left a mark.

She changed her grip on the scissors, holding them wide open, one of the blades clamped in her hand to drag the other blade like a saw. Back and forth, she dragged it across the tough leather, a high-pitched whine escaping from her lips. Her eyes glazed, she was lost in her anguish.

"Did you hear me?" Gee shouted, grabbing her bony shoulder.

Cracker raised the scissors beside her head, the glinting tip pointing toward Gee's face.

Something trembled in the back of Gee's mouth. He bit down on his bottom lip to contain it. An urge, almost compulsive— He mustn't let it happen. His tongue. His tongue quivering, taut, like an elastic wanting to snap. As if he held back a sneeze. But far, far worse. Wanting.

Cracker clutched the scissors so tightly her fist was shaking.

Plat. Plat. Plat. Her living blood, bright red, dripped from the heel of her hand onto the pale carpet.

"Your hand," Gee whispered. "You're bleeding." The rich scent of it hit him; sweet, complex, overwhelming. Hunger punched him in the gut. Gee crumpled with the intensity just as Cracker plunged the scissors toward his face.

The edge of the blade nicked his scalp, leaving a small gash. But he didn't feel it. The hunger writhed in his gullet like a beast. He panted through the contractions, on his hands and knees, like a woman giving birth. So powerful. The need.

Three droplets of Cracker's bright red blood. In the strands of the carpet. He wanted to suck whatever he could out of the threads. The delicious scent pulled at him. Worse than a dog. The strength of the longing, so intense, a thin white bead of saliva hung from his lips.

It looked like Elmer's glue....

Jesus! Gee dragged his mouth across his shoulder and desperately squeezed his eyes shut. Let it pass, he begged, as the pain of hunger racked his skinny body. Let this pass. Please.

Cracker gasped. "Oh!" she cried. The scissors fell from her bleeding hand and embedded in the carpet, point first, beside Gee's face.

Wearily, Gee raised his head like a drunk.

Cracker was clutching her sister around her waist. But not to lift her up. She held her as if someone were trying to take her away.

Her sister ... the solid edges of her were fading. Growing thin, transparent, flickering between material and unsubstantial. "Klara!" Cracker begged. "Don't go! Don't do this to me!"

Her sister, the belt, simply faded. The wardrobe was once more filled with clothing on hangers, and Cracker was left holding nothing.

Chapter Twenty-One

Cracker crumpled to the floor. She curled into a ball, wrapping her arms around the back of her neck. "Couldn't stop her," she whispered. "You're so stupid. You should have known. The signs were there all along. Why didn't you *do* something? Why? Why did this have to happen?" She hit the back of her head with her fists, clouting herself again and again.

Gee wearily pushed himself upright to sit on his knees. He stared at Cracker, caught in her psychological Half World.

He had scarcely enough strength to take care of himself. Groaning, Gee rose to his feet. He wrapped his arm around Cracker's middle and tried to get her to rise. She was floppy with despair. Mindless, useless. A burden. White Cat had said it was okay to leave her....

The image of Popo's face filled Gee's mind. The creases beside her mouth. Her dark knowing eyes that saw everything, and did not look away. Popo would never leave Cracker behind. Just as she had taken care of him his entire life.

What do you care? She's not here! And she's the one who told you nothing of your shocking past. Feeding you and housing you is not the same as taking care of you! What a joke!

Gee shook his head. That awful voice inside him—he mustn't listen. It was so very powerful. Every time it took him to the edge, to the tipping point. Because what it said was true. Popo wasn't here to help him through this terrible thing. Popo *hadn't* told him about his horrific background. But she had taught him many other things. She had taught him, through example, love, patience, discipline. She had taught him to think critically.... The monstrous voice inside him didn't lie, but its truth was a partial truth....

You must remember that, he told himself. Partial truth can manipulate. Partial truth can distort.

He hooked his arms underneath Cracker's and dragged her backward out of the room. She did not resist. She was like a person drowned.

As the scent of her fresh blood hit his senses Gee's deep hunger swelled anew. He gritted his teeth and continued dragging his friend down the hallway. Only I can control my compulsion, he thought. Not Popo. Not the evil thinking inside of me. I can do it. I *will* do it, he promised. They had to get out of there. White Cat had said.

Gee dragged Cracker to the top of the stairs. He propped her up, sitting against the wall, her feet on the steps below.

He looked to the ground floor through the rails of the banister.

He couldn't see anyone, but they could be hiding, waiting to pounce. Ilanna, or Karu.

Gee shuddered. Ilanna.... A shiver skittered down his spine.

You know you want her.... the voice crooned. *As much as she wants you. Just be honest. All else will follow.*

It was true. A part of him was drawn to Ilanna. He had to stay away from her. Not because he was frightened for his life. It was the way she made him feel....

Cracker's palm still seeped with blood. Gee licked his lips. The brilliant colour, the rich, complex odour—he could practically hear the cells tinkling their soft music. His tongue grew sticky with want. He breathed through his mouth so that the overwhelming scent was less intense. He ripped out the bottom of his T-shirt, a narrow strip, and used it to bind Cracker's wound.

She stared past him. "I was too late," she whispered. "I'm always too late...." Her voice crackled. Parched.

Gee stared at his hand. Smears of Cracker's blood. He wanted to lick it so badly that his fingers trembled. He closed his eyes and rubbed his palm against the rough surface of his jeans. "Let's go, Cracker," Gee said gently. "Now."

Cracker was silent. Motionless.

A jangle of metal against metal. Not Cracker's boots. From outside the front entrance. Someone was unlocking the door. Cracker raised her head.

The deadbolt turned and the door swung open. Klara entered.

Cracker gasped.

"Oh no," Gee muttered.

"Klara!" Cracker cried, her voice filled with hope, with joy.

Klara didn't hear her. There was a grey cast to her white skin, her eyes blank. She looked about a year or two older than Cracker. Her pale hair was soft and curly.

She would have been very pretty, Gee thought.

Cracker bolted down the stairs, almost tumbling in her haste. She threw her arms around her sister and kissed her cheek. "Klara! Oh, Klara. I've come to help you! You don't have to do this. It's okay now."

Her sister was motionless in Cracker's arms. Her eyes stared blankly toward the kitchen. Cracker, clasping Klara's shoulders, gazed lovingly at her face. Her joy and relief slowly faded, to be replaced with a growing fear. "Klara," she gulped. "Do you see me? Can you hear me?" She gave her sister a little shake.

Klara's head wobbled, but her eyes remained the same. Vacant. Senseless.

Gee's heart clenched with pain. "She can't hear you, Cracker!" he exclaimed. "She's dead. She already died. She's just caught in her Half World loop. Can't you see?"

"No!" Cracker vehemently denied. "She's right here! I can feel her. I can hold her. She's not dead! I just have to wake her up."

The hairs on the back of Gee's neck tingled. Wake her up.... The ones who "woke up" in Half World ... they turned into monsters.

Like you! Like youuuuuu!

Gee shook his head. No! No. He might have been a monster in the past. But he wouldn't turn into one this time. He would not.

Cracker shook her sister again, harder. Klara's head wobbled. Her eyes remained flat. Unseeing. Cracker slapped her. Her sister's face was whipped to the side. Her eyes unchanging, she faced the kitchen once more.

"Oh, god." Cracker's face began to crumble. Her shoulders slumped and her grip on her sister began to loosen.

Klara walked to the kitchen. They heard the clatter of a drawer being opened.

Cracker, unable to stop herself, stumbled after her. Cursing, Gee followed.

"Sssssssss." The sound was weak. Like the last bit of air leaking from a tire. Lilla was almost a pool of black ink atop the stool where he had left her. *"Eaaatssss,"* she begged.

Gee bit his lip. Was this the fate that awaited him if he continued to resist his hunger?

"No!" Cracker shouted.

Klara clutched a paring knife. She began digging the dull tip into the thin skin of her inner wrist. Cracker clamped her arms around her sister once again, pinning her arms to her side. Klara did not struggle. Her eyes stared.

"Stop it!" Cracker cried. "You don't have to do this!"

"Can't you understand?" Gee said, tiredly. "Her suicide can't be undone. You can't undo it, Cracker. And even if we did manage to wake her from her cycle, you realize that she'll turn into a cannibal like those little girls at the hotel? The ones who were going to eat you! Do you want her to turn into a monster? Would you rather her be 'awake' at any cost?"

Something rustled in the dark stairwell to the basement.

Gee spun around.

"I finally see," Karu rasped, as he stepped into the light. "I remember...."

Gee moved to stand between Karu and Cracker, his arms open in a futile attempt to shield her from the approaching bird man.

His heart thudded much too slowly. Still trapped in the trauma of her sister's cycle, Cracker seemed no longer to care about her own safety. She continued desperately trying to remove the knife from her sister's clutch. Klara simply held on to the handle as if she were a film on pause. Cracker sobbed quietly with desperation.

"Leave us alone!" Gee shouted at Karu. "If I've wronged you in my past life, I'm truly sorry. But I don't want anything to do with you. I don't want to fight you." He gulped, hard. Where was Ilanna? If only Cracker would snap out of it!

The bird man moved toward them.

"Shhrrrrr," Lilla hissed a weak warning from the stool.

Surprised, Karu glanced toward the unexpected sound.

Gee launched across the kitchen, smacking his palm against Karu's bird face. He would smother him. Just as he had the bully in the car park. The flesh of Gee's hand began to spread.

He hadn't considered the shape of the bird man's face. His beak protruded too far for Gee's skin to create a seal— Karu twisted his mobile neck and *snapped, snapped* his curved, razor-sharp beak, catching the thinning flesh from the heel of Gee's hand. White chunks, like soft bocconcini, dropped to the kitchen floor.

"Uh!" Gee cried out. He backed away, clasping the wrist of his maimed hand. It wasn't the pain. He felt no pain. Chunks were missing from his hand. His wound was bloodless, painless and white through and through. As if he were made of plaster of Paris.

A noise erupted from Gee's mouth. He slapped his unwounded hand over his lips. He didn't know if he was trying to hold back laughter or sobs. But if he started, he didn't know if he'd be able to stop.

"Did you not hear me? I said I understand," Karu rasped.

Gee shook his head. Had the bird man gone mad? He stared at Karu's muscled arms, his broad chest. He couldn't overpower him. And if he had gone mad, there was no reasoning with him. Gee shuffled closer to Cracker. The back door. They had to run for it.

She was gasping for air in a wordless struggle for the knife in her sister's hand. Dehydrated, despairing, Cracker's exhaustion overcame her will. Her hands fell from her sister's arms.

As if returning to autopilot, Klara took another futile stab at her wrist. The skin was marked, but not broken, the knife too dull. She paused. Tilted her head to one side. Klara returned the knife to the drawer and neatly slid it shut. She walked past the people in the kitchen as if they were no more than shadows. They could hear her soft footsteps climbing the stairs to the second floor. The soft thud of her bedroom door.

"Oh, god." Cracker's voice was small. Young. Her hands clasped the back of her neck. "She's going to do it again...."

"You are not meant to see this," Karu's rough voice throbbed. "The living aren't meant to witness the cycles of Half Life. No good can come out of it. You must return to your Realm."

Gee stared at the bird man. What kind of trick did he think he was pulling? "Where is she?" he demanded. "Where is she hiding?"

"What?" Karu croaked.

"Don't think you can trick us! Where's Ilanna? What do you want with us!"

Karu slowly raised his hands, palms outward. "She's not here. I've broken from her. I—I've changed. I haven't encountered her since leaving the hotel. I will aid you as I'm able."

"Liar!" Gee cried. "You're just saying that so we'll lower our guard. And then you'll eat us! Like all the other monsters in Half

World. I've seen only two kinds of beings here: they're either caught in a loop of their own suffering, or they're murderous cannibals! How can you prove to me that you're different?"

"I've stopped eating," Karu said simply.

Gee scowled. "And you think I'll just believe you?"

"Look more closely." Karu's voice was hoarse. He took a very slow step toward Gee, so as not to startle him.

Gee's eyes narrowed.

Karu's hands were shaking. And his body. His flesh. Somehow it seemed less substantial ... as if he were beginning to fade. Like Lilla.

Cracker, with her arms clasped around the back of her head, didn't look at the bird man. She was rocking a little, trying to soothe herself.

"I'm being pulled back," Karu said. "To the beginning of my cycle."

"Why?" Gee asked suspiciously. "Why have you stopped eating now?"

Karu dragged his palms over his bird face. "Millennia of this interminable Half Life. The interminable hunger.... To what end? After Melanie broke the bonds that divided the Three Realms, Half Lives have transitioned to the Realm of Spirit. Yet we, who continued to consume, have not. Does a monster know when to stop being a monster? Do you think a monster can change?"

Gee, deeply troubled by the questions, could not reply.

"Truth be told," Karu's voice was low, "I believed in the same things that Ilanna believes. I raged that we were trapped in Half World, and that if we were trapped, then all should suffer with us. Yet the taking of others' Half Lives began to pall. When we came for you in the Realm of Flesh, when I saw you with Cracker, something shifted. I followed you here from the hotel because of your friend."

"Because of her Life!" Gee accused, backing closer to Cracker so that Karu's way was blocked. "You would take her Life!"

"So I thought. But it wasn't her Life that drew me."

"What, then!" Gee hissed.

"It was her love for her dead sister."

"Klara," Cracker whispered, crossing her arms protectively over her chest as if she cradled her sister. "Why does my love for Klara have anything to do with you?"

The feathers atop Karu's head ruffled with agitation. "Hearing you speak of your sister, watching you seek her in Half World, led me to memories I had long buried. Memories of a brother who came from the Realm of Flesh to save me after death."

"What happened?" Gee couldn't help asking.

"My brother found me, and he forced me to eat."

"Oh, god," Cracker whispered.

"His intentions were not ill," Karu said grimly. "He sought to release me from my pattern so that he could take me home. But when I awoke to the awful hunger, I turned and consumed my brother."

A small cry escaped Cracker's lips.

"After a time, in my madness and pain, I was discovered by Mr. Glueskin." Karu looked at Gee with unreadable eyes. "And Ilanna."

Gee couldn't stop himself. "What happened to your brother after he died?"

Karu closed his eyes. The feathers atop his head ruffled with agitation. "I don't know," he said, his voice hoarse. "Only that he was gone." He turned his gaze toward Cracker. "I don't know where my brother's Half World is; it may be that he's already passed to Spirit. But all that I knew, until seeing you, was that I must not return to my cycle, or a tremendous evil would happen." There was no warmth in his avian eyes, but neither were they cruel. "I was wrong. No matter how awful the cycle, we can't flee from it. It must be faced, and faced again."

"No." Cracker's voice was small. "It's not fair. It's not right."

Gee was very still. What the bird man had said resounded like a bell inside his chest.

"There's nothing you can do for your sister now." Karu's voice vibrated with his conviction. "Your love and loyalty are admirable, but you must accept her death and return to the Realm of Flesh lest your actions lead to even greater suffering."

A hollow wooden *thump-thump-thump-thump-thump* echoed from the second floor. A staccato of desperation, vibrating through the floorboards. Oh god, Gee thought, staring at Cracker's face. It was her sister—her final struggle in the wardrobe.

Cracker's amber eyes widened. With realization.

Her face collapsed. Her eyes dimmed. Her indomitable will finally swamped by her exhaustion, she crumpled to the floor.

Chapter Twenty-Two

Gee caught her just before her head hit the ground. Cracker was groggy. She wasn't unconscious, but her pupils seemed overlarge. She kept on blinking, slowly, as if she were trying to focus. Gee tried to raise her to her feet, but her limbs were slack and he couldn't do it. Too weak, he thought. Too hungry. Despair washed over him, as unstoppable as the rising tide. And the faint sweet strum of Life, seeping from her sweaty scalp, rising from her skin....

Doesn't she smell gooooooood? his vile voice crooned. *Don't you waste it! You better eat her up before it's all gone!*

No! Gee shook his head, biting his lower lip. No!

The thumping of Klara's feet inside the wardrobe continued, awful and horrendous. How long did it take for her to die, only to cycle again and again and again? He'd tried to tell Cracker about the futility of trying to change Klara's Half Life. But she hadn't listened. He should have tried harder. He should have forced her not to follow. He should—

Something was lodged in his throat. He swallowed, hard. Had a part of him hoped it might be possible? Maybe he'd led her to her doom because a part of him wanted to see if Half World could be altered. Not for her sake. But his own....

Cracker had asked him to keep hold of her if she fell too deep. The girl was half-slumped against Gee's chest. Her Life force was so leached that her intoxicating scent was waning. The horrendous urge to consume her would not overwhelm him. But even this boon was too little, too late—he had scarcely the energy left to continue moving, let alone care for a fallen friend.

And he hungered, still.... He just didn't want to eat her any more than anything else that moved and quivered. Not to worry! Gee's lips quivered. Laughter. Tears. He didn't know. Popo, he pleaded. I don't know what to do.

Keep her! When you finally accept your heritage, she will nourish you well! his other voice gleefully advised.

Karu reached down and plucked Cracker out of his arms. Her head lolled against the bird man's upper arm. Gee struggled to his feet, alarmed.

"She must be taken back to the Realm of Flesh. Before her Life runs out," Karu declared.

"Put her down!" Gee said. "How can I trust you now? Just because you say so? We can't go back yet. We still have to find my parents."

"Continue with your journey. I'll carry her out alone."

"No!" Gee cried. "How can you prove that you won't just eat her!"

As you want to do, the voice inside him giggled. *The only reason you don't trust him is that you don't trust yourself!*

Gee shook his head. No. It was because he had no reason to believe the bird man. He had no proof.

The thumping sounds from the second floor were slowing, quieting. An awful silence. Gee looked up at the ceiling. Cracker, eyes dim, didn't seem to notice. "We go together," Gee said.

"Even if it means her Life runs out before you've found what you seek?" Karu asked. "If you value her Life, you—"

The bird man's eyes narrowed. "Maybe you value her Life the most only when it's within your reach." His voice was a low rasp.

"No!" Gee shouted. "That's not why!"

Cracker's arm flopped toward Gee. "Staying," she whispered. "With Gee. We promised. Not dying. I'm just tired."

A small warmth surged inside Gee's heart. He gripped Cracker's weak hand.

She tried to smile. "You stayed with me. I'll stay with you."

"We'll make it," Gee promised. "We have to. It won't take long. We can hurry...." Gee's breath caught. His grip went slack, fell from Cracker's hand.

"What?" she whispered.

Gee's head dropped. "I don't know where they are." His voice was barely audible. "I don't remember anything. I have no connections to them. Not like you had for your sister. How can I find them if I have no memories?"

White Cat.... Gee crammed his hand into his pocket. Sitting the stone statuette in the centre of his palm, he whispered intensely, as if he were praying to Spirits, "Come back. Please, we need guidance! We need your help. Please!"

White Cat ballooned so quickly, all eighteen pounds of him, that his thick fur hit Gee's face before the cat's weight overwhelmed his hand. The cat landed on the floor with a heavy thud.

"Nice," White Cat remarked.

"Sorry!" Gee said. "Help us. I need to get to my parents. And Cracker's growing too weak."

White Cat stared at Cracker in Karu's arms. "Well!" he exclaimed. "What's been going on since I've been resting?"

"He says he's switched sides," Gee said.

White Cat's expression was dubious.

"Help me," Gee said. For a brief moment the lights in the ceiling seemed to make a slow swirl above him. He closed his eyes. "Guidance."

White Cat sniffed. "About time," he muttered, before yawning so widely they could almost see down his gullet. He flicked the air with the tip of his tongue and closed his eyes. "Unfortunately, I have no idea where they are."

"What!" The cat's words were a punch in Gee's gut. He tottered backward, slumping against the counter.

The cat shrugged. "I've never had the pleasure of meeting them." He turned his head to the side to cough quietly. "*Eh-hem!* Yes. Well. I wish I could be of greater assistance."

Gee stared at the cat with disbelief. "Why are you *here*?" he said through gritted teeth. "What *good* are you? You haven't done a thing for us since we arrived in Half World!"

"Maybe he's not our friend," Cracker whispered.

"The eel," Karu rasped.

They all stared at the grim bird man.

Karu gestured with his beak. "Lilla was with Ilanna and Mr.

Glueskin when they went to see if his parents cycled, still, without him. Maybe the eel remembers."

Gee lurched to the tall stool where he'd left Lilla.

The eel could no longer raise her head. She was virtually a thick black puddle, as if her body could no longer maintain its shape.

"Lilla?" he whispered. He knelt beside the eel and gently picked her up, cradling her in one arm against his chest. She felt like a loose skin of water, yet much lighter than she'd been before. Sloppy, her skin felt soft, as if his fingers would slip right through her. "Can you lead the way?" Gee asked, desperate. Was it too late? He looked about him. She needed to eat. That's what she said. He—

White chunks on the floor. His flesh. His glueflesh.... Gee shuddered. Was there some Life in those pieces?

He snatched up a small chunk. It felt like firm tofu.... His skin crawled. Yet Gee held the flesh in front of Lilla's mouth, and prayed that she would eat.

"Interesting," White Cat murmured.

The eel's jaw slowly opened. Gee tucked the white chunk into her mouth. The hair on the back of his neck quivered. This is grotesque, he couldn't help but think. This is so, so weird. Please let it work.

Lilla slowly closed her jaws. She was very still.

"Come on," Gee pleaded, giving her a little jostle.

Lilla shuddered. Jerked back her head. She opened her jaws once more. The piece of flesh was gone.

Gee snatched up another piece and tucked it inside the eel's mouth. She ate the second piece more quickly. "Yes," Gee hissed with relief. He fed her all the pieces he could find.

Lilla slowly raised her head. *"Eaaatsss,"* she whisper-hissed.

"Ratttssssss." She felt a little more substantial, but was still very weak. And her eyes still dull.

"Rats," Gee said, "we need to find her some rats." She needed more lively flesh. Just this once. If only enough to see them to his parents, he rationalized. We kill rats all the time. What does it matter?

"Backyard." Cracker's voice was hoarse. "By the composter. There were always rats." She looked up at Karu's harsh face. "I need water. Even if it's not real."

White Cat leapt atop the counter and padded toward the window. He stared out intently at the darkness, the tip of his fluffy tail twitching.

"I'll be right back," Gee said. He glared at the bird man who held Cracker in his arms. "White Cat, keep an eye on Karu," Gee demanded as he unlocked the back door. White Cat grunted. Gee could hear the sound of water rushing from the faucet as he stepped outside.

The backyard was dim, the far edges dark. Uncannily still. He didn't want to look too closely—didn't want to learn what lay beyond. Gee spotted a raised vegetable garden, and beside it, two slatted containers with lids. He crept quietly toward them.

Lilla extended herself so that she was a little closer to the composting bins.

"Only a couple," Gee whispered. So that she had energy enough to help them.... He could hear the scrabble of small claws against the walls of the container. The slurry of dragging tails. He gently lifted one of the lids.

It was black inside. Empty.

"Oh," Gee sighed.

The blackness writhed.

Undulating, heaving, the bin wasn't empty—it was so full of rats they moved like dark liquid. Several leapt from the bin, their white teeth bared, glinting with black blood.

Lilla launched from Gee's arm. She flew through the air, jaws open wide, to plug a rat's head into her gaping mouth. They both fell to the wet lawn.

The rat frantically scrabbled with its claws, scraping at the edges of her mouth.

Gee held his breath. His heart thudded unbearably. A sour sweet saliva pooling in the back of his mouth.

The rat, plugged inside Lilla's maw, scratched wildly at her cheeks, her throat, but its claws only slicked off the dense slime the eel was exuding in her excitement. The rodent tried to yank its head out, but Lilla's inward-pointing teeth only dug in deeper. They flipped about on the dark lawn to the sounds of the rat's muffled screeching, the wet *thwap*, *thwap* of the eel's body.

Gee giggled. He slapped his hand over his mouth. What was he *doing*? It wasn't funny!

Yes it is, it is, it is! It's hilarious. It's delicious. It's fucking brilliant!

The eel whipped back and forth and the rat was tossed about, its long naked tail snapping loudly.

Gee's lips began spreading into a loose grin.

The rat shuddered, its tail quivering. Lilla bit down and jerked her head backward, stripping the fur away from the rodent's body as if she were pulling off a sweater. The rat's raw torso, glistening pale grey like an oyster, fell out of her jaws. Its lower half was still intact and matted with slime. It looked like it was wearing wet fur trousers.

Saliva filled the back of Gee's maw. He didn't know if it was nausea or hunger.

The eel flung the fur out of her teeth and fell upon the fresh meat. The scent of flesh hit the air and the other rats began leaping, scattering from the bin.

It lashed out of Gee's mouth with the crack of a whip. White, gooey. His chameleon tongue. The bulbous tip engulfed an entire rat, and Gee could feel its futile struggles down the horribly extended white length. His tongue snapped back into his mouth, the captured rat encased in the taut gluey tip.

Gee swallowed.

He could *feel* the rat sliding down his esophagus.... Writhing, clawing. Gee giggled. Shocked, he clapped his left hand over his mouth.

The rat churned, heavy, in Gee's gut like a greasy chunk of pizza. A slice of pizza that was half alive.... Twitching, twisting, clawing for escape. Gee could scarcely contain his giggles at the unfamiliar tickling coming from inside.

He'd swallowed a rat, whole. He'd fucking eaten a living rat! Gee wanted to smack his hand upon his thigh, bend over, hoot with laughter.

He wanted to vomit.

"Eaaaatsss," Lilla hissed. *"Sooo gooooodssssss."*

Gee squeezed his eyes shut.

Grandson.... The sound of Popo's voice. A small warmth filled Gee's heart.

The image of Popo's crinkled face, her keen bright eye, filled his mind. She looked so real, so close, his heart spasmed with emotion.

You're a good boy.

A good boy.... Was he hearing her voice because she had died?

No. He didn't believe it. Not Popo. Not yet. Oh, Popo.... Gee's lips twisted with self-loathing. What have I done...? He wrapped his arms around his middle. What have I come to?

The rat's movement inside his stomach grew still.

It hit him. A surge of energy rippled from his belly outward to all his extremities. Delicious shivers of power shot through his nerves, faster than electrons, finer than light. His very cells vibrated with the sensation, a harmonics beyond sound. His hair felt as if it were standing on end, quivering with intense delight.

And then it was gone.

Gee stared at his shaking hands. They glowed, white, in the dim grey light. "Oh, god," he quavered.

"Seeeeeee," Lilla chided.

The hunger burst.

Like a monster breaching his skin, his need roared, unleashed. Gee ripped off the lid of the second container and his long white tongue snapped and snapped and snapped again, snatching the leaping, twisting rats out of the air and swallowing them whole.

Lilla plunged into the container. She tore through the rats in a frenzy of feeding, and wet fur flew, sticky with blood, reeking of fresh flesh and iron.

"So." White Cat's voice was low. Furious. "This is what you've come to."

Faster than thought, Gee's tongue shot out from between his lips, the fat tip whipping at the cat.

White Cat twisted and leapt, and Gee only ripped out a patch of soft fur.

Mindlessly, his tongue snapped back into his mouth only to whip out once more. As the cat arced and dove, Gee's tongue snapped and splatted a hair's breadth behind. With a yowl, the cat dashed to the edges of the yard, beyond Gee's reach. He leapt atop the fence and, with great dignity, slowly sat down. The tip of his tail twitched.

"What would Popo say?" White Cat asked. "She did not raise you to turn to this!"

"POPO ISN'T HERE! POPO KEPT SECRETS FROM ME! IT'S HER FAULT THAT I'M LIKE THIS NOW! IT'S NOT MY FAULT!" Gee bellowed.

His eyes bulged, his hair standing on end as his body stretched ever taller, thinner, growing monstrous. His tongue hung down to his chest as he panted like a dog. His rage consumed him and he could no more control it than he could a firestorm.

"MY ENTIRE LIFE! TREATED LIKE SHIT! BECAUSE I'M DIFFERENT? POPO SHOULD HAVE TOLD ME THE TRUTH! AT LEAST THE TRUTH WOULD HAVE SET ME FREE!"

White Cat stared at him, saying nothing. He turned and leapt off the fence.

And disappeared into darkness.

Chapter Twenty-Three

"Bravo!" a familiar voice cried out, ecstatic. "Bravo! Encore! Marvellous!"

Gee slowly turned around. His mind was empty. A tinny noise rang inside his ears.

Ilanna stood in the glow of the light from the kitchen window, a dark silhouette, Rilla undulating by her side.

Gee's gulper mouth began shrinking as his rage slowly receded. Horror and shame began swelling inside him like a rotting carcass. What have I done?

What have I *done*!

"Oh!" Ilanna exclaimed. "You're trembling. Don't be frightened, my darling." She drew closer, bringing with her the eternal reek of the sea.

Before she reached him the energy of the rats' Half Lives surged through his body, and he vibrated with the mind-blowing effects. He felt as if he would burst apart. As if he were a god.... Potent, saturated with possibilities. Primal. He tipped back his head and roared at the skies like a beast being slain, a beast born once more. And just as quickly the fire flamed out and he was left panting.

Hunger began lapping at him again.

"You see how it is?" Ilanna said gently.

Rilla, writhing eagerly at her side, snickered with malevolent delight.

Lilla had gone very still inside the container, partly covered by tufts of wet fur, torn flesh. Rilla strained toward the bin but Ilanna jerked her shoulder, reining her back. "You just ate!" she hissed. She smiled at Gee. "We just ate," she repeated, as if she were turning down an invitation for lunch. "A trio of security officers. *Mmmmm. Mmmm!* Thank you for having them delivered to us, darling...."

As his hunger swamped him anew, weakness crept upon him once more. Gee's head slumped and he turned away. "How do you keep finding me?" he asked wearily. "Why can't you just leave me alone?"

Ilanna tipped back her head and her laughter trickled like water. "Leave you alone? *Darling*, you're the one who made me who I am today. I *owe* you my loyalty and commitment forever. We're drawn together, through our experiences, our desires, our memories. Our love...." She giggled playfully. "I'll never let you go," she hissed.

Swish, swish, swish. Her cold, lean torso pressed into his back, and Rilla slipped around his waist to hold him closer. Her deep, cold wet sank through Gee's skin. His teeth began to chatter.

"You don't know how pleased I am to see you behaving like your true self, my darling Glueskin," Ilanna whispered. "We can lead Half World back to its glory. Then dissolve the barriers between the Realms."

He closed his eyes as her lithe length writhed against him. She felt so good.... To want her. To be wanted. When his entire life no one had shown interest.... The longing burned colder than ice, burned as deep, as strong, as his compulsion to feed and feed again.

Ilanna was lipping the lines of his shoulder blades through the thin material of his T-shirt.

Gee shuddered with wanting. Please, he thought. I'm so tired of this struggle. Maybe this is my destiny. It would be such a relief not to have to keep on fighting. Just to give in to my desires, my needs....

I'm conflicted. It was Cracker's voice, ringing inside his head. The tinge of sneering and affection that was so utterly Cracker. *That's the human condition.*

Gee's lips trembled. His body stilled. Maybe he wasn't alone in his struggles.... His smile, unseen by Ilanna, was small. Scarcely discernible, but a smile after all.

"I don't know why you've continued to flee from me. I've only ever wanted the things you've wanted for yourself—for you to meet your poor, dear parents who long to have their son returned to them," Ilanna murmured against his back. Her breath was so very cold.

"Gee?" It was Cracker. Her voice, small and exhausted, quavered with disbelief. Her silhouette stood outlined in the lighted frame of the doorway, Karu's imposing figure slightly behind and to the side.

Gee closed his eyes. He swallowed. The aftertaste of wet rat fur and blood thick upon his tongue. The path he must take was clear.

He twisted around to slide his arms around Ilanna's cold waist.

"And so you shall take me to them, Ilanna, as you have tried for so long," he said loudly. "My thoughts have been confused by my time in the Realm of Flesh. No more."

Ilanna's laughter vibrated with triumph. "I knew you couldn't hold out against me, against your very nature! Come!" her voice rang. "Rats aren't enough to sustain you. You will eat of your little friend, and then we shall come full circle, and return you to your parents."

"No!" Gee shouted. "No," he said, more deliberately. "My need to see my parents immediately presses upon me. We'll leave Cracker here, with Karu to hold her until our return. You and I will go now, without them, and return later. To celebrate." Gee let his hair sweep over the doubt in his eyes. This was the gamble he was forced to take. He had to believe Karu spoke the truth when he said he would take Cracker back to the Realm of Flesh on his own. She was at greater risk near Ilanna.

He was at greater risk near Ilanna. And White Cat, gone. Let me do the right thing, Gee thought. While I still can.

"Oh, Gee." Cracker's small voice was barely audible.

"Shhhrrrrrrr," Rilla hissed suspiciously. She rose up to gaze into her mistress's eyes.

"We leave, now," Gee demanded.

"Ooooh," Ilanna purred. "I love it when you're so forceful. Karu!" she cried. "You will keep the girl, unharmed, until our return, you hear! If you start eating without us I'm afraid we'll be having chicken for dinner!"

The bird man made a rasping sound. He drew Cracker back into the house, and she did not resist him. The door was closed.

Something wet trailed down Gee's cheek. He hadn't said

goodbye.... The wetness dried quickly, pinching his skin. He brushed it off and it fell from his face like a piece of dried wax.

"Idiot bird," Ilanna hissed. "He's stopped eating. Maybe we should eat him first, before he fades back to the start of his idiot cycle!"

Gee's heart bloomed. Maybe Karu had been speaking the truth. And if he was, he would take Cracker back, before her Life was completely leached. Gee could go see his parents, and then return to Popo on his own. He would not have failed his friend.

"Take me to my parents," Gee said.

Ilanna nestled her wet head underneath his chin.

Her cold was sinking into his body, and Gee's neck grew stiff even as hunger howled from his belly. "You better stand to the side. Your cold is making it difficult for me to move."

Ilanna clicked her eel tongue, but pulled away from him. "It's not far," she clipped. "Nothing is far in Half World, unless you've forgotten. You're lucky that I remember!" she spat. So volatile. So vicious. So exciting....

Gee shook his head. He caught a brief glance of Lilla before she ducked silently back into the bin. Even Lilla didn't want to stay with her former mistress. And if her long-time eel companion feared and rejected her....

Gee linked his elbow around the remains of Lilla's eel tail that still dangled uselessly from Ilanna's left shoulder. "Lead me to them now, and I'll follow," he whispered into her ear.

Rilla strained once more toward the composter. Ilanna slung her shoulder in the opposite direction and began striding toward the back fence, pulling Gee along with her.

"Finally," she gloated. "Full circle. To rip asunder and start anew...." She gestured imperiously at the gate. Gee opened the latch and pushed it outward.

Their footsteps crunched upon the gravel. Gee didn't look back to see whether Cracker watched them.

As the opaque darkness began to thicken, the *crunch, crunch, crunch* began to sound like something being chewed by enormous teeth. Gee fought back an urge to giggle. He was giddy with hunger. And desire....

And if he were honest, it felt strangely liberating to walk away from Cracker—away from responsibility. From obligation. The only person he had to worry about was himself. A bubble of curiosity, even eagerness, began to expand inside Gee's chest.

His parents.... He would finally meet them. What were they like? Maybe they were rich! Maybe they were important people. Were they self-aware, like Ilanna and Karu, or were they still trapped in their cycle of death, like Klara...?

Gee didn't know which was better. Maybe, if their death hadn't been so awful, a recurring Half Life wouldn't be so bad....

Maybe.

Maybe not.

Maybe, maybe not. Yes, no, maybe so....

The other children had chanted the refrain when he'd asked if he could play with them. They'd run away, laughing. The mantra rang inside his head as they stepped deeper into the darkness. Gee didn't know where the memory came from. He'd forgotten all about it.... That made me sad, he remembered. When those classmates had run away.

"'The time has come,' the walrus said, 'to talk of many things,'"

Gee softly quoted. He began to giggle as a residual bubble of giddiness expanded inside him.

"What's so amusing, darling?" Ilanna asked carelessly.

The swishing of her wet dress sounded so cold Gee couldn't help but shiver.

"I'm thinking about oysters." Gee gulped at the saliva pooling in the back of his mouth. "Stupid oysters are just as delicious as clever ones...."

"Don't talk to me about oysters," Ilanna snarled. "I was so long tormented in the ocean, I would gladly tear out my own eyes before seeing it again!"

Rilla rose up to stroke her mistress's cheek, hissing sympathetically.

How awful, Gee thought, to have to give up seafood.... He giggled again.

So dark. The streetlights had gone out, or had disappeared. The lights from apartment buildings and mansions, the flash of distant explosions. "Who turned off the lights?" Gee tittered.

"Shhhhhht!"

Gee didn't know if it was Ilanna or her eel.

When had the city grown so dark? He couldn't say when it had shifted, only—

The air *gave*, like moist fabric. Gee stumbled—and pitched forward to the ground that was farther than he'd expected.

He stumbled. Into a space stinking bitter with smoke, pungent with the odour of burnt rancid fat, scorched bread. The oily sweetness of dirty animal fur. The gravel had turned into a hard-packed dirt floor. In the centre of the smoky space was a small pit glowing with a low fire that was turning to embers. Above the fire, suspended from a tripod, was a worn cauldron. Gee looked up. The peak of the circular roof had been left with a gap to let the smoke out, but much of it still pressed heavily upon them. The crumbling wattles were black with years of smoke. Along the dark edges of the roundhouse he could see baskets, mostly empty, a few clay pots. A sleeping area, slightly raised, covered with what looked like animal hides.

"Welcome home, darling...." Ilanna's voice quivered with laughter.

Gee's heartbeat thudded slow and heavy inside his head. "This is *it*?" His voice was hoarse. Incredulous. The home was nothing but a stinking, disgusting hovel.

"Rather modest, shall we say," Ilanna sneered. "It's no wonder you felt compelled to go out on your own. From such humble beginnings...," she cooed, Rilla hissing with her. "But you must know that your parents have been *dying* to see you."

Stumping footsteps, heavy and careless, drew toward them. A hunched form entered through an opening Gee hadn't noticed before. Something small fluttered inside his chest. I'm just excited, he thought. Nervous. What did Cracker call this feeling? Nervousing....

All was silent, except for the rustling of the person who had returned, hanging something up on the wall. Too far away from the dim glow of the low fire, Gee couldn't see the person's face. The fluttering rose from his chest to the base of his throat.

Ilanna, as if sensing his agitation, stepped on his foot with her barnacle-encrusted heel. "Just wait!" she whispered.

The figure, a woman, stumped toward the fire. Though

Gee and Ilanna stood inside the circle of the dim, pale glow, the woman didn't seem to see them. She crouched beside the fire and laid several sticks of wood on top of the embers. Flames flickered upward, bringing more light into the roundhouse. Shadows licked the walls.

She was dressed in a rough tunic, her feet wrapped in pieces of hide. Posture bent, as if she'd spent her entire life carrying buckets filled with stones. Her sharp nose was like a blade upon her face. Dirty creases lined her black eyes and her cheeks were gaunt, rendering her face almost skull-like. Her dark hair was tangled, an oily mess.

One of her arms was curved beneath her belly.

Gee didn't know he was shaking his head.

"Behold." Ilanna swept out her arm dramatically. "Say hello to your *mommy*!"

Rilla frothed gleefully, twitching, jerking with delight.

Gee took a faltering step backward. He found himself pressed against crumbling wattle and daub. No. He shook his head. Not her.... His real mother was lovely. His real mother was clean. His real mother would know her son as soon as he entered a room. Not her. Not *garbage*....

Popo had said he was special.... Popo was a LIAR!

His hands were clenched so tightly that gluey flesh began dripping from his fists, hanging in long thin strands, *platting* upon the filthy floor.

"Stop that!" Ilanna banged him with her shoulder.

"Her!" the voice inside him seethed. "She!"

The woman turned away from the fire. She shuffled to the baskets and picked up a clay pot, then carried it to the fire and poured something into the cauldron. When the liquid hit the sides of the hot metal it *whooshed* in a dense wet cloud. The reek of watery old bones billowed upward. The stink of onions gone bad. The woman picked up a wooden spoon and stirred the contents.

The woman—she was younger than he'd thought. Scars, upon her face; they shone in the flickering light, a pucker of tissue distorting her cheek, rucking it upward toward her ear. She kept turning toward the entranceway as if she was waiting for someone.

The room was bright enough that she ought to have seen them. But her eyes slid over their forms as if they were no more than shadows in a perpetually shadowed place. Just like the lady in the pillbox hat, Gee thought. She hadn't seen them either. She saw only the quintuplets she murdered in her tight little cycle of violence.

Gee shook his head. This person before him—he had no feelings for her. She was nothing to him. The word "mother" meant *nothing*.

A dull *thud* from outside the walls of the hovel.

The woman jerked.

Thud! Thud! Something was being struck. Or kicked.

Gee's stomach turned. It sounded like it was a body.... An animal bleated with pain. Gee prayed it was an animal.

The woman raised both arms to cover the back of her head.

Run away! the small boy inside of Gee pleaded. *Before it's too late.*

And go where, do what? Return to Popo, only to draw Ilanna back to fetch him? Live on with the unbearable knowledge of his disgusting tongue? Continue with his life knowing that every day he would fight the compulsion to consume his best friend?

You know you want to, his nasty voice whispered. *You know you will.*

Gee's shoulders slumped forward as he loosened his clenched fists. He closed his eyes.

"It's already too late," he whispered. The truth of his words, spoken aloud, bloomed like reeking night flowers. He slowly nodded his head. "It's always been too late. For some people, there's no second chance. For some people, there was never a chance."

He smiled a small sad smile.

Chapter Twenty-Four

A tremendous *thud!* Dust, soot drifted down from the roof. The ragged woman moaned.

Scraping, slapping at the entrance.

"So close," Ilanna whispered, excitement throbbing in her voice. "Very soon, my saviour. My hero monster."

"What's going to happen?" Gee asked.

"Your destiny." Ilanna's voice was sweeter than ambergris. "And with your destiny lies mine…."

The thing outside bellowed, a roar of rage. He had to bend to step through the doorway. Lean, hard, reeking acrid.

Gee's hand crept up to cover his lips. This man—he was so familiar and unfamiliar…. Like the face of someone he knew but whose name he could not recall. Shivers prickled up the back of Gee's neck. Fluttered next to his heart.

The woman uttered a low moan. She clamped her arms around her middle as if cradling something precious. Her dark, sunken eyes were as expressionless as stones.

Ilanna began to laugh, her voice throbbing with exultant glee. "Behold!" she cried. "The child has returned!" She pushed Gee toward the open doorway. "They, your parents. Your true family of origin. Your legacy." She laughed and laughed, triumphant and malicious.

Gee scarcely heard her. He took one faltering step toward them. They were so poor. Wretched, filthy and ugly.... His mobile lips twisted with distaste. How could *he* come from *them*? Sour phlegm fluttered in the back of Gee's throat. He swallowed the mass down. But if it were true, he thought. He would finally truly belong.... His feelings were disgusting. Writhing, one entwined atop another, like a mound of worms.

Conflicted, just as Cracker had said....

He wanted to see their faces, up close. Would he see himself in their features? He boldly took one more step, and the firelight flickered upon them. Gee stretched out his long, thin fingers. "Mother." His voice did not quaver. "Father."

His mother was shaking, her arms still clutching her middle. She stared past Gee, her eyes flat and unseeing.

Gee frowned. Beneath the grime, beneath the scars and the suffering, the woman was still young.... Surely not old enough to be his mother. He turned his gaze to his father.

The thin and reeking man, covered in tattered clothing, had a face ravaged by bitterness, poverty, rage. He glared past Gee, down at his wife. Why, he's not old either, Gee thought. A balloon of relief expanded inside his chest. "They're not my parents," he said wonderingly. "They're not old enough to be my parents. You've made a mistake," he chided Ilanna. "I'm displeased." For some reason he couldn't stop smiling.

The man didn't seem to hear him, didn't seem to see him. As if the strangers inside the house were only shadows cast by the flames.

Gee stuck out his tongue. He plunged his thumbs into his ears and waggled his fingers beside his head. *"Booga, booga, booga!"* he shouted. But the man and woman looked through him as if he weren't there.

"You're the one who misunderstands," Ilanna hissed from behind. "You've been living time in the Realm of Flesh, but Half World turns in cycles. Your mother and father are the age they were when they suffered their greatest trauma. And you should be part of that trauma, but they've been cycling without you."

"What…." Gee's voice faded. Rilla slowly stroked his back, gliding up and down. Gee didn't know if Rilla was doing it to goad him, or if Ilanna was trying to be kind….

Gee's father raised his fist above his head. His mother curled around her middle, instinctively tucking her chin into her chest, turning her shoulder slightly.

"Don't you look away from me!" Spittle flew from his father's mouth.

"Your mother," Ilanna whispered. "Your mother who does not see you—she was pregnant with you."

The woman, unable to control her fear, turned even more so that her back faced the trembling man.

"You make me do this!" his father screamed. His raised fist dropped hard upon the crown of her head. She was felled to her knees.

"She was giving birth to you when your father killed her." Ilanna's voice might have been sad.

"And after he finished murdering her, he murdered you."

"No—"

Gee couldn't breathe. A blow. As if he'd been struck with an axe. Cloven in two. He suddenly folded in half and gagged. White, elastic, like heated mozzarella, he vomited his tongue because there was nothing in his stomach. But as he continued retching it kept on pouring outward, each convulsion triggering more until a white mound began forming at his feet and his body began shrinking.

I'm going to vomit myself inside out, he thought. I'm going to vomit myself empty. And still he retched, unable to make it stop.

"Stop it!" he heard Ilanna screech, but she sounded very far away. Or maybe she sounded too close … he couldn't say. He felt so very weak. Insubstantial….

Rilla, a crackling luminescence. She snapped her jaws and her rows of glinting needle teeth sank through his extended tongue. She snapped and slashed, ripping the thick white strand in two.

Gee gagged once more, and the small stump retracted into his gullet like an elastic band. Grit, rubbish dug into his palms, his knees. His arms and legs lost inside his clothing. The floor stank of urine and rancid oil.

In the background, dull thuds of a body being struck. Cries of pain.

Between Gee's hands was a mound of steaming white glue.

"Take it back in!" Ilanna shrieked. "Don't waste yourself!"

Gee nudged a new tongue into shape inside his mouth, even as he stared at the part of himself that he'd vomited onto the filthy floor. He shuddered, almost on the verge of retching once more. The thought of taking it all back inside him was repulsive.

"Do it!" Ilanna screamed. "Don't you realize how many centuries went into growing your potential? How many people you inhaled to leach their power? Don't waste it! Look at yourself!"

Gee struggled to his feet. When he stood upright the room spun for a moment, and he held out both arms for balance. His eyes slowly regained focus.

What—

The room … it had grown larger, Ilanna taller. His eyes were at the level of her enraged lips, and his clothing hung off his smaller frame. His jeans barely stayed on his hips, and the hems puddled around his feet. His ripped T-shirt oversized and loose.

He was no bigger than a twelve-year-old child.

So very weak. The edges of the raging hunger roared, stronger than ever before. "Oh no," he murmured, his voice high-pitched and slightly husky.

"Hurry!" Ilanna screamed. "Before your glueskin hardens! Take it back in!"

Gee pulled his lips inside his mouth, creating a tight seam. He slowly shook his head.

His mother staggered and crashed against the wall. Slid to the floor.

His mother. His father was beating her to death.… His father gripped his mother around the neck with one hand and forced her to her feet. He shoved her across the room and she stumbled over the empty baskets and skidded to the ground.

His mother was eerily silent.

Gee stared, his lips sealed shut, his dark eyes wide and uncertain.

Why didn't his mother fight back? he wondered. Why did she not speak?

Ilanna prodded Gee's vomitus with her toes. It had cooled and hardened swiftly, like plaster of Paris. She screamed with rage. Batted the back of Gee's head with Rilla's muscular eel body. "You stupid rotten piccc of SHIT!" she shrieked. "All wasted! Centuries and centuries of power! A millennium of growth! How could you let this happen? You don't have rage enough to do what must be done!"

"What must be done?" Gee asked in his childish voice. His jeans were so loose they threatened to fall off his skinny hips and drop to his ankles. It would have been hilarious anywhere else.... Cracker would have laughed.

Succumbing to gravity, his jeans slithered to the ground. Gee stepped out of them, leaving his too-large sneakers behind as well. Hollow, he thought. Empty. He'd felt so *powerfully* hungry before.... Now the hunger felt like a creeping weakness, spreading from his belly, jittering inside his legs. He stood, barefoot, in the decrepit hovel as his father grabbed his mother by the hair. He watched them as he'd watch something on television. He felt nothing for them. It seemed unreal.

"After your father kills your mother, you must kill your father!" Ilanna screamed.

Gee held very still. His temples beat overloud, overslow, in time with his half-dead heart.

"That is how you first broke your original cycle," Ilanna spat. "Your father beat your mother, and she birthed you as she lay dying. Even as you took your first breath of Life, your father murdered you. An eternity of birthing and dying, at the hands of your father, until you began to remember—through pain and death, through betrayal and evil, you remembered each time, growing, feeding your rage, until you were birthed, whole, come to term nourished on hate, powerful enough to finally kill the father who had killed you a million times before."

Gee's dark eyes were unfathomable.

Across the room, his mother groaned. His father was kicking her in the back. I am not a part of them, Gee thought. They are not a part of me.

"Now, they cycle without you. Unless you kill your father, you will never realize your true power, you will never be free. Destroying the destroyer determined your destiny! If you fail to kill your father now, you'll be pulled back into a cycle that still seeks to return you into its pattern. Back into your mother once more. To begin a new age of suffering. Perpetual victim once again."

Was it true? Gee wondered. His mother had both arms around her middle, even though she wasn't pregnant with him, helpless to the nature of her original cycle.

His fa— That man. He kicked her and kicked her, with measured strength to prolong her suffering. Gee lowered his head so that his hank of hair covered his eyes.

To have sought his true parents—

To have to see them like this.

Black blood dripped from his mother's scalp onto the floor. Her nose running, thick with mucus and blood. Her eyes dull, flat, dead from eternal suffering.

Do you think she feels nothing? asked the part of him that still remained a child. *Do you really?*

That man was killing her. Killing her on repeat for uncountable years. And he was Gee's father? From death to death to death. Child of a murderer. Child of the murder victim. Gee gagged again, barely able to hold in his horror.

"Do it!" Ilanna screamed. "Kill him! You must kill him!"

The space around him torqued with excruciating slowness, sound stretching, twisting beyond words, beyond meaning. As if air were thicker than water and he was sinking, falling.

Gee clamped his hands over his ears. What was he supposed to do? If he killed his father, he became the monster Ilanna wanted. If he didn't kill his father, he was doomed to die and die again.

His mother ... she clasped both arms around the dim memory of her unborn baby and curled tightly onto her side. She guarded her baby as if it were her own life. His father was kneeling beside his mother's prone body. His father was weeping, with hatred and a twisted, hideous love. "You see what you make me do!" he screamed as his hands began squeezing her throat.

She batted feebly against his wrists.

Gee stared down at the tableau. He is killing my mother....

Gee raised his skinny childish arms, the sleeves of his too-large T-shirt almost reaching his elbows. He wrapped his own fingers around his father's neck, his glueskin elongating, stretching to form a perfect circle. He sealed the tips together.

Gee began to squeeze.

His father's neck was sticky with sweat and filth, his skin loose with poverty. Half Life trembled in his throat like a sickly sparrow. The small flutter made something deep inside Gee quiver with delight. Small seams cracking, spreading outward, the darkness he'd held contained his entire life breaking apart to swamp his senses, his body, his mind.

Yes! It burst full bloom, like a carcass flower. *YES!* Gee tipped his head back and roared at the universe that had made everything so wrong.

"YES!" Ilanna screamed. "You are Mr. GLUESKIN!" She pealed with exultant laughter, shrieking with triumph. "My powerful, beautiful Mr. Glueskin returned to me!"

Free! Finally free! Glueskin shuddered with the intensity. Vibrating. His dark hair began floating, eddying around his pale face, rippling from root to the tips, the strands turning from black to white.

"I'm FREE!" Mr. Glueskin howled. "AWOOOOOOOOOOO!" His childish, monstrous laughter filled the air.

Chapter Twenty-Five

Mr. Glueskin bent in close to whisper tenderly in his father's ear, "Like father, like son." He giggled. "It's only right that a child surpasses the parent. Don't you think, Father? Isn't that every parent's wish?"

His father, still choking his own wife, could not turn to see his attacker.

"It should be," Mr. Glueskin gritted.

His father's grip around his wife's neck slackened as he struggled for air. She fell from his hold onto the hard dirt floor. He half-turned his body to meet the eyes of the one who strangled him....

"Oh, Father," Mr. Glueskin cried out, with operatic pathos. "Only now do you see me. Only now you cast eyes upon your son." He smiled too wide, his childish lips stretched to his ears, his dark eyes glinting like black marbles. "In death truth is born."

His father began to flail desperately as his Half Life was slowly squeezed from him. Mr. Glueskin was faintly aware that his mother had rolled to her side. She was coughing. She was yet Half Living. Does it alter my destiny? he carelessly wondered.

His father's eyes were beginning to bulge, black blood vessels spreading inside the whites.

"Death of the father," Mr. Glueskin crooned. "Birth of the son. . . ."

"Stop it, Gee!" a girl's voice cried.

Pain seared. Razor-sharp. Across the back of his thighs. Startled, Glueskin dropped his hands from his father's crumpling neck. The man slowly pitched, face down, upon the ground. He began whooping for air.

Mr. Glueskin stood still for several seconds, as if confused.

"No!" Ilanna shrieked. "No! No! Nooo! Finish it! Finish killing him off, you idiot!"

Mr. Glueskin slowly shook his head. Who had dared to attack him?

"You pathetic, hopeless fool," a gritty voice rose from the ground. "I told her it was a waste of time." White Cat sat calmly. The cat's tail slowly twitched from side to side. His grey eyes were narrowed in distaste.

Mr. Glueskin's mother had curled up into a fetal position. Still half alive. His father was on his hands and knees, his head hanging, gasping for air.

White Cat flicked one paw as if trying to shake off something dirty. "I send you to seek your past, and you devolve to *this*."

White rage bulged inside Mr. Glueskin's chest. "HOW IS IT MY FAULT THAT I COME FROM THIS?" he screamed. "I DIDN'T ASK FOR ANY OF IT!"

White Cat's voice was cold. Unrelenting. "There is no *fault*! No one has control over the circumstances of their birth. Can you not see this? You have forgotten too quickly what I have told you: *your past does not have to become your future!*"

Mr. Glueskin began to laugh, from deep within his belly. The sound, the fury, too dark, too awful, coming from his childish face. His preternaturally white hair. "You would deny me my birthright?" he asked. "You would deny me my legacy?"

"No, Gee." It was Cracker. Supported by Karu's arm, she stumbled into the circle of firelight that shone fitfully from the middle of the roundhouse. They were both wretched with exhaustion, though the bird man's posture remained straight and proud.

Cracker clutched Lilla in one hand. The eel slowly wove from side to side, hissing softly.

The eel—she must have led them back to him. Why? It was too late. Too late.

"You don't have to kill him." Cracker's voice was hoarse. "Leave them to their Half Lives. Now you know. You've seen them. We can't do anything to make them change. Remember? Like my sister.... It's too late for them. We can go home now."

Mr. Glueskin smiled at the humanity shining from Cracker's golden eyes.

"So full of care. So much feeling," he admired. "As if anything actually matters. Do you think our lives matter? Look at this place! Even if we go back, we'll only end up in Half World. And maybe your worst is yet to come. Maybe your worst isn't failing your sister."

Cracker cried out as if he'd stabbed her.

"What if your worst is *far* worse than you've already experienced?" Mr. Glueskin gloated.

Ilanna laughed at the look on Cracker's face. "That's right, stupid child!" she hissed. "So naive. Still having faith in Life, in hope. Freedom comes when we have no ties to Life, when we've killed hope!"

"Yessssss." Mr. Glueskin smiled wide, his grin stretching from ear to ear. "Hope is the pathetic dream to which the desperate cling. Mewling. Whimpering. Pathetic!" As if their Lives mattered! It was charming, really. After he was done with his father, he'd have to eat Cracker up, all by himself! He wasn't sharing with Ilanna, no! If the Half World rats felt so delicious, imagine how he'd feel when he consumed what was left of Cracker's Life! White drool began pooling from his mouth and a bead dribbled past his lips to hang, suspended, from a long thin thread.

His father was shambling toward his wife with his hands outstretched, still caught in his recurring nightmare, knowing nothing else. His mother had only managed to push herself to her hands and knees.

"Don't you feel sorry for them?" Cracker whispered. "They're stuck like this, suffering. Even your father...."

Did he pity them? Mr. Glueskin wondered. He supposed a part of him did.... A terrible smile began spreading across his face. But feeling pity didn't mean it stopped you from killing. Sometimes, killing was the most compassionate thing to do....

"Isn't it such an archetypical act—to kill one's father?" Mr. Glueskin asked, conversationally. "Our English teacher, Ms. Park, would agree. I'll write a sonnet about it afterward—no, a tragic play. A musical! I'll hold auditions at the lobby of the Mirages Hotel. It's going to be a Half World hit production! But first things first." He turned tenderly toward his father.

Something slammed into the square of his back. Air knocked out of his lungs. He was so much smaller, lighter than before that he staggered forward, crashing into his father. His father seemed not to notice. Dark eyes blank, he was reaching out his gnarled and filthy hands once more.

Mr. Glueskin turned, incredulous. Who would *dare* try to impede him?

White Cat stood with his back arched, fur standing on end, making him twice his already formidable size. "Control yourself!" he hissed. "If not for your sake, then for the sake of your popo!"

"Popo!" Mr. Glueskin cried. "POPO!" he bellowed. "POPO IS NOT HERE! POPO CANNOT SAVE ME NOW!" His chameleon tongue snapped out from between his elastic lips.

White Cat leapt, twisting through the air to avoid the sticky, bulbous tip and landing on his paws metres away.

Gee's tongue whipped back into his mouth only to lash out again.

"I'll deal with the cat!" Ilanna snarled. "Finish your father!"

Rilla shot to the end of her length, snapping her terrible jaws. She ripped out a clump of fur and White Cat yowled with rage.

Karu squawked as he moved toward Ilanna. She whipped her head around, mouth wide open. Her eel tongue shot out, straight for Karu's eye.

So noisy, Mr. Glueskin thought. So very calamitously busy. Distracting him from the most important thing! Smiling, he turned toward his appalling father. Mr. Glueskin tapped his finger upon his chin. Instead of throttling his father first, perhaps he should just eat him up instead! No need to waste his Half Life. Not a nutritious starter, perhaps, but so richly symbolic! Ms. Park would find it meaningful, like a Greek myth. "Ahhhh, Ms. Park," Mr. Glueskin murmured, "one day, you too will have your tragedy in Half World." He smiled and began unhinging his jaw, his mouth dropping, gaping wide, down to his chest, like a gulper eel.

A weight clamped upon his back.

Two arms encircled his upper arms and clutched at his chest, two legs wrapped around his upper thighs. Cracker. Leapt onto his back. Because he had shrunk in size, the sudden weight almost threw him face down, but he staggered at the last minute and regained his balance.

"You can still stop," Cracker whispered in his ear. "It's not too late, Gee."

Cracker was latched onto him like the Japanese ghost story. She clung, tight as a tick, and her weight seemed to grow. His knees wobbled.

"You don't have to stay on this path. You can have a better life."

Mr. Glueskin frowned, even as he spun to the left, to the right, to dislodge the girl on his back. "Gee is dead, stupid girl. And there are no paths in Half World. There are only cycles! You can't change a cycle!" Unable to weaken her grip on him, Mr. Glueskin began elongating his arms, noodling them backward. They looped around to come up behind Cracker's back.

"That's right!" Ilanna shrieked. "Don't listen to her! Your true cycle is the one that includes the death of your father by your hands!" Her words ended in a scream as Karu used his beak to rip Rilla out of her shoulder socket.

"She lies," White Cat said calmly. He sat beside the dying fire, somehow still managing to look clean. "Your original cycle contained *your* death, not your father's. You tore free from your Half World cycle only by becoming a murderer."

Mr. Glueskin went very still.

The original cycle.... His original cycle, ended in his death. As a baby newly born, only to die.... Yes, that's what Ilanna had said. He'd been trapped in this unfair cycle, never to live, only to die and die and die again. Until his rage and fury grew strong enough to kill the killer. *In order to have a better Half Life, he had to kill.* That was the lot that had been given to him. His fate. His destiny.

He *deserved* to live. Everyone deserved to live. It WAS NOT HIS FAULT!

"Don't do this," Cracker whispered. Her hoarse voice was full of tenderness. "Let's just turn around and go home. It will be okay. We can make it okay, somehow."

Realization was a sickly toxic light, the morning after the bomb had exploded.

Cracker was wrong. He could not go back to the Realm of Flesh. His cycle was here, in Half World. Melanie had taken him out of Half World, out of sequence, out of sync.... It was the wrong time for him to be in the Realm of Flesh. Popo should have been smart enough to realize! How could they have done this to him? It would have been better not to know that there was a better life, only to have it taken away....

Love had made Popo stupid. Mr. Glueskin shook his head. It had made *him* stupid. Stupid and weak. No longer. He glanced down at Cracker's hands that gripped so tightly at his chest. As if she would never let him go. Mr. Glueskin's lips trembled. It was so very clear.

"Did you come back for me because of your feelings of loyalty and affection?" Mr. Glueskin asked.

"Yes!" Cracker cried, the pitch of her voice rising with hope. "We came to Half World together. You helped me find my sister. And now we've discovered your past history. We can go home now. I'm not going back without you."

Mr. Glueskin smiled tenderly, though Cracker couldn't see him. "Let me liberate you from these feelings," he said gently, his obscenely noodled arms circling entirely around her so that the sticky pads of his fingers settled upon her neck from behind. Mr. Glueskin's expression was dreamy, and white stringy tears began dribbling down his face as he sealed his fingers into a single thick strand.

Instinctively, Cracker tried to prise her fingers beneath the tightening elastic band around her throat.

Mr. Glueskin raised his arms high, lifting the struggling girl above his head, her legs vainly kicking the air.

A harsh cry escaped Karu's beak when he caught sight of Cracker. He held Ilanna from behind as she whipped her head from side to side, far enough for eel tongue to snake back and bite the bird man's face. Puffs of small feathers whirled in the disturbed air.

Rilla chased White Cat, followed closely by Lilla. White Cat yowled. In the twisted knot of black against white it was impossible to tell which eel was which. They rolled about the filthy floor in their desperate struggle.

"Dirty, dirty," White Cat's voice could be heard growling.

Mr. Glueskin focused only on what he had to do. Lovely Cracker first, and then he'd be free to deal with his father.... He retracted his elongated arms as he gently lowered Cracker onto the ground before him. His white hands around her throat were taut, like rope.

She didn't have energy left to struggle. But her eyes.... She was not frightened.

Her eyes were brilliant with furious Life. And in her eyes still, faith and hope shone as gold as honey.

Stinging. His face.... Streaming from his eyes, the moisture seeped into his lips and the taste of salt bloomed upon his tongue.

Salt. Tears.... He was weeping human tears....

Mr. Glueskin shook his head, but the mortal tears fell and fell, streaming down his face, filling his mouth, as he'd never cried before. Why now? *Why now?*

Something was wrong. What was it? WHAT?

"Kill her!" Ilanna cried desperately. "Finish her off, and then kill your father!"

Mr. Glueskin slowly turned his face toward her. Ilanna was held, immobile, in Karu's taut arms. Lilla and Rilla had torn each other so ragged that they lay upon the dirt floor, strands of exposed bones, black skin, white flesh, twitching.

"Not long ago, you asked me what the point was in 'being good' when everyone ultimately ended up in Half World." White Cat's voice was dry, measured. He sat calmly beside Cracker's head, his tail curled composedly around his paws. The cat stared at Mr. Glueskin's fingers wrapped around his friend's neck.

Cracker gazed up at Mr. Glueskin's face. Fearless. She followed the flow of living tears that streamed down his childish white cheeks.

In the cycling of the Realms, where everyone passed through Half World, there was no reward for being a good person. Mr. Glueskin had seen the truth of that in his passage through this Realm. There was no angelic chorus for behaving well. No reward for not inflicting hurt upon others.

“It’s not just what we choose to do,” White Cat intoned, “but why.”

Mr. Glueskin’s hands were still.

“Why we choose what we do....” Mr. Glueskin repeated. His voice lowered to a childish whisper. “Not for a reward. Not for redemption....”

His little voice was as brilliant as a winter star in the darkest night. “Even after having chosen to harm. When the choice is before me again—choosing not to harm over harming ... makes me human,” Gee whispered.

His breath shuddered through him.

Such relief. As if the weight of a million years had been lifted from his shoulders.

Let him float away.

His fingers fell from Cracker's neck.

"No!" Ilanna wailed. "The cat lies! Choosing power over weakness makes you human! Choosing our lives, on our own terms, makes us real!" She struggled to break out of Karu's hold, but the bird man held her tightly. "We don't have to be victims, trapped. Look at your pathetic parents! Look at their *humanity*!" she snarled. "Is that what you choose? That's no choice! It's failure!"

Gee's childish skinny arms hung loosely at his sides. Cracker's eyes were closed. A terrible red bruise around her pale neck. And she was very still.

A ragged cry escaped Gee's lips. What had he *done*!

Chapter Twenty-Six

Salt tears burned his face, filling the back of his mouth. Gee placed a tentative hand on Cracker's bony shoulder and gave a little shake. Please. It hadn't been him. Not him....

"I am so pissed off at you, Gee," Cracker said hoarsely.

Gee's voice snagged in his throat, halfway between a sob and laughter. And his heart ... his heart felt a joy so sweet it pierced him to the core. It was going to be okay. He wasn't a monster.

A grotesque *crack.*

His mother—her head tilted at a terrible angle. His father was staring, as if confused, at the palms of his hands. He had killed her again. As he'd done uncountable times before.

Gee shuddered. How could this suffering continue for so very long? How could such suffering be borne? His mother whom he did not know, whom he'd never know. Her horrendous cycle of pain. How torturous their Half Lives. How grotesque that they'd cycled through this for so long, trapped in suffering. And he'd almost joined them back in Half World. If he'd killed his father he would have returned, the son who killed his killer father, and become the monster that Ilanna wanted him to be. Powerful, cruel, yet trapped to kill and feed for eternity.

Eternity....

Cycles. Broken. Unbroken. Something ... something not quite right. Gee frowned, confused, as unease began forming, growing inside him like a dark tumour.

He had stopped himself from returning to that cycle! I'm not going to be that thing! I chose! Gee implored. But the dread continued to swell inside him like rotten fruit.

White Cat caught his eyes. The cat's gaze was piercing, as if he could see every little secret Gee held dear to his heart.

Please! Nothing else! Because how much more could he bear?

"No!" Ilanna's voice was thick with pain and denial.

Rilla, and Lilla, in tatters upon the filthy ground, were beginning to lose solidity. Too broken, energy spent, they were beginning to fade.

"I need you!" Ilanna screamed. "I hate you! Feed them something! Feed them so they stay here with me!"

Rilla, completely lifeless, faded away before their eyes, the pools of black blood evaporating with her.

"Lilla, thank you!" Gee cried. He didn't know if the eel heard him before she disappeared.

Gee's father, still compelled by his own terrible pattern, rose to his feet and lurched outside. Toward the remainder of his cycle, until his own Half Death, to return to murder his wife once more.

Gee had nothing to say. Only a small frown etched into his childish forehead.

His mother. Her body began fading. Gee stretched his hand toward her hair. Just once ... to touch the mother he'd never known. "Mother," he whispered. She dissolved before his eyes, and his fingers slid through empty air. Gone. To return to the start of her terrible Half World cycle.

But not me! Gee thought. Not me!

Ilanna wailed with rage. She writhed inside Karu's hold, flip-flopping like a frenzied fish, her fury so great it would burst out from inside her skin.

Gee slipped his arms beneath Cracker's armpits and pulled up so that they could sit, shoulder to shoulder. The effort had them both panting.

Karu. Something was happening to him. Gee blinked and blinked to rid his eyes of tears.

The bird man seemed to flicker with golden flames. Gee rubbed his forearm across his eyes.

With a triumphant cry, Ilanna writhed herself out of Karu's weakening grip and rolled onto her side. Armless, she sought the wall for leverage so that she could rise to her feet.

"Yesssss." Karu's voice was a throaty purr. He sounded almost like a cat. The bird man's perpetually taut muscles were loose, relaxed. He opened his eyes. They flickered like orange firelight. "I never thought it could happen to me...." The feathers on his head ruffled, soft, then lay down slowly. He turned his head toward Cracker. "Your presence, your actions reminded me of my brother. And I remembered it all—my awful death, how my brother came to seek me in Half World. My monstrous betrayal of his love. But

most importantly, I remembered what it means to love.... Little Sister. Live," he said, as if bestowing a benediction.

Growling, Ilanna propped herself against the wall, using her back to inch her way upward, to stand upright once more.

Karu made no attempts to stop her. He remained seated. But he was full of calm as he gazed upon Ilanna. His matter was beginning to break apart. He wasn't fading, as the others had.... It was as if his flesh was turning to motes of orange light. Warm, the colour of flames, the flecks of light held the form of the bird man.

Oh, the Spirits welcome me! Karu's voice rang inside their heads.

The orange motes began to rise.

Our cycles. We must accept our cycles, Karu's voice rang. *Ilanna, even you.... I'm free!*

The tiny motes expanded, filling the dirty hovel with a brilliant orange light. The sparks swirled wildly, though the air was motionless, and converged to form one glowing orb the size of a heart.

The hinotama floated weightlessly above their heads before it slowly bobbed down to gently alight on Cracker's forehead. The light glowed upon her face, warm and kind.

Some of Cracker's weariness lifted. And she looked more like a teenage girl.

Karu's Spirit shot up through the ceiling and disappeared.

"He is free," White Cat said, surprise tingeing his voice. "Not bad for a bird." He lifted his front paw and began chewing off chunks of dirt caught in the fur between his pads.

"Fool! Traitor! Coward!" Spittle sprayed from Ilanna's lips, her black seal eyes enormous in her maddened face. She kept her back pressed against the wall as she circled the room, her eyes fixed on Gee. "Karu is an idiot," she hissed. "Weak and stupid! He has betrayed our vision. Only *we* are left to return Half World to its glory. To spill into the other Realms, to turn them all to Half World. We, the powerful. We, the depraved. We, who are not bound by conscience and humanity! Half Life for eternity!"

White Cat, paw half-raised, turned his gaze between Ilanna and Gee.

The lingering taste of tears was salty upon Gee's tongue. To think that Karu could attain Spirit. After all that time. Gee hadn't noticed that he'd risen, that his hand was outstretched toward Karu's last golden light.

"My darling love," Ilanna whispered with terrible desperation. "My beloved Glueskin. Come away with me, and we can build our power once more. I will show you the most wondrous creatures to eat. The most delicious, nutritious babies and children." She giggled playfully. Desperately. "The best ones are the freshly arrived, the ones who've just come over, still reeking of Life." She began to slaver, ever hugging the walls. "We'll begin by feasting on your false friend and your evil cat. Their Life will feed your transformation. We'll squeeze the last living juices out of them—"

"No." Gee's childish voice rang.

Ilanna froze.

White Cat closed his eyes. Cracker began to smile.

"I will never eat again in Half World," Gee said. A wave of weakness washed over him, dark, heavy. The hunger was still there. Despite his resolve. The sudden *squeeze* of screaming need almost had him howling. He fell to his knees, then to all fours. His white hair flopped over his face as he panted through the spasm, like a woman struggling through labour. His breathing slowly calmed. "I will not," he whispered.

Weariness pressed upon him, the weight of ten thousand years. The face of a child, the hair of an ancient....

Cracker reached to stroke Gee's cheek with tenderness.

"Let's go home," Gee said in a small voice. "I'm ready to go home."

"Yes," Cracker said gently.

Gee could feel someone staring. The cat, he thought. That shrewd, unrelenting, demanding cat.... With great effort, Gee opened his eyes.

Ilanna began laughing. From deep in her belly, low and awful, growing louder even as the pitch veered into a terrible shriek. She pelted toward them, her leg swinging back to kick Cracker with a killing blow to the head.

Gee only had time to extend one hand, palm outward. His arm shot out, looped once around Ilanna's leg. He yanked upward and she crashed to the ground, hard.

She began shrieking, flipping, twisting, jerking like a maddened eel.

Gee looped the length of his elongated arm around and around both her legs, binding them together, immobile. She hissed, enraged, frothing with spit and fury.

Gee sealed the binding and pinched off his arm. His energy spent, the distended limb fell to the ground like a limp garden hose. He couldn't even keep it raised. Gee slowly dragged it back to his side, across the rough ground. With great effort he reshaped himself a new hand. It scarcely held its form, and the white skin was smudged and lustreless.

Glumly, he stared down at his chest. He was even smaller than before. Every time he cast off his flesh, he became smaller.

Ilanna's shrieks of rage turned to sobbing.

"Come on, Gee," Cracker said. They helped each other to their feet. Gee tottered with weakness.

Some of Cracker's vigour had returned since Karu's Spirit had touched her. Her hands were firm. Steady. She stared down upon Gee with dismay. He was almost a head shorter than she was.

"What's happening to you?" she cried.

"I think it could fall under 'regressing,'" Gee muttered.

Cracker, unable to help herself, giggled.

"I have to leave," Gee said. "Before I have to see my mother return."

Cracker, blinking hard, nodded fiercely. They turned toward the opening, White Cat following behind them.

"Wait!" Ilanna cried. "Don't leave me here like this! How will I eat? I have no eels to aid me!" She flipped-flopped wildly, like a grub. Unable to break the white binding around her legs, tears of rage and fear began streaming down her face. "Do you understand what will happen to me?" she screamed. "I am thrown into the sea, alive! I am ripped apart, consumed, alive, by creatures in the deeps! I am betrayed by my love, by my own family, to this nightmare. And you will send me back again!"

Feelings writhed inside Gee, so mixed he couldn't begin to untangle them. To leave her, to leave her suffering, felt monstrous. He gasped, the edges of his Half World fading, as his own hunger washed over him again. He swallowed hard, panting, until the awful need faded into a bruised ache.

"The hunger is terrible, Ilanna. Almost unbearable." Gee's voice was dull. "I'm sorry. The only way to move beyond the cycles of suffering in Half World is to not eat. And to accept your cycle. As Karu did."

Did White Cat emit a soft purr? Gee wasn't sure.

"How *dare* you!" Ilanna screamed. "Telling me what to do! Do you think you're better than me? You're nothing! You're an abomination. Who are you to tell me to accept my cycle! What about your own? You unwanted git! I'll make you pay! I'm coming back for you! I'll never forget. And you'll be sorry! Because I'll start with your grandmother first. I'll make it last a long, long time. My eels. They'll eat her alive, they'll make it last for years! Years! And you will watch her. And you will turn back to me, and eat your grandmother with me! Do you hear!"

"Let's go." Cracker's voice was firm. "There's nothing we can do."

Wearily, Gee followed his friend out of the terrible place.

They trudged away into the darkness as Ilanna alternated between screams of rage and uncontrollable sobbing.

"Untie me! Don't leave me! I'll devour you! I'll flay your ugly little friend! I'm coming to get you both! You'll be sorry!"

They could hear her for a very long time.

They didn't turn back.

WHEN HER VOICE finally faded Gee felt dirty, guilty and relieved at the same time. Some part of him still wanted Ilanna. A part of him felt sorry for her. Maybe he had done her a wrong, in his own way. But he couldn't undo what had been done. And he couldn't give her what she wanted. Soon exhaustion overcame thought, and he could concentrate only on placing one foot in front of the other.

White Cat bounded before them.

Sometimes the cat sat, waiting, until they caught up, before bounding ahead once again.

"Are you cold?" Cracker asked, glancing down at Gee's bare legs, exposed beneath the hem of his torn T-shirt. His bare feet. "Doesn't it hurt?"

Gee shook his head. "It doesn't matter. Don't worry, I still have my underwear on." He managed a faint smile.

Cracker grinned in return.

"I want to get out of here." He looked about anxiously at the grey dregs of Half World. The rubbled streets, the mounds of smouldering, stinking fires. The press of rounded shadows that suggested forests, or fallen clouds. Darkness was heavy upon them. They could hear the rustle and click of small claws, beaks, the sound of something enormous being dragged over pebbles. The uncanny laughter of too many children dead before they'd had time to live.

They caught up to White Cat once more.

"Do you know the way home?" Cracker asked him. Her voice had gone hoarse again. She still needed water, Gee thought grimly.

"Melanie returned by taking the elevator at the Mirages Hotel," the cat stated.

"Is there any other way?" Gee asked. "A faster way?"

White Cat sniffed. "Maybe for cats," he said, as if they were the only people who didn't know. "But not for the likes of you." White Cat bounded into the greater darkness.

"How insufferable," Cracker muttered.

Gee almost grinned.

They struggled after the cat.

Gee and Cracker walked the nightmare distance that seemed

to unravel before them with no end. With no change of light, no measures of time, they could only continue as best they could, trusting the cat's guidance.

In the stretch and pull of space and time, Gee sometimes wondered if they were still alive. Maybe they had died altogether and were actually reliving their Half Lives, thinking that they needed to go back to the Realm of Flesh. What if their Half Life was this?

I should feel happy, Gee thought. I'm not a monster. I'm going home. But something churned deep inside of him. A small worm gnawed.

Something still undone.... Gee vehemently shook his head. No! It was done! He had passed the test. He had chosen to be human, after all. Please....

Gee was glad that White Cat walked in the lead, so that he didn't have to feel his eyes so cool and weighty upon him.

Gee's scalp prickled.

Cracker's bright eyes widened.

Something ill, powerful ... the air vibrated with it. They both looked back.

In the distance, movement. A swell of darkness was moving toward them, and as it drew nearer the noise began to grow. At first, like the sound of water, it trickled and murmured.

The noise began to roar.

Giggling, weeping children, the howl of crazed feral dogs, leap-frogging shadows, bounding ever closer. Laughter, the sound deep and liquid. Tinged with monstrous power. Ringing wider, farther, expanding until it engulfed them.

"Now I'm *really* cross with *youuuuuuuuuu*," a voice cried out playfully.

Completely mad.

Ilanna's voice, but changed. Deeper, resonant, as if she'd grown enormous. Vibrating with rage.

Gee's heart was a panicked bird. How could she have broken free? He had nothing left to fight her with.

"Haste!" White Cat snarled.

Gee grabbed Cracker's hand. They broke into a staggering run, the pounding of their footsteps terrible, painful, reverberating through their fragile bodies.

"All this exercise has made me hungry," Ilanna called. Her voice, drawing nearer, trembled with glee. "*Mmmmmm. Mmmmmm.* I wouldn't mind starting with a bit of CRACKER!"

White Cat yowled with triumph. They watched as he leapt into the air and disappeared.

"He's found it!" Gee gasped. "This way!"

They plunged into something transparent, at once viscous and opaque. As if they leapt into a wall of water and disappeared. The city bulged and pulled them in.

Chapter Twenty-Seven

Sound overwhelmed them. Screeching, grinding of rusty metal. Cabs careening, clip-clopping horses, the creak of wooden wheels over wretched cobblestones. White neon lights flickered, punctuating the dusk. The distant blast of improvised explosive devices, the *crunch, crunch* of mortar, the wail of an old-fashioned siren. Somewhere high above them the wind whistled with the heavy beat of enormous wings.

Hooooonnnnnk! Headlights pinned them, paralyzed, in the middle of the street. They stared as the driver repeatedly pressed on the horn.

"Idiots!" White Cat hissed from above.

They looked up as one.

The opulent lights of the Mirages Hotel glowed behind the cat, who sat waiting for them at the top of the semi-circular stairs. As if cued, a fountain began spouting behind him, a cascade of light and water. A tinny orchestral recording surged.

White Cat narrowed his eyes with pleasure, enjoying the dramatic display for a brief moment before he leapt toward the hotel entrance. They ran after him.

Gee gasped when they spilled through the circular door. He couldn't help being overwhelmed by the opulence—the brilliant chandeliers in high-arched ceilings, the gleaming expanse of marble floors, the centrepiece of black and white flowers as large as a city bus. Employees stood at attention, numerous bellboys and attendants. The check-in counter glittered as if encrusted with jewels. In a spacious lounge area where drinks were served several guests stood or sat in easy chairs, waiting for someone to join them.

Gee shook his head. It all looked so *normal*.... Not filled with monsters as it had been for Melanie.

Fear pressed upon him from behind. He looked over his shoulder. Ilanna had not yet reached the city.

"White Cat," Gee whispered. "Didn't *The Book of the Realms* describe this lobby as a goblin market?"

"That was in Melanie's time," White Cat stated. "But since the Three Realms were reunited, many have gone on to Spirit. This is a less frightful place now. But 'ware! Danger is still everywhere. Quickly now. To the elevators."

"Keep your head down," Gee reminded Cracker, linking his skinny child arm around her elbow.

They walked across the great lobby as casually as possible. Gee couldn't help double-taking when a chicken with lady's legs darted past. But for the most part, the guests were Half Worlders trapped in their trauma cycle. Their eyes drifted past them as if they weren't there.

Gee glanced back at the revolving doors once more.

"Oh!"

He'd almost run into her. A whippet stood upright on her two hind legs, dressed in high heels and a bikini. Her spine was horribly arched backward to compensate for the bulging mound of her rib cage, and she tottered precariously upon five-inch high heels. "What *is* that gorgeous aroma?" The dog snuffled compulsively as her tail swung a frantic beat. Her excitement was so great she trickled urine.

"Delightful! It reminds me of something … it's on the tip of my tongue!"

A few of the guests began drawing closer. A cloven hoof trod upon Gee's foot and he staggered.

Their glittering eyes with strangely formed pupils, like those of goats and chameleons. Some of them had snouts and beaks. Nostrils quivered, inhaling, sucking in deep their odours.

Cracker had her head low as if she were avoiding demented paparazzi.

"*Ohhhh*, sweet mother of god," an older woman groaned. "She smells so *gooood*. She smells of Life!" A monitor's tongue flicked out from between her human lips to taste the flavour in the air.

"Life!" the creatures cried. "Life! Give us Life!"

Gee, so much smaller, could only catch glimpses of White Cat through the gathering crowd. The cat had reached the elevators that were raised higher than the lobby. Standing on his hind legs, propping one paw against the frame of the doors, White Cat reached out with his other paw, a single claw extended, to press the call button.

As one of the two cars began to descend the cat glared impatiently at Gee and Cracker. "Hurry!" he mouthed, his whiskers pointed in their direction as they tried to squeeze their way through the small crowd.

Cracker was yanked away from Gee's side. She didn't even have time to cry out.

"Oh!" Gee gasped. He was jostled farther and farther as the crowd circled around Cracker. He reached out, trying to force his way back to her side, but the crush of their scaly bodies, their bulging forms—he couldn't break through. And he had little strength remaining.

"Mine! All mine!" voices cried.

"Give us a piece."

"I got here first! I need it the most!"

Cracker would be torn to pieces.... Too small, powerless, Gee was lost inside the press of bodies. He jumped up and down like a little child. He could see nothing. There was nothing he could do. Shame twisted inside his chest.

A large man, his torso naked, like a faun, only his two legs—they were the thick stubby limbs of an elephant.... His eyes whirled, as if intoxicated. Finding Gee in his way, he knocked him aside as if he were a doll.

Gee fell face forward onto the cold marble floor. Someone stepped on the middle of his back, forcing out all of the air. The high heel punched a hole into his lung. Gee screamed.

Pain. Pain as he'd never known it. Why now? When he hadn't felt it before? His lung burned. Whistling. Whining. He would be trampled to death. And it hurt. It hurt so very much. To death....

The Half Worlders were after Cracker because she smelled good. She smelled of Life. But they had let White Cat pass. He was made of stone. And Gee? What was he that they passed him by?

I am not alive.... Gee moaned.

No! It couldn't be. But the truth of the knowledge refused to fade. Not alive, as Cracker lived....

The woman tried to dislodge her shoe from the middle of Gee's back by giving it a little shake. Gee screamed again.

Desperate to reach the beguiling aroma, she abandoned her footwear.

He could feel his slow heartbeat throbbing around the heel that pierced his back. It hurt so much. Things only hurt if you're alive! Gee railed.

Cracker cried out.

No! What was happening to her—

A boot kicked the side of Gee's head. White light exploded behind his eyelids. He could scarcely breathe. "Someone," Gee mouthed, his lips moving against the cold polish of the floor. "Please, someone help."

Cold, slickness gently twined around Gee's ankles. The gelid length moved lovingly across his skin and a rush of shivers trickled down his spine. In a daze, he began smiling, because it felt so nice—

He was yanked upward into the air. The jolt of his own weight and gravity wrenched his ankles and neck. He gagged, simultaneously biting his tongue.

Gee dangled upside down, a metre above the heads of the tallest creatures crowding around Cracker. He swayed slowly, his

T-shirt bunched around his neck and armpits. He twisted from side to side to catch sight of what had saved him from being trampled. His movements dislodged the shoe that was stuck in his back and it fell to the floor with a clatter.

Gee sucked his breath. The pain, whistling in and out. He could feel wetness sliding down his back. Cracker. What was happening to Cracker?

He began twisting frantically. The thing holding him gave him a little shake. A warning.

Gee stopped moving. Still upside down, he was slowly turned around.

It took a moment to recognize Ilanna's inverted smile, but when her eel tongue darted, Gee couldn't keep a small sound from escaping his lips. What she had become….

Her legs … her smooth, pale human legs, they'd melded together and grown thicker, longer, into the body of an enormous white sinuous eel. Muscular and thick, a vestigial crease remained, the seam running down the entire length to the tip of her tail. Like Nu Wa…. It was her long tapered tail that held him aloft.

Gee's eyes widened. It wasn't just her legs … her body stretched, long and sinewed, all the way up to her head. She no longer had a neck or shoulders or a human torso; the only part of her that remained human was her head.

"Maybe I should thank you," Ilanna hissed. "Your betrayal tipped me into a most *transformative* rage and loathing. I have reshaped my destiny. As you once did. And now I no longer need you." Feigning sorrow, she widened her beautiful seal eyes and her voice wobbled. "I really wish it didn't have to end like this between us. But you've betrayed me in the worst way possible. And I've simply outgrown you." She slicked her tail even farther along his legs, past his ankles, so that her tail bound him all the way from his knees to his toes.

Gee slowly swayed back and forth.

The din below him sounded far away as pressure grew inside his head. He could feel his eyes beginning to bulge against the sockets.

Gee closed his eyelids. It wasn't fair. He hadn't done anything to deserve all these terrible things. But they still happened ... whether you deserved it or not. And did anyone truly deserve it? He had no answers.

"To be human," Gee mouthed. "Or not...." He almost laughed. How he'd hated Hamlet, the sniveller, when they'd studied the play with Ms. Park....

He opened his eyes.

Ilanna's face was mere inches away from his own, Gee's eyes parallel to her quivering lips. They parted, and her eel tongue slowly began slipping out, the waft of the winter seas a blast of brine and icy death.

And her teeth. Jagged, glinting and so many. She smiled broadly and pulled him closer even as she slowly turned him around. Her cold breath hitting the wet on his back. She pressed her mouth against his bleeding wound, and began to suck.

Gee screamed with pain.

From a great distance, he could hear Cracker's muffled shouts. White Cat's cursing.

"We could have been friends," Ilanna whispered moistly. She spun him around so that he faced her once more.

His black blood was smeared around her pale lips. Gee fought his revulsion.

"We could have been lovers. I would have been your mommy, your older sister. Your teacher, your torturer and your saviour...." Ilanna whispered. "I would have been everything for you."

"You offered so much," Gee rasped. His smile was sad. Resolute. "But it was an offer I will never accept."

Ilanna's eyes narrowed into slits. The tail that bound half the length of Gee's legs squeezed so tight that his white glueflesh shot out in streaks.

Now! Gee thought.

"Karuuuuuu!" Cracker's voice rang out, as pure as a bell.

Gee pinched off his flesh at his knees, leaving Ilanna holding the amputated remains. He began to plummet. Gee shot his two palms upward. They splatted upon Ilanna's face, and even as she reared back, he willed his palms to spread, thin, elastic, to encase her entire head.

Trapped in a web of skin, Ilanna reared desperately, stretching even more glueskin away from Gee's body. He was still stuck to her, and he hadn't the strength to pinch off his arms so that he could fall away. Before nothing of him was left....

Ilanna writhed and weaved in her struggle for air, each movement pulling more matter away from Gee's body.

I'm like pull taffy, Gee almost giggled, as a wave of hysteria washed over him. He shook his head. Stop it! I have to pinch free from her, he thought desperately. He was so weak. Yet gravity continued to work on what remained of his body, and Gee stretched and sank to the ground. He was caught in the folds of his overlarge T-shirt, his arms stretched as thin as string, his mass so depleted he was scarcely larger than an infant....

Dazed, Gee stared up at the chandeliered ceiling. The ornate mouldings were so pretty, he thought. Very soon, someone would step on him, crush him, and he would just be a large wad of gum sullying the beautiful marble floor. At least he hadn't succumbed.

He had not!

Relief, pride, even sorrow—a small human ember deep inside.

Ilanna, looming high above him. Without hands or eels to assist her, she couldn't tear away the asphyxiating skin of glue. She thrashed back and forth, stretching Gee's string arms even thinner into threads. Her thick muscular tail began banging the ground, knocking over the hotel guests, in her desperation for air. Tables tipping, chairs flying, the shatter of crystal smashing. The sounds of Ilanna's choking gurgle horrible and pitiful. She reared, whipped her body in the opposite direction, and the thread of Gee's arms finally snapped. Free.

He could not even crawl.

Ilanna began to sway in a giant circle.

"I'm sorry, Popo," Gee whispered. "I tried my best...."

"Pathetic," a snide voice growled.

Gee weakly turned his head.

A paw smacked him, hard, on the nose. A burst of white light bloomed behind his closed eyes. Gee shook his head sluggishly and blinked, trying to focus.

White Cat loomed over him, his malevolent eyes filled with spite. The cat hadn't even used his claws. Look at that, Gee thought sluggishly. I've lost so much of myself that I'm no bigger than a cat.

"Gather your wits!" White Cat demanded. "Reshape your legs at the very least! Idiot!"

Gee stared down at his body. His legs ended at his knees. The cat was right. He had to make an effort.... His head fell back onto the floor.

Ilanna, smothering beneath the skin of glue, began weaving back and forth dangerously.

"The things I'm forced to do," White Cat muttered. He placed his forepaws on Gee's side and began to knead.

"Don't help me," Gee cried, "help Cracker!"

"Cracker doesn't need my help!" White Cat seethed. "She's rather adept at having her best interests met. Not unlike a cat," he said begrudgingly. "But you are a different matter!" He treadled the boy across the floor as if rolling a log.

White Cat rolled him so quickly that Gee grew dizzy. Yet he clung to one thought: Cracker was okay? "Wait!" he cried. "Stop!" He wanted to see. Where had the crowd gone? What was happening?

"Haste, not waste," White Cat muttered. "If you have energy enough to bellow, reshape your legs!"

Gee gritted his teeth, and tried to stretch, s-t-r-e-t-c-h, the glueskin farther down his legs, but the dizziness overwhelmed him. "You have to stop," he pleaded. "I can't—"

He thudded against something so hard that his teeth clacked, barely missing his tongue.

"Oops," White Cat said, having rolled him into the first stair by the elevator entrance. He didn't sound very sorry.

Ilanna's monstrous body stiffened above him. Rigid, a gargantuan eel statue. Gee couldn't look away. She teetered so very slowly that he felt as if he could catch her somehow—and then crashed to the ground with an impact so great that the floor shuddered. She'd landed a hair's breadth away from where he'd been lying moments before.

Gee stared, paralyzed by the near miss. He would have been crushed beneath her. "Thank you, White Cat." His voice trembled.

Ilanna's long, thick, muscular eel body twitched with the final throes of her Half Death.... The slick white gleam of her skin began to fade and the taut muscles to slacken.

The glueskin Gee had used to cover her head was still intact. It lay flat upon her beautiful features. A thin mask. He had killed her.

Once, she'd been a human. A girl. An infant born in the Realm of Flesh.... A human who'd been betrayed by the ones she loved the most. To end up in Half World. To suffer. And he had killed her.

Gee turned his head to the side and retched. A thin wad of white glue bobbed from his quavering lips. He spat and spat. Wiped his mouth against his shoulder. "I'm sorry, Ilanna," Gee whispered. His eyes burned. Please. He had to get out of this place. He wanted to go home.

"Pah!" White Cat batted Gee's head with his paw. "Ready yourself!"

Gee squeezed his eyes shut, hard, to rid himself of the last of the dizziness.

"Oooooh," the crowd sighed. *"Ohhhhhhh."*

Something was glowing, a warm and beautiful colour in the dim and monstrous world. Moving, the reflections of orange light flicked around the walls and the great ornate ceiling.

Orange, Gee thought wonderingly. Ohhh....

"So pretty," the crowd cried, staring upward, transfixed.

A hinotama, the size of a human heart, flared like an orb of firelight. It bobbed weightlessly above the guests' heads, weaving, diving playfully. The orange-yellow glow was vibrant in the grey Realm, and the creatures and monsters, the maimed and the suffering, raised their hands, trying to touch the brilliant orb as it wafted just beyond their reach. Bewitched, they seemed to have forgotten what they'd been doing....

As they chased after the beguiling light, Cracker was left behind.

Flee now, Karu's Spirit urged. *Leave this Realm. Live your life fully as you are meant to.*

Karu. He'd come back. Gee stared, his mouth fallen open, as the flame-orange hinotama floated above the heads of the Half Worlders.

"Catch it!" the creatures cried. "So beautiful, the light...."

Karu's flame was a blossom of hope. Gee couldn't look away. He found himself half-raised up, and his desire was so great that two small baby arms had formed without his knowing. He reached out with both hands instinctively, his chest aching for something he could not say.

"Oh-hoh." White Cat's voice was quiet, almost gentle. "Do you recognize, young Gee, what you truly long for?"

Before he could reply, Gee was snatched up underneath his arms and clutched against Cracker's chest. His T-shirt dangled loosely like a swaddling cloth.

Gee was swamped by embarrassment—I'm sixteen years old! he thought indignantly. A man!

"Jesus, Gee," Cracker muttered. "What the hell!"

His relief was so great he wept. Tears, salty, sharp upon his tongue. He couldn't help peering over Cracker's shoulder to gaze at Karu's brilliant Spirit.... Ilanna's white sinuous body lay in a large S-shape on the marble floor.

Ting. The elevator had arrived.

Cracker carried Gee inside the open car. He twisted in her arms so that he could see the lobby before the doors closed.

Karu's Spirit seeped through the glass window and the enthralled creatures all churned through the rotating doors, fighting, yanking each other back, until they became jammed. The Half Worlders who'd made it outside were as gleeful as children as they ran and leapt after the bobbing orange light.

The creatures stuck inside the rotating door wept.

Movement. Ilanna's body quivered. No, not quivering—she was beginning to fade away. Patches fluctuating between opaque and transparent, she was breaking apart into nothing. Pulled back to the beginning of her cycle. The cycle she had denied for so very long.

Did Ilanna deserve to return to her horrible suffering? Did anyone? Gee looked away.

Thankfully, the doors of the elevator slid shut.

Chapter Twenty-Eight

"Could you press four, please?" White Cat asked in a perky voice, as if he'd just checked into the hotel and was starting his holiday.

"Shut up, cat," Cracker muttered. She sighed.

Gee heard a finger jab, once, against the button. His heart sank. A keycard. They didn't—

The elevator began to rise.

"We didn't swipe," Gee whispered. "Why is the car moving?"

"No one needs a keycard to reach the fourth floor," White Cat said enigmatically.

"Gee!" Cracker gasped. "Your back! It's bleeding!"

He'd forgotten about it. The pain wasn't as bad. "I think it's stopped," he said. "It doesn't hurt that much."

Gee peered over Cracker's shoulder. "Am I too heavy?" he asked. What was the point of acting embarrassed at this point?

"I'll manage," she said. She began to convulse.

"Are you okay?" Gee cried.

She shook once more. She convulsed again. *"Hahahahahahaaaa!"* she bellowed. *"Hohohohohohoooo!"* Tears streamed down her face as she laughed and laughed, unable to stop.

"Thank you." Gee's voice was clipped. "For your sensitivity. And for not making me feel self-conscious."

She laughed even harder. "I'm sorry," she gasped. "I'm sorry! I really am!" She broke into peals of laughter again. "No, really," she managed, between guffaws, "I think it's kind of hysteria. Because everything is so fucked up."

"I'm touched," Gee said. "You're so thoughtful."

"I'm sorry," Cracker gasped. "Sorry." She wiped her nose on his swaddled T-shirt. "Your white hair is awesome. I think I'll do that when I get home."

"Are you two finished?" White Cat asked icily. "The fourth floor requires all your wits!" He stared, sourly, at Cracker's boots. "Those weigh you down. You should take them off."

"What?" she asked. "That's like asking a witch to give up her spells! Like asking a warrior to give up her sword!"

Gee almost smiled.

"Never mind." White Cat rolled his eyes. "I guess you made it across with them on."

"Jesus," Cracker muttered indignantly. "The nerve! Give up my boots!"

The elevator *sagged*, briefly, and their stomachs dropped.

"Let this be the final time," Gee whispered.

The doors slid open.

The darkness was so thick, so complete, that it spilled into the elevator. It was as if the car was suspended in nothing, in nowhere, and they the last of the living. The silence was so heavy it pressed upon their chests like night haunts stealing their breath. The lighting inside the elevator flickered, began to buzz. It flared brighter, then, with a *pop*, quickly faded.

Gee could see only the blue after-image of light before that too disappeared.

The darkness was utterly complete. As if light had never existed.

"Spirits grant us safe passage," White Cat intoned, with none of his usual attitude. "Everyone—hold on to each other so that we don't become lost. Darkness tries to lead astray. You may hold on to my tail," he said through gritted teeth.

Gee felt Cracker shifting him to her opposite shoulder. She leant forward to blindly reach for White Cat's fluffy tail.

"Okay," she said in a small voice.

They stepped out of the elevator and into darkness.

One, two, three, four … darkness began to roar. Like a flash flood careening down a bouldered riverbed. The thunderous noise drowning heartbeat, breath, cries.

We are so tiny, Gee thought, we are motes in a vast universe.

I want to live.

As if the waters had parted, the noise veered away, and with the movement came the light.

"Ah!" The cry burst out of him. Emptiness yawning all around them, and only Cracker's steady pace across the ever-collapsing bridge of crows. The birds flew hard, their vast number bridging the abyss that separated the Realm of Flesh from Half World.

"Shitshitshitshit," Cracker chanted, clutching White Cat's tail.

"Don't you dare close your eyes this time!" Gee shouted.

The air whistled and flapped, hoarse caws filling the air. The crows' wings glinting like black water in the grey light.

There! The mountain ledge, the Gate to the other side.... Cracker ran steadily upon the ever-shifting backs of crows, across the open air, with a sureness that Gee couldn't fathom. Did faith keep them aloft? he wondered as they drew closer to the rocky ledge.

The texture of her steps shifted. A lurch. A ledge.

Cracker's strength finally gave as she reached solid footing. She collapsed forward, but used her forearms to absorb her fall so that she wouldn't crush Gee. The surface, littered with dry finger bones, crackled and crunched beneath her. Cracker rolled away to lie upon her back.

They both stared upward at the sky, breathing hard, unbearably grateful.

The sky was blue. Beautiful. They'd never seen such an intense and luscious blue, and it filled their hearts with joy.

White Cat batted away parched white bones before sitting calmly, gazing at his companions' exhaustion and relief with a look of distaste. His fluffy tail slowly rose up and down.

The hoarse cries of the jubilant crows fading away.... Their gasps for air began to ease. A cold thin wind keened. Gee shivered.

Almost there....

A sudden sense of urgency pressed hard on his chest. Gee sat up abruptly. Startled to find himself so very small. He'd grow again, once he started eating real food in the Realm of Flesh, he reassured himself. He would grow fleshly again. Because he had, once before, when Melanie had brought him out of Half World as a baby. He'd grown into a tall teenager, fed so well on Popo's delicious cooking....

Gee stared at his baby hands, soft and weak. A surge of tears filled his eyes once more, and he angrily swiped the emotions away with the back of his hand. Why was he crying now? He'd become so emotional. A crybaby, he thought, a sad, wry grin twisting his small lips.

The cliff face began to shake, a low rumbling of granite. Small rocks rained upon them, and Cracker rolled over, groaning with pain, her weary muscles. She rose to her feet even as the ledge lurched beneath them.

With a terrible groan, the giant Gatekeeper tore herself out of the cliff face and stepped onto the ledge. Her timeless granite face that had weathered more years than they could imagine stared across the great divide with an implacable gaze.

Gee, able only to sit, had to tip his head back in order to see her face.

"The toll," the Gatekeeper groaned, her voice creaking with the terrible weight. "You must pay the toll in order to pass."

"Fucking toll." Cracker shook her head. "Still asking for it. After everything. I can do it this time. I'm pretty sure."

"The *tolllll*," the Gatekeeper groaned.

"Don't," Gee told Cracker. "Let me. It doesn't hurt me."

The rock face began grinding.

A small opening that continued to widen....

Gee stared at the stone giant's face. Had she opened the portal for free? Was that even possible?

The Gatekeeper's thick neck creaked as she turned her head toward the Gate. The portal was opening. And they hadn't paid the toll. The crescent continued to grow.

There was someone on the other side. A waft of lemon grass, the musky sweetness of ripe fruit.

"Popo?" Gee whispered. "Popo!"

The opening widened further to reveal a second person. Compact. Skin browned by the sun. Long hair tied back in a low ponytail.

"Older Sister?" Gee mouthed, his eyes round with wonder.

"Grandson!" Popo cried. Tears streamed down her wrinkled face and she held out her arms toward him. Her warm brown eyes shone. "Oh, what has happened to Grandson? We've come for you! Come through. Quickly!"

Gee's heart stilled. They were so full of life. They were brilliant in their mortality. He touched his face with his soft baby hand.

Even as the portal waxed gibbous, something unfurled inside Gee, and he could not make it stop. Like a flower opening to the light. He knew. He finally understood.

"I can't go back."

"What! What are you talking about?" Cracker practically screamed. "It's okay now! We did what we had to do! We can go home!"

Popo's eyes had widened. She began shaking her head.

"You know," Gee said. "Popo, you know. The cycles. The cycles need to flow as they flow. We can't try to alter the path before its time. Or we put everything at risk again. I wasn't born into Half World. Older Sister carried me out.... And the Realms were reunited. I got to live with you for a while...." His smile wobbled. "But I'm not meant to stay in the Realm of Flesh."

"Bullshit!" Cracker shouted. She reached down to pick him up.

Gee scuttled backward, close to the cliff ledge.

"Go through!" he shouted at Cracker. "You're meant to go back. Not me. Hurry!"

Cracker's eyes darted back and forth between the open Gate and Gee. Her instinct to save herself warring with loyalty.

Gee glared at Melanie. "Take her out!"

Melanie, eyes fierce, pinched her lips with determination. She leapt through the portal and threw Cracker over her shoulder.

"Stop," Cracker cried. She began sobbing with rage, with sorrow. "Take Gee, too! It's not fair! Let me go!" She tried to struggle but she was no match for Melanie's strength.

Melanie carried her to the other side.

Popo had closed her eyes. She continued shaking her head. Resolute, she stepped across the Gate to be with Gee on the bone-strewn ledge. She picked him up and held him close, as if she would never let him go.

"If Grandson must stay here, Popo will stay with Grandson." There was no fear in her voice. Only enduring love.

"Oh, Popo," Gee quavered.

"Hurry!" Cracker sobbed. "Gee!"

The portal was beginning to close. Gee could feel his grandmother's mortal heart pounding against his chest.

Gee bent his neck and bit his grandmother's shoulder, hard.

"Oh!" Popo cried, instinctively releasing her hold.

Gee fell and his heart plugged his throat. Only to be caught inside the arms of his older sister.

Melanie hugged Gee close for a brief moment. "You're very brave," she whispered into his white hair. "I was wrong about you. I'm sorry."

She set him down on the ledge.

Gee stared, eyes dry, as his sister tried to drag his beloved Popo through the shrinking portal.

The old woman fought back, shaking her wrist free from Melanie's hold, turning for her grandson.

"Hurry!" Cracker screamed.

Melanie slung her grandmother over her shoulder and leapt through.

Gee caught a glimpse of his popo's face as she reared up, her hand outstretched.

"What?" Cracker's muffled voice sounded incredulous. "No!" she shouted from behind the women.

Tears streamed down Popo's wrinkled cheeks.

"Grandson!" she cried.

"Thank you," Gee whispered.

The cliff face was solid once more. The wind whined, cold, and Gee's white hair ruffled against his dry face. The stone giant was silent.

Gee stared at the dry little finger bones that surrounded him. He was sitting on several of them and it was terribly uncomfortable.

His back was beginning to ache once again.

But the sky.

How brilliantly blue, the sky.

Chapter Twenty-Nine

"That was all rather unnecessarily NHK morning TV melodrama," a dry voice remarked.

Gee slowly turned his head.

At the great stone feet of the giantess sat White Cat, his fluffy tail curved elegantly around his paws.

Pain torqued inside Gee's chest. He wasn't alone.... Tears filled his eyes. Unconsciously, he raised his baby arms toward the cat.

White Cat stared incredulously. "You cannot be serious," he enunciated.

Gee lowered his arms, a small smile tugging at the corner of his lips. He heaved a great sigh, and it broke apart into shudders. "You stayed with me...."

"I can't *stay* here, of course. Nor do I want to," White Cat said loftily.

"How will you return? Now you'll have to pay the toll." Gee didn't ask the cat when he would leave.

"You must pay the toll in order to pass," the stone giant intoned.

"For the love of—" White Cat glared upward. "We are so utterly done with the payment of tolls. Surely you can see that. *Such* a base demand." The cat closed his eyes with disgust. He sneezed emphatically.

The Gatekeeper shifted, creaking ominously with the weight.

Gee wondered when the final parting would come. It might have been better if the cat had just left with everyone else. To go through that pain again.... "How will you get back now?" he whispered.

"Cats have ways." White Cat blinked. "More ways than humans have."

Gee stared at the rounded stubs of his baby knees. Had Popo, Melanie and Cracker made it safely out of the Cassiar Connector? Were they on their way home?

"I don't think she heard me thank her!" Gee burst out.

"She knows." White Cat's voice was gentle. "Fear not."

Fear not.... A choking sound escaped from Gee's lips, but he swallowed hard. If he started laughing he didn't know if he'd ever be able to stop.

The keening mountain wind turned into a low howl, and Gee's lanky white hair whipped his small face. He didn't doubt his choice, but he was so frightened he could scarcely bear it. His teeth began to chatter.

"You surprised me." White Cat's voice held grudging respect. "How did you come to understand that you had to remain in Half World?"

Gee dragged the sleeve of his overlarge T-shirt under his nose and wrapped his arms tightly around his middle. “It all clicked into place. Like the final pieces of a puzzle.” He shrugged. “Everything works in cycles. Or it’s supposed to. People like Ilanna and Karu.” Gee gulped. “People like Mr. Glueskin— They did everything they could to keep themselves out of their awful cycle. But Karu turned to Spirit, because he stopped eating people, because he finally accepted his cycle. It set him free from suffering. Free to pass to the Realm of Spirit.

“Ilanna couldn’t accept her cycle, and she just faded, to start her suffering all over again. And me....” Gee looked across the abyss.

Halfway between them and the mountainside of Half World, the sky leached from blue to grey.

“If I went back with Popo I’d be just like Ilanna, denying my suffering, but in trying to escape it, being trapped by it. Melanie carried me out of Half World, and I got to live, for a time, with Popo.” Gee dragged the back of his hands over his eyes. “But that wasn’t really a part of the cycle I’m supposed to be in. Avoiding my cycle means being trapped in Half Life. It means never attaining Spirit.”

A second realization bloomed inside of him. “My birth mother, too.... If I’m part of her Half World cycle, and I’m missing, she won’t ever be able to attain Spirit either.”

Gee could feel White Cat staring.

“Why should you care what befalls her?” White Cat asked.

“I don’t know if I really do care,” Gee had to admit. “But my birth mother suffers. And that— The man who is my father ... he suffers doing evil.” Gee’s eyes were fierce. “I did evil too, as Mr. Glueskin! Popo knew that! But she still gave me a chance! She still loved me!”

"Calm down." White Cat's voice was dry.

Gee took a long shuddering breath. "I'd do almost anything to go back home, to live with Popo.... But it wouldn't work. I'd be disrupting the cycles. And even if Ilanna didn't come for me again, Half World would send someone or something to take me back. I won't do anything more to have Popo risk herself again."

The cat settled down onto his haunches and half-closed his eyes.

Gee's eyes widened. "You knew!" he exclaimed.

The expression on White Cat's face remain unchanged, but the tip of his tail twitched.

"All along. From the very beginning. You knew I had to return to Half World...." Gee's chin slumped to his chest. "Why didn't you tell me? Us? We wouldn't have had to suffer like this. You should have said."

White Cat made a noise as if he were bringing up a hairball. "It's not the kind of thing a person would believe. You needed to learn, to grow, and that meant you had to live through the experience. Everyone did. Difficult though it was," White Cat conceded.

"Grow," Gee scoffed, gazing at his baby arms, the remains of his legs.

"Unpleasant as the change may feel"—White Cat's voice was gentle again—"this is your true size in Half World. You never grew out of infancy."

"I hadn't thought of that," Gee said.

White Cat closed his eyes. "You learned to stretch the limitations of your cycle, first by turning your rage and fear into a way to control your body. Then you fed it with borrowed energy from the Half Lives of other creatures. But your body's growth in Half

World wasn't organic growth. Impressive though it was. It was a distortion."

"How did I grow in the Realm of Flesh?"

"You were still half alive, after all. And Popo fed you well." White Cat's ear twitched.

Gee sighed. "Popo is an amazing cook...." He blinked fiercely.

"I meant she fed you with love," the cat snipped. "She makes a fine steamed sablefish with green onions and ginger, however," he couldn't help adding with a little quiver.

White Cat tipped his head back and stared directly upward. "How long do you intend on eavesdropping?" he asked rudely. "You can go away now."

The great pillar legs of the stone giantess groaned as she shifted her great weight. "The *tollllll*," she moaned.

Gee gazed unhappily at the Gatekeeper's worn face. "And how long have *you* cycled, asking for this terrible toll?" he asked. "When will you be free?" He shook his head. "I don't know why Life and Half Life must be so hard." His small hands squeezed into tight fists.

White Cat set a soft paw atop the back of one fist. For once he said nothing.

Gee exhaled and opened his hands. "Can you tell me that one day there'll be more than just suffering?"

White Cat patted with his paw, once, twice, a third time with the prick of claws before he drew away. "Has that not happened for you already?"

Gee's lips trembled as a faint smile flickered across his face. "Yes," he whispered. The relief that washed over him was so very sweet. "Yes, it has."

He closed his eyes. Just one last thing. Though the mountain was so cold. He wanted to do this last thing.

Gritting his teeth, Gee willed the flesh he had left to stretch once more … to grow elastic, to ripple from his torso, down his thighs, past his knees. Quaking with the effort, the tendons in his neck taut, he formed shins, calves, ankles, feet and all the toes, those numerous toes….

"Paws would have been easier," White Cat remarked. "Perhaps without the fur."

"Pah-hahaha!" Gee burst out laughing. Before he could finish the last toe. He fell back, panting, and watched a slurry of grey clouds slide across the intensely blue sky. He chuckled weakly. Stupid cat, he thought, with resentment and affection. *Ahhh,* he didn't need that last toe. He would make do with what he had.

Gee rolled to his front and placed his hands flat on the rock ledge, underneath his skinny little chest. Pushing his butt up in the air, he walked his new feet toward his hands, like a baby learning to stand. He pushed up with his hands and wobbled as he adjusted to the limbs of a gaunt baby. Much too large, his T-shirt and underwear slid off and puddled at his feet.

Perfect, Gee thought. Naked, to top it off. Figures.

"Planning on going somewhere?" White Cat asked. "Streaking, maybe?" He rose gracefully and stretched his back, extending one paw and his tail before padding silently around Gee's unsteady form. As he passed by, he let his fluffy tail slide across Gee's back.

It was almost enough to topple him.

"Shut up," Gee muttered. "Don't touch me. I have one thing left to do. And it's going to take everything I have, so don't distract me."

"What, pray, is there left to do?"

"I'm returning to my cycle." Gee's throat was so dry he could no longer swallow.

White Cat shrugged a cat shrug. "You needn't do anything to get there. You can rest on this ledge until you fade away, as everyone does in Half World. And you'll automatically be taken back to the start of your cycle." The cat's tone shifted. Softer. "You don't have to do anything else. It's enough."

Gee's eyes shone. "I want to return on my own terms. I'm going to meet it halfway."

The Gatekeeper was staring at him with her unreadable stone face. "Why are you still here?" Gee asked her again. "Why haven't you reached Spirit?"

The stone giantess took a crashing step backward.

"One day," Gee whispered. "You will one day." He turned to the edge of the ledge. Resolute. He tottered toward it, unsteady on his newly formed feet. His certainty was a solid core inside him.

He looked down, down; so far and deep it fell away that he couldn't see the bottom, only swaths of clouds wisping white and grey, texturing the immense distance.

If you fell forever, would it stop feeling like falling?

"Tell Popo I...." Gee's voice faded. "She'll know." He smiled. "She knows."

He did not look back at White Cat. "Thank you. Until our cycles overlap once again."

Gee dove.

The air roared.

Cold. Fast. Tears stripped from the corners of his eyes. Hair a white flame forced back from his face. Arms extended, fingertips tearing through icy sheets of clouds. A falcon's majestic plummet. A superhero.

Try "naked baby." A snide voice filled the inside of Gee's mind.

Startled, he looked to his side.

White Cat, ears pressed flat to his skull, plummeted beside him.

What are you doing? Gee screamed, appalled.

I'm just joining you. For a little while. I've never tried this before.

Are you crazy? What about your cycle!

I'm not going with you to the end of this journey. Just partway. Shut up. You're ruining the experience.

Gee shook his head. That cat. That awful, awful, infuriating cat!

The edges of the roaring wind growing darker. Gee could no longer feel his fingers, his toes.

It was so cold, so fast.

Turning to heat.

Gee closed his eyes.

Like a meteor.

Roaring.

Faster.

Now.

Chapter Thirty

Ming Wei, Melanie and Cracker sat around the large wooden table in the open living room. The air was still. The weight of their words would not dissipate and the burden of it pressed upon their shoulders.

Face washed clean, Cracker was pale and gaunt in the folds of Melanie's old green housecoat. She looked hardly old enough to be in junior high school, let alone sixteen. Cracker glanced about, wide-eyed, as if she could scarcely believe that colour had always existed. The tall potted tree with brilliant miniature oranges hanging from the branches, the nap of the red velvet cushions, the golden glow of sunset blazing through the large windows.... She marvelled at the beauty.

Ming Wei's palm rested on one of two books lying on the table. One of the tomes was ancient, with a thick leather cover, cracked and stained with age. A faded circular symbol was engraved in the middle. The book beneath Ming Wei's palm was newer. The edges of the pages were gilded in gold and the leather cover was smooth, a rich deep blue.

Melanie's long hair hung loosely. Movement on her shoulder; a dark red rat muzzle poked past the curtain of her hair. It twitched its whiskers as it sampled the air, and then looked upward.

A small object dropped out of the ceiling and landed with a clunk on the wooden table. It clattered across the surface until it came to rest against the spine of the blue book.

The three of them stared at the statuette, looked up at the ceiling for a hole that wasn't there.

"Well." Ming Wei's voice was dry. "He's never done that before."

The white statuette shivered, some force within its nucleus shifting, the fine moment between inert and living. Shimmering, it burst from stone to flesh.

White Cat's eyes bulged, his pupils enormous. His tail puffed and perpendicular, his fur crackling as if he'd been caught in a storm of static. "Spirits light the way!" he yowled.

They stared at the cat, aghast.

The cat's pupils slowly narrowed in the yellow-green of his irises. His fur settled and he calmly lowered his tail, wrapping it around his paws as he sat down.

"Gee. . . ." Ming Wei whispered. "And what of Grandson?"

White Cat was sober. "He has returned to his cycle. Bravely. His Spirit true."

Ming Wei stroked the cover of the blue book. Her fingers brushing the embossed letters of the title, *The New Book of the Realms*. She smiled, a little sadly, but no longer wept.

White Cat's eyes narrowed. *"Ahhh,"* he said. "A new book. I wondered if that might happen."

"What does it all mean?" Melanie's voice had an edge. "What now?" She started laughing, a small, bitter sound. "How many times must people go back there? First, to seek my mother, only to lose her. Then end up saving Baby Glueskin. Only to have him returned to Half World!" She was standing now, her hands on the table, breathing hard. "He's gone back to his cycle, a cycle that produced a monster! It's going to start all over again!"

"Gee's not a monster," Cracker said.

"Cracker is wrong," Ming Wei said gently. "Gee *is* a monster, but if he is, so are we all."

"We're nothing like Mr. Glueskin!" Melanie cried. "I am not!"

"No," Ming Wei agreed. "Melanie has not turned into Mr. Glueskin. Yet Melanie has a propensity to be him. Everyone does." She raised the new book and set it atop the old, pushed them both to the middle of the table. Ming Wei rested her hands on the curved arms of her wooden chair. Melanie sat down.

Through the closed window they could hear the hoarse caws of the evening crows returning to the mountains. The house rattled slightly as a bus drove past. Someone pressed long and hard on their car horn.

"It's still not fair," Cracker whispered.

Ming Wei shrugged with great eloquence. "It is not fair that your sister died so young. It is not fair that Ming Wei's lover was killed during a burglary. It is not fair that Melanie could not have more time with her mother. It is not fair that Grandson could not return with us to Life." She shrugged once more. "And so, the cycle continues, fair or not."

"But Popo." Melanie's voice was soft. "Won't it start all over again? Gee's in Half World to stay, and he'll turn back into Mr. Glueskin. He'll find Ilanna, and they'll start their work to dissolve the binding that separates the Three Realms. Someone will have to go back and fight him all over again!"

Ming Wei was stern. "Youth seeks immediate and visible outcomes. And if they don't see it with their eyes, they believe nothing has changed. Yet change is often slow, and it is often subtle." The old woman took a deep breath. "Gee had to return to his cycle, as he discovered he must, so he accepted. But he returned on his own terms. And he returned to the cycle changed, did he not? For he lived here, with us, for sixteen years. He experienced life and love, friendship and family. He had a home. These things he had which he never had before. He is changed, even as he returns to a cycle he did not ask for." Ming Wei nodded. "What kind of effect this will have upon his cycle we have no way of knowing. But change has been wrought."

"So, you really think things have changed for Gee? Do you think it's going to be okay?" Cracker asked.

Popo turned her head toward the window. To the gathering darkness outside.

White Cat flicked his ear.

"As night follows day," Popo said. Her eyes shone bright.

The tension fell from Melanie's shoulders, and Red Jade Rat climbed down her arm to nestle in the cup of her hands on the table.

Cracker sighed, her breath breaking into shudders. "So what do we do now? What are we supposed to do?"

Ming Wei smiled. "We carry the memories of our loved ones forward. We honour their memories. And we live well. That is all."

Her eyes glinted. Her matter-of-fact tone was belied by the tears in her eyes.

Cracker dragged the back of her hand across her face. "Live well...," she muttered. "After what I saw in Half World, I'm scared to death of dying!"

Melanie grinned momentarily before it faded. "I'm frightened, too. To have to return to the moment when I lost my mother.... I still have nightmares."

Ming Wei clicked her tongue. "Cannot Melanie and Cracker see?" she asked impatiently. "They have already confronted and accepted their worst moment. Just as Ming Wei accepted that Nora Stein was killed, Ming Wei chose to live and continued to grow. So Melanie and Cracker have accepted, and will continue to grow. If you live your life well, without rage and denial, if you live with patience and compassion, you have nothing to fear in Half World. Inside every one of us there exists already our own Realm of Flesh, Half World and Realm of Spirit. Inside of us! When we understand this, there is greater balance. Melanie, you chose to live. You have moved forward. You are not trapped in your Half Life here, and so you will not be trapped when your time in Half World comes. It is the same for Cracker."

"I think I understand what you mean," Cracker said slowly. Her head dropped and a lock of black hair fell across her pale face. "It still hurts so much that Klara killed herself, that I couldn't help her." She took a deep breath and dragged her fingers through her hair to push it away from her forehead. "But you're right, Ms. Wei. I've accepted that I couldn't undo her suicide. And hearing Karu's story, and what happened to his brother..." Cracker shuddered. "There are worse things than death."

"Poor Gee." Melanie's voice was low. "I-I didn't treat him well. I was too frightened to give him a chance. And then I left as soon as I could." The red rat scurried up her arm to nestle against her neck, its tail hanging down over Melanie's chest. Melanie automatically raised her hand to gently stroke the curve of the rat's back. "I'm sorry, Popo."

Ming Wei stared intently at her adopted granddaughter. Melanie did not look away. "Popo was sad and angry," Ming Wei stated. "But Popo also understood why Melanie did what she did." She half-rose and then leant across the table to gently tap Melanie's cheek with her rough, work-worn hand.

Cracker tilted her head to one side. "Weren't you in hospital, Ms. Wei? Gee was worried about you."

"Pah!" Ming Wei scoffed. "Anemic, they said. Low blood pressure." She flapped her hand. "The doctor was younger than Melanie! What can a doctor that young know about an old woman's health! Ming Wei needs to sell her store and start dating again!"

Melanie's eyes crinkled with laughter. Cracker's mouth fell open with awe.

White Cat rose to his paws, arching upward in a slow stretch, ending with a dramatic quiver of his tail. He padded to the far end of the table and turned so that he faced them all at once. "I'm bored. And I'm hungry," he yawned. "No one has bothered to ask me about my well-being, to offer me sustenance after all the things I've done, everything I've suffered for no personal gain. I'm ordering takeout. I don't know why but I fancy broiled eels drizzled with teriyaki sauce on rice."

The three women stared at the cat.

"You're unbelievable," Cracker muttered.

White Cat began to purr. Once he was certain everyone was watching, he leapt gracefully and landed upon the velvet cushion of the easy chair. Draping his paws over the armrest, he batted the phone receiver out of the cradle and began tapping out numbers with a single extended claw. He nosed the mouthpiece and cleared his throat. "Hello? Yes. I'd like to order for delivery," he purred.

"Order for everyone else as well, wretched creature!" Ming Wei called out. "And White Cat is paying." Ming Wei stood and gestured to Melanie and Cracker. "Come."

She went to the filing cabinet. Atop it was the latest framed school photo of Gee. Next to it was Melanie's university convocation photo. Ming Wei took her grandson's photo and carried it to the altar she'd made for her long-dead lover. She moved Nora's photo a little to the side. "Please take good care of Gee, dear Nora," Ming Wei said as she placed Gee's photo beside it.

Cracker gazed at his image. The long hank of dark hair, falling diagonally across his face, covered one eye. His other eye stared directly at the camera. Dark, intense, unreadable. The long lines of his pale face.... His thin and mobile lips were pressed tight. As if he held something back. He's beautiful, Cracker thought. And now he's gone.

Ming Wei picked up three sticks of incense. She handed one each to Melanie and Cracker, and kept one for herself. Producing a lighter from her pocket, she flicked it, raising the flame to the tip of the stick. It began to burn, and the musty, rich scent filled the air. Handing the lighter to Melanie, Ming Wei faced Gee's photo, raised the incense stick and bowed three times. She placed it in the holder and closed her eyes, her hands pressed together. Her lips moved as she mouthed words Cracker and Melanie could not hear.

Maybe Gee hears them, Cracker thought.

Melanie and Cracker lit their incense and sent their own messages as the rich, sweet smoke twined toward the high ceiling.

"Thank you, Gee," Cracker whispered. "I miss you. And I'm still pissed that you choked me, you asshole." She dragged her forearm across her eyes. "I hope we catch up with each other some time. I think we will." She felt a gentle tugging at the bottom of her bathrobe. It was the dark red rat. Its almost human hand patted her lower calf reassuringly.

"So it may be," Red Rat said in its funny low voice. "The cycles continue to turn, and we with them." It scampered back to the table.

"Just imagine two different-coloured socks in a dryer," White Cat said drolly. "A very *common* analogy, but it is adequate. The socks spin around, it all looks random, but eventually they will come into contact. Like that, if you will."

A small smile touched Cracker's lips. "Ms. Wei?" she asked.

"Hmph?" Ming Wei's eyes were closed.

"Can I come and visit you sometimes? When you're not busy?"

"Hmph," Ming Wei responded. "You can dust the tins in the store and sweep the floors."

Melanie shook her head. "I'll put on the kettle."

"You have to pay me minimum wage," Cracker countered.

Ming Wei widened her eyes, outraged. "Ms. Wei is doing Cracker a favour by offering work experience! This she needs to graduate from high school!"

"High school!" Cracker scoffed.

"No school, no visits with Ming Wei!" Ms. Wei said sternly.

"Geez." Cracker slouched. "You're such a hard-ass."

"And no more swearing! Wahhhh! Such a mouth on this one!" Ming Wei, shaking her head, returned to her chair at the table. "She has too much heat. Yin deficiency. She needs a soup. And lessons in manners."

A warmth began glowing inside Cracker's chest. She found herself standing beside the large window that overlooked the street outside. The purple sky was turning indigo, the street lights glowing orange.

She could hear Ms. Wei and Melanie murmuring at the table. The rise and fall of emotions and familiarity. It sounded nice.

She ran her fingers down the curve of White Cat's furry back.

His tail lashed. "The nerve!" he exclaimed. But he didn't leap away. He began to purr, a little unevenly, as if he were ill-practised.

Cracker continued stroking the cat as the night bloomed around them. His fur was very soft.

Epilogue

A haphazard cluster of roundhouses stood upon a small open field near a dirty stream. The dung heap, piled high with offal, excrement, broken pottery and bones, filled the air with a tremendous stench.

Packs of hairless animals, glowing with larval luminescence, slipped from shadow to shadow, the sound of trickling childish giggles following after them.

From the opening of one of the roundhouses a dim, pale grey light flickered. The perpetual dusk was torn by the sounds of a woman's screams.

Pain, suffering, she screamed, off and on, for several hours. She continued screaming until she was ragged.

Then … laughter … weak, weary, but laughter. Her voice, happiness tinged with sorrow.

A baby squawked. Gasped for air. Breathing, the newly born began to wail.

The grey light flickering from the entrance began to gutter. Dimming. The roundhouse fell to darkness.

"Oh, no." The woman's voice was anguished.

Out of the darkness, sapphire motes began to shine, one after the other. A myriad glow of minute lights, cascading shards of blue inside the home. Deep-blue rays escaped through cracks and seams, shone upon the ground outside. The rich saturated light throbbed with intensity and poured out the opening of the roundhouse.

The rays that spilled out of the shelter began to shrink as a brilliant blue hinotama, the size of a human heart, floated out through the hole in the ceiling and hovered above the decrepit shelter.

"Oh!" The weak voice was tinged with wonder.

The sapphire hinotama floated back down through the hole in the roof, re-entering the roundhouse. The blue light shone out from the seams and the opening of the home once more.

Small shadowed figures crept toward the shelter, creeping, hopping, drawn to the wondrous glow.

A second light, pale green, the colour of spring leaves, flared into being.

The dark shadows gasped with delight.

Two vibrant hinotama, sapphire blue and leaf green, floated outside. Their brilliant light was miraculous and the creatures raised their hands above their heads as if they were children trying to catch the stars.

The two orbs of light zigzagged across the dark sky, chasing each other, spiralling up to fall back down, so that the sapphire and green light would play upon the creatures who reached for them with such longing.

The brilliant hinotama shot across the dark skies and disappeared.

ACKNOWLEDGMENTS

The transformation of an idea to a published book is, simultaneously, miraculous and mundane. But it is always accomplished because of the support, kindnesses and professionalism of so many people. I am capable of writing books because of the many communities that sustain me. I am so very grateful.

I am blessed with the presence of Koji and Sae in my life. The most amazing and beautiful things I've learned, I've learned through you. My writer-guardian angels: Chris and Nozomi, for sending me a laptop, eternal gratitude. Chris, thank you so much for early story feedback. And to ever-supportive Naomi and Kyoko; thank you for being there when my creative process falters.

My dear beautiful friends, comrades-in-writing, feminists, activists, bad-asses & community family; thank you for laughter, passion, attitude, comfort, sharing meals, raising of cups and all that spilleth over. Blessings to Susanda Yee, Larissa Lai, Rita Wong, Joy Russell, Christine Stewart, Ivana Vukov, Graeme Comyn, Eva Tai, Edward Parker, Tamotsu Tongu, Kyo Maclear, David Bateman, Janice Williamson, Kris Calhoun, Nisi Shawl, Eileen Gunn, Roy Miki, Baco Ohama, Jean Baird & George Bowering, The James Tiptree Jr. Award Motherboard, Powell Street Festival Society, and Jeff & Ann VanderMeer.

Call-out to the Writing Cheerleading Squad: Nalo, Jennifer, Pamela, Larissa, Martin, David!

I am so thankful for the many people who ensure that the professional side of writing is as fruitful as the creative side. Gratitude to my amazing agents, Sally Harding, and everyone else at the excellent Cooke Agency! I'm also so very blessed with the wonderful people at Penguin Canada: thank you so much to Lynne Missen and (interim editor) Caitlin Drake, Vimala Jeevanandam, David Ross, story editor extraordinaire Jennifer Glossop and keen-eyed copy editor Karen Alliston. Rapturous joy-gratitude to Jillian Tamaki for the gorgeous cover art and interior illustrations, and a special thank you to photographer Kiely Ramos.

For generous funding/support during the long process of seeing a book come into fruition I am ever so grateful to the University of Alberta Department of English and Film Studies Writer-in-Residency Program, Canada Council for the Arts, and BC Arts. Tasukari mashita.